Songs of the Dead

Derrick Jensen

Flashpoint Press
An imprint of PM Press

Cover design by Beth Orduna and John Yates
Text design by Michael Link

Edited by Theresa Noll

10 9 8 7 6 5 4 3 2 1

ISBN: 978-1-60486-044-3
LCCN: 2008934204

Jensen, Derrick, 1960–
Songs of the Dead / by Derrick Jensen.
p. cm.

Fiction

Flashpoint Press
Published by PM Press
Flashpoint Press Box 903 Crescent City, CA 95531
www.flashpointpress.com
PM Press Box 23912 Oakland, CA 94623
http://www.pmpress.org

Printed in the USA on recycled paper.

Also by Derrick Jensen

Songs of the Dead
Derrick Jensen

Table of Contents

That we come to this earth to live is untrue:
we come but to sleep, to dream.

Aztec Poem

one

the cannibal sickness

Each night, I walk the line that wends between unconsciousness and terror, between forgetting and remembering, between present and past. Each night I do not fall asleep but instead stumble through time, falling into deep impressions—like five-pointed handprints on soft clay—of past on present, living in house after house after house of imagination, each one an edifice of events uncompleted. Does the land dream so, too, carrying with it the weight of thousands of years of nights on nights, remembering salmon that were and are not, caressing them in the infancy of their evolution and caring for them in their absence? Does the land mourn these losses as I mourn my own, and does she—it, he, pieces of moist soil between my fingertips, the orange bellies of ponderosa pine four arm lengths around—dream as well of times unwounded, and of woundings? Does time wind and unwind for her—for I know now it is her—each night as she sleeps beneath snow, stars, cold wind, trees sighing sadly or giving up their own ghosts before meeting what we have become, beneath a moon that night after night sees all, yet keeps remembering?

I know now that there is and always has been a heart that beats beyond the grasping of our mechanical fingers, unfound in the claws of our braced backhoes, slipping away in the face of our too-coarse bulldozers. The past resides in the soil, and though we believe it blows away and is lost, that is not true. It is there all the time, though we do not see it.

Our dreams carry with them the perfume of this soil, and will not without a fight let go of that which beneath it all makes each of us who we are. So each night I walk that fine line, and sometimes awaken to freeze before all that has happened to me, to her, to each of us, and to wish that things could be different than they are.

He touches the still-warm skin of her belly with the first three fingers of his left hand. Almost on their own, his fingers trace tiny circles toward the tented skin over her pelvis. Her skin is soft, pale. Her scent fills the room.

He stands between her legs, leans over slightly, then more. He touches the scalpel in his right hand to the skin just below her navel, and draws a line to her pubic hair, pink of skin, thin white layer of subcutaneous fat, light brown layer—so thin—of muscle, then the yellow wall of the abdominal cavity itself. The geology of skin. Which layer came first?

He remembers how she was a short time ago, still breathing, gasping, clinging tight to whatever she could grasp. Her clawed fingers opening and closing, wrists twisting beneath metal holding her to the table, skin tearing, and beneath the skin muscles tightening, rising up, trying to leave her body.

Dying, she'd terrorized him more than ever before. Again and again he'd asked her the one simple question he always asked, and again and again she'd pretended not to know. She'd kept up that feigned ignorance to the end, when with her last words—more a sigh, really, a gurgle, a retch, than any sort of sentence—she'd been able to convince him her ignorance might be real. "Nothing, nothing. Not at all." That's what she had said.

The scalpel. So small. Sharp. Bright. He breaks into the peritoneum. The first time he had done that he'd been surprised there was no stench. Some animals stink when you open them up. Most people don't. He sees the intestines, long tubes sheathed in fat, lifts them up and sees the bladder. It's also white. So much white. The size of a fist. Beneath that, what he's looking for. Pale pink, white, another fist. He slices at the ligaments, then pulls at the uterus. It doesn't come out easily. It never does. He reaches behind and beneath to sever the attachments, and finally the organ is liberated. He brings with it the ovaries.

His fingers are red. Cherry. Burgundy. Darker. Almost black. He looks at his watch. It's late. He puts down the scalpel.

This time he burns the body. He puts it in the back of his pickup and takes it south of town. It rides wrapped in blue plastic beneath the shell. The ride is smooth until near the end, when he drives across railroad tracks, up a slope, around a corner, and into a small quarry. Fractured rock on three sides, and trees on the other. Good cover. Here he can watch, just a little. He wants to see the fire. He's never done that before.

He stops the truck, hears the click of his door opening and the soft catch as he slowly shuts it. Walking to the back of the truck, he hears the gravel grind beneath his feet. He opens the shell and rear gate, then reaches for the tail of the blue tarp and pulls it toward him. The tarp is heavy, but not so heavy that he isn't able to carry it.

Then the unwrapping. He rolls the body free of the tarp, but doesn't look at it until he returns from the truck with the gasoline. Now he looks at her. Dark blonde hair, soft, tangled. Pockmarks on her face. Missing a tooth. That wasn't his doing. It was already gone.

She was not a pretty woman, he thinks, not very pretty at all. But at one time she had been. She'd had a picture in her wallet of a younger woman, standing next to a man. The woman was beautiful: slender, long blonde hair, smooth skin. He had asked her who that was, and she'd said it was her. "What happened?" he'd asked.

She hadn't answered, but she hadn't needed to. He'd known the answer. He'd seen the tracks on her arms when he first picked her up. Scabby, scarred, bruised. Abuse, drugs, alcohol, and sunlight had all worked together to harden the muscles of her face until she could no longer remove the mask of impassivity that protected her from customers, and from everyone. Or almost everyone.

He pours the gasoline, sets the near-empty gas can a safe distance away, lights a match, then uses it to ignite a twisted piece of newspaper. The flame describes a soft arc toward the body, then flashes outward in a concussive wave he feels in his belly. For a short time the flames seem to hold themselves above the body, but as he watches the skin begins to darken, then split away from the muscles tightening and becoming dark themselves, braiding to look like nothing so much as jerked meat. He follows the smoke up and realizes he needs to leave. Too much smoke, more than he anticipated. Someone could see. Still not too worried, though, he watches a few more moments before retreating to the truck, and afterwards driving back to the highway, back to the town.

two

p o s s e s s i o n

For the past few years, I've been working on a book called *Possession*. It is, like all of my other books, an attempt to provide at least preliminary answers to what I perceive are some pressing questions. *A Language Older Than Words*, for example, is, among other things, an attempt to explore the relationships between silencing and atrocity, and between remembering and healing. In *The Culture of Make Believe* I wanted to ask and attempt to answer questions like, What is hate? What are the relationships between hatred, perceived entitlement, objectification, and atrocity? What are the logical endpoints of this culture's way of perceiving and being in the world? And *Endgame* was centered around the questions, Do you believe this culture will undergo a voluntary transformation to a sane and sustainable way of living? If not (and almost no one I ever talk to believes it will) what does that mean for your strategy and tactics to defend the places you love?

It's always easier to articulate the questions that drive a book long after that book is done. During the writing itself, it often seems as though I'm slowly feeling my way forward in the dark, arms outstretched in front of me to warn of obstacles, as I attempt to follow some almost entirely unseen path toward some entirely unseen goal. Often this goal is not only unseen, but literally unimagined—that is, after all, one of the points of writing a book: to imagine and articulate that which before, you could not put words to or sometimes even conceptualize—but it feels like *Possession* is yet another attempt to understand the incomprehensible destructiveness of this culture. We can talk all we want about silencing, perceived entitlement, and all that, but none of it could ever be sufficient to explain how any group of people, no matter how stupid or arrogant, could kill the planet they live on so that they can make money. *Possession* is about more than that, though. It's also about our relationships to various parts of the world about us. And this is where *Possession* veers slightly away from the other books; in this book, far more than in the others, I ask about our relationships—sometimes beneficial, sometimes harmful, sometimes neither, sometimes both—not only with those others we can see and feel and hear, like trees and dogs and cats and rivers, stars, mountains, and so on, but even moreso with those we can't: muses, fates, the dead, and so many others. Asking these questions is then leading me, shuffling as always and sometimes stumbling, toward questions concerning free will, or put more straight, toward questions about how I make decisions, or put straighter still, toward the question: when I do make a decision, who is making that decision? Who's in charge? And further, who—chance, physics, fates, God, the gods, or any (and maybe all) of a myriad of others—determines the results of that decision?

On November 8, 1939, Georg Elser tried to kill Hitler. Elser knew that each year on that date, the Nazis commemorated their failed putsch of 1923 with speeches and a dinner. For several months prior to the 1939 gathering, Elser was able to spend the night unnoticed in the Löwenbräu restaurant in Munich, where the meeting would be held.

Elser's plans were meticulous. He had long-since taken a job in a quarry for the express purpose of stealing explosives. Task accomplished, for thirty-five nights he carved a hidden chamber into a concrete post next to which Hitler was to give his speech. A pair of timers would trigger the explosion not long before Hitler reached his crescendo.

I've often wondered how many times over the next six years—the last of his life, all spent in a concentration camp, perhaps noticing day-by-day his bones jut more from his skin, perhaps watching the white marks of malnutrition march down his fingernails—Elser must have asked himself why he chose to set the timers late and not early in Hitler's speech. Was he worried that Hitler would not be prompt, or that preliminary festivities—the playing of the Badenweiler march and the saluting of the Blood Banner—might take longer than anticipated? Or was there no good reason for the timing? Do you think that in the long years afterward he ever considered how many lives were lost because of that one simple and virtually meaningless—by itself—decision? Perhaps more to the point, do you think there was ever an hour in which he did not consider the unfortunate effects of his choice?

I don't ask this to blame Elser for his timing. At least he made the effort. And there was no way for him to know that fog—nothing more substantial than fine droplets of water hanging suspended in air, so unpredictable, an act of God—would save Hitler's life.

The assassination attempt nearly did not come off. Because Hitler had already brought the country to war, that year's service was to be abbreviated, with Rudolph Hess delivering the speech instead of Hitler. But on November 7, Hitler changed his mind and decided to fly down from Berlin to participate in the ceremonies.

Each year the speech began at 8:30, and lasted until 10:00. But this year was different. Because November in Munich frequently brings with it fog, Hitler faced a decision: should he spend the night in Munich, should he chance flying back and risk being delayed in the fog, or should he return by train? Hitler would have to finish early so he could catch his train at 9:31. Georg Elser did not know this.

By six o'clock that night, the hall was packed with the cream—such as it was—of Nazi society: Himmler, Rosenberg, Frank, Goebbels, Ribbentrop. A band played the Badenweiler march while the Blood Banner was brought in. Hitler arrived to massive applause, and began his speech at precisely 8:00.

His speech ended at 9:07, and he was out of the building by ten after. The bomb exploded at 9:20, causing the roof to collapse and killing nine people. Elser was later arrested trying to escape into Switzerland. He was sent to a concentration camp, and was murdered by the SS on April 5, 1945.

◉

three

places we do not see

A couple of years ago I had a dream that wasn't so much a dream as it was a visitation, a conjuration of the sort I'd somehow thought only happened in books and movies, in which you speak some demon's name and the demon appears. I've since come to understand that these visitations—of demons and many others—are a part of life no more unusual, and normally no better perceived, than the stones on the ground, and the speaking of these stones.

In this dream that was and continues to be even more than a dream, I was fighting with rebels against corporations, against the forces I fight in waking reality, only this time I was using guns instead of words. In this dream we were losing horribly, just as we are in waking reality. We were, and the parallels continue, drastically outnumbered by the military and the police. Many on our side were being shot. I lay flat on my belly behind a lip of concrete. It was small cover, but with bullets ricocheting around me, it was far better than nothing. The firing of guns—mainly theirs, but a few of ours—merged into a constant roar. Then the roar lost its continuity, first to tiny gaps not yet filled with silence but still carrying echoes of the explosions, and then with silence in which I could hear my own gasping breaths. The firing became more and more sporadic, then stopped altogether.

I glanced to my right, to one of my fellow rebels, and I saw that the reason he no longer fired back was that he was dying. In this dream that is even more than a dream, that is a visitation or a conjuration, I saw a vampire fastened to the man's neck sucking out his blood and his guts. The vampire dropped the husk, looked, found someone else, attached himself. Then I looked at the enemy and I saw that there was not one vampire, or even a hundred, but thousands, and more than thousands. I saw, in this dream that is more than a dream, that these vampires were killing every human they could find. They were sucking out their blood and their guts. They were having a feed. The vampires—or demons, or whatever other name we may wish to put on these others whose real name I don't know—were neither angry nor evil nor in any way malevolent. They were famished, and they were eating. They began to chase me, as they were chasing everyone else. I evaded them, at least temporarily. I stopped. I looked through a glass window in a steel door. Thin metal mesh reinforced the window. Beyond the mesh, beyond the glass, beyond the steel, I saw a vampire who was not chasing, not feeding. He was standing. He was watching. He had pale skin, smooth scalp, grotesquely long fingers and a just as grotesquely long, curved nose. In this dream I knew he was the director. I did not and do not know what this means.

I woke up. I tried to convince myself that this dream was and is "no more" than a dream, and that these vampires represent those forces we are fighting against, that they represent those who are killing the planet, that they represent this culture as a whole, this culture of napalm, toxic wastes, deforestation, rape. No. I tried to convince myself that they represent something much more specific: the biotechnology industry, for example, and its creation of monsters. No. The dream, which really was and is even more than a dream, would not allow those interpretations. The vampires are vampires. And they're hungry. And they're waiting to be released, waiting to feed on humans.

There's a fire somewhere. I can smell more than see it, but my eyes trick me, with a slight sting, into pretending that I see the smoke. I don't, of course, except when I do, and even then, like all of us, I'm never sure if what I see is what I see.

There *is* a haze in the distance, but it's just the sky settling back to earth at the end of the day. It's July, and it's hot. I'm sweaty, wet beneath my arms, on my lower back where my shirt touches my skin, and under the elastic band of my underwear.

I'm in Hangman Valley, in the western part of Spokane. I'm walking, as I often do, near Hangman Creek, which used to be Latah Creek before any of this began, and certainly long before any of it began with me.

Or maybe not. That's one of the things I often have difficulty with. Before. During. After. Sometimes I don't understand what any of it means.

But it's hot. I understand that. It's hot enough that the leaves on the trees hang limp, except when a hot breeze makes the air quake with their paper rattling. Edges of these leaves are turning brown, and the grasses beneath have long since died or gone dormant, used up for and by the summer, and dry as tinder. Even the needles of the pine trees seem to have lost their strength and their shine.

It's cooler by the creek, though not as much cooler as I'm sure it once was, back when the creek was a creek, deeper, wider, stronger. I go there often. It's a reasonably long walk from my home—probably a couple of hours—and a longer walk back since I have to go so much uphill.

I sit by the creek, take off my shoes and socks, roll up my pants, and put my feet in. I lean forward to search for tiny fish. None. I close my eyes, then open them again quickly, just to see if this will make the salmon appear. I know that's not how it works, but it's never stopped me from hoping. And sometimes I do see them. They haven't been here since the Grand Coulee Dam was built back in the thirties, but sometimes I still do see them.

Every fire has a life of its own. I've known this as long as I can remember, since long before any of this began. The flames speak, not so much to me as to each other. Sometimes they do speak to me, although I never can be sure what they are saying. But I do know that each flame is alive, individual, as much as any other being.

There is a woman. She takes a shortcut through an alley. She is thinking, or not thinking, but seeing inside of her what she saw that morning, which was a puppy she gave her son for his birthday four days before. When the puppy wagged his tail he did not so much wag his tail as wag his whole body when he squirmed toward her son, who in turn did not smile so much with his lips and teeth as he, too, smiled with his whole body. This is what she is seeing when she hears the sound that is not a sound but the movement of a sound throughout her whole body, the sharp cracking of lightning as it strikes inside her brain, but does not stop after the bolt has gone; it keeps expanding outward until there is nothing left of her skull and of what was inside her skull, and she is flying, having been struck, and there is nothing but the sound that keeps expanding, and no longer can she see the puppy or her son or anything but the sound that is no longer a sound, but everything she knows.

That is what I hear. When I walk where the car struck her, that is what I hear.

Not every time. But often. And if the truth is that while I see salmon not nearly often enough, this I see far too often.

I haven't always seen like this, and even now I often do not. I used to not see anything more than anyone else, or maybe I should say not more than any of my neighbors, or maybe I should be even more precise and say not more than any of my human neighbors. I think nonhumans—and some humans—see this all the time.

For example, just a few days ago a huge submarine earthquake caused a tsunami that rocked parts of Indonesia, Sri Lanka, Thailand, Malaysia, and India, killing more than a hundred thousand humans. Just today I read a news report saying, "Wildlife officials in Sri Lanka expressed surprise Wednesday that they found no evidence of large-scale animal deaths from the weekend's massive tsunami—indicating that animals may have sensed the wave coming and fled to higher ground. An Associated Press photographer who flew over Sri Lanka's Yala National Park in an air force helicopter saw abundant wildlife, including elephants, buffalo, deer, and not a single animal corpse." The response by one person was, "Maybe what we think is true, that animals have a sixth sense."

I'm not saying I have a sixth sense. Sometimes I'm not even sure about the other five, and my girlfriend Allison will tell you I sure don't have much of the common one. But I see things, and hear things. No, I see places, and I hear places. Places where I'm standing. Places where I'm sitting. Places where I'm sleeping. Sometimes I hear what the place says to me.

It's not something I can force, by any means. It just happens. It used to scare me more than it does now, but even now I do not understand it, and even now sometimes it terrifies me.

The first time was in a forest. It was a couple of years ago. I was driving our old yellow pickup, and Allison was in the passenger seat. We were going to collect firewood from slash piles in clearcuts left over from logging in the national forest. We did this often.

I wasn't particularly tired, but somehow with no discernable transition I fell asleep behind the wheel. I've done that a few times driving late at night, only to jerk awake as I slip onto the shoulder, but this time there was no sliding onto the shoulder, and no jerking awake. This time I didn't even close my eyes. But I was asleep, and I began to dream with my eyes open. I saw a logging truck come down the road toward us, and I pulled over slightly to let it pass. I saw Allison shift and start to ask something, but then stop. I saw my hands turn the wheel to the right to maneuver around a corner, and then bring themselves back to ten and two o'clock for the straightaway. Another logging truck, and again I pulled slightly over. Again Allison shifted, and this time she asked, "Are you all right?"

"I think so."

"Why are you swerving?"

"What?"

"Swerving."

"The trucks."

I looked at Allison, and beyond her to the beauty strip, and to the old clearcut on the other side. I remembered that clearcut because we had been there a couple of years before to pull wood from those slash piles, and we had stopped in our work to make love. In the time since, that's become part of our woodgathering ritual, but that time had been the first. I felt my foot ease off the gas pedal and onto the brake. I felt my other foot push in the clutch, and my hand slide the gearshift into neutral. "Allison."

She looked at me.

I heard the crunch of tires on rock. "Look at the forest."

She turned to look outside. "I know," she said. "I hate those fuckers who do this."

"No," I said. "The clearcut. It's gone." It was. There was no thin beauty strip of trees masking a clearcut. There was nothing but a thick forest quickly turning dark from shade and crisscrossed branches and leaves and trunks.

She looked back at me. "Derrick," she said.

"I don't understand." I felt the car roll to a stop, felt my foot leave the clutch, felt my other foot stay on the brake. I saw Allison looking at me.

Do you want to know why I love Allison so very much? She did not tell me I was wrong or crazy—I was thinking both of these things quite well on my own. She did not tell me that the forest was gone. She said, "Tell me what you see."

I'm awake, but my eyes are closed. I don't know how long I've been lying here. I used to sleep with the drapes shut, but not anymore: I don't know many feelings more delicious than drifting with the morning sun on my shoulders. I hear footfalls, that seem to be more from the dream side than the waking side, then a voice, definitely from the waking side. It's Allison.

"Good morning."

I smile and open my eyes. "How's the painting?"

She smiles—like the puppy, like the little boy—with her whole body. "It is *so* good. I'm doing the dagger. I'll finish today."

It's my favorite painting of hers. Perhaps I was wrong when I said I love Allison so much because of what she said to me. Perhaps it's because of paintings like this one. It's a stroke for stroke reproduction of Peter Paul Rubens' *The Rape of the Daughters of Leucippus*, with one small change. And as is so often the case, one small change changes everything. Instead of the two women being defenseless, they're fighting back: the first is raking her attacker with her fingernails, and the second is about to plunge a small dagger into the breast of the other man. Her new title: "The Attempted Rape of the Daughters of Leucippus."

"Your timing was perfect," I say. "I was just about to get up."

She smiles slyly, "This isn't the first time I checked."

"Can I see it?"

"In a while." She stands near the edge of the bed. I know she wants to sit, but is wearing her workclothes. I notice her breasts beneath her shirt, the way they move slightly with every breath. I notice the sun on her hair and her hair falling over her shoulders. I notice her hands, long slender fingers smudged with paint. I move up to her face, and let my eyes follow the smooth line of her cheek down to the slight square of her jaw, and then up to her lips. She's still smiling.

"You have the face of an angel," I say.

Her smile broadens. I can see it in her shoulders, and in her hips. "Would you like to see god?" she says.

"Of course," I say. "And you?"

"Always."

"Look at me."

"I want to come home."

Allison says again, "Look at me."

"I'm scared."

She grasps my hand, places it in the middle of her chest. "Look. Feel. I'm right here."

I'm still dreaming, and my eyes are still open. I shake my head, stare at her eyes. My head clears for just a moment. I see the clearcut behind her, and know where I am. But then I begin to slide back into the dream. The forest rematerializes. I see it. I do not see the clearcut. I still see the inside of the truck. I still see Allison. But everything beyond has changed. Again I shake my head, stare at Allison. Again I return. Again I slide back into the dream.

I hear a voice—not Allison's—say, "Don't fight it." But I do, shaking my head.

I take my hand from Allison's chest, and slap my own face to wake up. No, that's not true. I focus on my hand, will it to move itself from her chest, will it to recoil and strike. It complies, slowly at first, and then with force. I don't wake up, and suddenly Allison is holding my hand between her own.

I hear the voice again, still not Allison's. I don't know whose it is or where it comes from. "Don't fight it."

I hear my voice say, "I'm slipping."

I hear Allison's voice, saying to no one I know, "Let's get you to ground." She squeezes a hand at the end of an arm I see coming from a shoulder at the edge of my vision, then lets go. She opens her door, walks around the front of the truck. I will my eyes to follow her. She opens my door, leans across to unfasten the seatbelt, grabs the keys, takes a hand I think is mine. I am watching this dream, this movie of a dream, as a left foot that looks like mine comes into view. It reaches for the ground. A right foot follows. I seem to stand. She shuts the door. She leads, and I see my feet take step after step following her.

"Here," she says. "Sit down. Lean against this." She lays her palm flat against the gray trunk of a big cedar.

She helps my body sit. I feel the texture of the bark through my shirt against my back. I stare straight ahead, away from the road, into the forest.

I am neither so stupid nor so arrogant as to believe that what we see is all there is, nor that the world is so simple as we insist on pretending.

To pretend, for example, that trees don't want to heal; or to pretend trees don't feel angry, scared, joyful, grateful; or to pretend salmon do not speak, or to pretend they do not feel all these things, is to be willfully unaware.

To pretend there are not places we do not see, unseen folds in the fabric of what we call reality, hideaways and homes into which plants and animals slip as surely and secretly as they slide into holes in ancient snags, to pretend there are not places these plants and animals go to get away from us, places they go anyway, places that are as much their homes as are the forests, rivers, mountains, deserts that we normally see, is to suspect them of living in only a tiny portion of their habitat. It is to confine ourselves to a tiny portion of our own habitat.

four

p o w e r

I know where and when the sickness began. Anybody who thinks about it knows the answer to that one: several thousand years ago in the Middle East, the cradle of civilization, with other irruptions of the sickness in other civilizations in Asia, Central America, and a few other places. As to why it began I can't say. I've written several books on this culture and its destructiveness, and I still can't even pretend to understand the genesis of these horrors. Sure, we can recognize that many indigenous cultures did not and do not destroy their landbases, and we can describe the differences between this culture and those that might lead to these widely disparate behaviors. We can recognize that many indigenous cultures had and have very low to nonexistent rates of rape, and that in many indigenous cultures both women and children are treated well. We can describe the differences between those that lead to the rapes and mistreatment on one hand, and the relative egalitarianism on the other. We can know that many indigenous cultures had no rich and no poor. Many practiced relatively nonlethal (and downright fun) forms of warfare. We can ask what it is that makes this culture promote certain behaviors and other cultures promote other behaviors. We can be clear about all of this.

But where did it start?

Jack Shoemaker stares at the table, at the tools arranged on a white towel folded once lengthwise. Handcuffs. Duct tape. Rubber gloves. Blackjack. Knife. Scalpel. Hypodermic and syringe of ketamine. He's already laid plastic over the basement floor, and a plastic tarp is in the back of his truck. He looks at his watch, then back to the table. He won't use the rubber gloves or the scalpel till he gets back, and might not have to use the knife at all, but it's always better to be prepared. He pats his shirt pocket: cash. Everything's ready.

He slides the scalpel into a cardboard sheath and blinks twice. His lips slightly relax into the barest open-mouthed smile. He'd read somewhere that the word *vagina* is Latin for *sheath*, a sheath for a man's sword. So he looked it up.

Jack tears off several small pieces of duct tape and attaches each tool to the towel. He rips off two more pieces and returns the roll to its spot. He uses one piece to attach the roll to the towel and sticks one corner of the other to his left hand. Then he steps to the end of the table and rolls up the towel. Holding it tight with one hand, he pulls the tape free with the other, then attaches it, securing the bundle enough to prevent accidental opening without hindering accessibility.

He looks again at his watch. It's almost time to go.

Kristine looks at her watch. Time to go to work. She opens her wallet to look at the mirror inside. Not great, she thinks, but good enough. She runs her hand through her hair, feels the slight stickiness of her scalp and the texture of her hair made thick and brittle, like straw, by dirt, sweat, and hairspray. She looks again at her watch. Yeah, there's time, she thinks, there has to be time. Otherwise she's never going to make it. She rummages through her canvas bag of clothes, but can't find what she's looking for.

"Fuck."

Kristine keeps digging. She sees a black tube top and realizes she hasn't worn it for a few days. She remembers the tip she got the last time she did. She could use the money. Maybe it's a lucky shirt. She puts down the bag, unbuttons and pulls off her fuchsia blouse, stuffs it into the bag, and shimmies into the tube top. She looks again in the mirror, and again she runs her hand through her hair.

Back to the bag. She finds a small black chunk of heroin wrapped in plastic, along with a pocketknife, syringe, bent spoon, and a lighter. She unwraps the heroin, and the stench makes her salivate. She uses the pocketknife to scrape a little into the spoon. Not much, just enough to remove the edge. Then she pours in a little water and stirs the mix with the tip of her needle. She flicks the lighter, holds it under the spoon. The tar dissolves. Using the cotton ball as a filter, she fills the syringe. She sits cross-legged on the ground, then extends her right leg while keeping her hips open so she can see the back of her knee. The needle finds its own way into her vein, and the plunger finds its own way down.

She feels good. Not so good she can't move or do anything but stay here under the bridge—just good enough that now she can go to work.

Nika is awake, but the apartment is silent, so she lies in bed with her opened box of memories. So long as she keeps her eyes closed and doesn't move, doesn't hear anything, she can pretend she's in bed at home, that she is somewhere and someone else, a world away from where and who she is now. This is how she gets through each day. She takes each memory out of the box, holds it, turns it around and around in her mind, tries to re-create its feeling in her body. There's her little brother Petya playing with his dog in the field behind their home, and there are the flowers in the field. There is the sun on her shoulders as she watches. Even the sun somehow felt different then: it's hard to believe it's the same sun shining now. There is her mother giving her the pendant cross given to her by *her* mother, whose mother gave it to her. There is the feeling of her mother's fingers on Nika's neck as she attaches it, the smell of her mother, the smell of the kitchen. There is her father's smile as Nika tells him her marks at Lyceum.

She lies there comfortably, almost drifting, almost smiling, as image after image bubbles up. Blood sausages with her grandmother. Bathing her great-grandmother, cutting her hair, clipping her toenails, listening to her stories of the German occupation and holding her when she got confused over what year it was and thought the Nazis were coming to the door. Nika remembers her first kiss with her boyfriend Osip, how neither had known what to do but had learned so quickly and easily. She remembers watching Petya practice ballet.

She hears steps on the stairs outside the apartment, and starts to put the memories back into their box, starts to shut it up tight and lock it. But then, as so often happens, another memory forces its way before her. An advertisement in a newspaper. She sees the newspaper as though it's before her now, sees the ad circled in red pen. A secretarial job in Vilnius. She remembers begging her mother to let her have this adventure the summer before she begins her college, and her mother and father finally approving. She wishes she would have not chosen that day to look in the newspaper, wishes she would have listened to the dreams that told her not to go.

The steps are closer on the stairs, and she needs to conjure another memory before she can shut the box. She cannot bear to end on this one. She searches, her eyes moving below her eyelids. Seven years old, she thinks. Eight. She needs to find something good. And then she remembers. Six years old. Christmas. A gift from her parents. Normally the gifts were simple and necessary, like pencils or notebooks. But this time she rips apart the paper to find a toy drum. Her parents smile as she bangs on it. She almost laughs now as she wonders whether a few days later they were still smiling, or whether they regretted bringing all that noise into their home.

The footfalls cross the hallway outside the apartment. The front door opens. She locks her box of memories, closes her eyes tight, then opens them wide. She's not in Russia. She's in the United States. Spokane, Washington, in a shitty apartment just off East Sprague. The door slams shut. She hears Viktor's voice, in Russian, as he shouts, "Nika, you lazy slut. Get up. It's time for work."

Kristine gets out of the car, done with her first john of the day, a regular who likes things, as he says, vigorous. She walks to the corner, sees Nika putting her pendant around her neck. That means she must have just finished a job, too: she never wears it around men.

"Hello, Kristine."

Kristine nods, smiles. "How are you doing?"

"I'm making some money."

"Viktor letting you keep any?"

"He says I'm not making enough to keep him happy."

"Fucker." Nika makes more than anyone else Kristine knows. She's what men want. She's young, blond, pretty, slender but not crack-thin. She doesn't use. She's quiet—you have to strain to hear her speak.

Kristine doesn't know much of Nika's history—the woman doesn't open up to anyone, at least to Kristine's knowledge—but she presumes from the accent and the shared apartment that Nika was part of a big shipment of women from Russia by way of Lithuania and then Amsterdam.

Kristine envies Nika. Certainly not her being so far from home, but half a world or half a continent, does it really matter? Besides, "home" was the last place Kristine would ever go again. At least here she gets money for her services.

Nor does she envy Nika's looks or figure. She knows how long they'll last. No, she envies Nika's ready access to a shower. In order for Kristine to bathe, she has to convince a john to rent a room, then afterwards take a quick shower and put on makeup before heading back out to the street. She sometimes fantasizes about a long hot bath, with soap and bubbles and bath oil in those squishy, slippery marbles that slowly dissolve. She could live in a house or apartment—and she has spent a fair amount of time in squats, though of course that doesn't solve the shower problem—but then she'd have to put up with the other women, and especially with the pimp.

Kristine asks, "How much does he say you owe by now?"

"I'll never see the end of this. The more I make, the more I owe."

"You and me both, sister."

"Who do you owe?"

"My dealer. You've got Viktor, I've got heroin."

Nika looks at her for a long moment, then to the ground.

Kristine continues, "At least the heroin makes me feel good."

"And it won't kill you if you run away."

Kristine laughs. "Oh, it will kill me all right if I try to leave. I've done that a couple of times, and it came right after me to bring me back."

Nika is silent.

Kristine says, "I don't know how you do all of this sober."

"The tricks?"

"All of it. Look around. Do you ever actually look at the people? Not just the johns. All of them. They're as dead as we are. Only we've got the sense to know it. And the cars. Do you ever notice the air? It tastes like shit. No, it doesn't. I grew up on a farm, and this smells far worse than shit."

"I grew up. . . ." Nika trails off.

Kristine doesn't look at her directly. She wants to know more about her friend, but knows if she says the wrong thing she'll scare her away. The silence stretches longer.

Finally Nika says, "In the country."

More silence. Kristine wants to ask where, what it was like, who was her family, but doesn't know where to start. So she does what she knows is best. She lets the other be.

Nika says simply, "I'm never going home."

Kristine knows better than to disagree directly. She says, "It has happened before. Some women have made it." A pause before she continues, "Do you want to go home?"

"More than. . . ."

A car slows, pulls up to the curb. It's one of Kristine's semi-regulars. Kristine says to Nika, "Fuck. I'm sorry. Maybe later?"

The man opens the passenger window, leans across, says, "Hey, Kristine, who's your pretty friend?"

Kristine senses money slipping away, and wouldn't mind if it were slipping to Nika. She would mind it going to Viktor.

Nika comes over to the car. The man looks from her face to her breasts and back to her face. He does the same to Kristine, then says, "I'd forgotten how much your shoulders turn me on. Same price? Get in."

The street is hot, and empty. No people, no cars. Nika paces back and forth, facing then going with the nonexistent traffic. She doesn't see the truck pull up next to her, and jumps a little when she hears it close by. She turns, looks at the man inside. His passenger window is already down.

She walks to his vehicle.

He says, "Would you like to party?"

"What do you have in mind?"

"Depends on the price."

"First," she says, "you've got to show me something I don't have."

The man has done this before, knows the game. Cops can't expose themselves. He unzips his pants, pulls out a nondescript penis.

She licks her lips. "Very nice," she says. *Make the sale*, she thinks.

"Well?"

"Makes me want to drop my price. For you I'll do a blow for twenty-five, a lay for fifty, half and half for sixty, and for a hundred you get me for an hour."

"That's a discount?"

"That's *my* discount." She pushes back from the truck.

"No, wait, here." He pulls a couple of fifty dollar bills from his shirt pocket.

She puts the money in the front left pocket of her tight shorts, pulls the pendant from her neck, puts that in the other pocket, and gets in.

The man says, "Buckle up. I don't want to get a ticket."

She does. He begins to drive. They make small talk. He asks her name. She tells him. She asks his name, and he gives her one she knows is false. He asks her other questions and she lies, too. He doesn't pull into an alley like she was expecting, but drives around, as though uncertain what he wants to do next.

Finally she says, "You'll need to pull over if you want me to do you."

The man just says, "We've got time."

She thinks, *It's your money.*

Then the man says, "Do you believe in God?"

She doesn't say anything. She tries to read what he wants, give it to him. It is safest—and makes the most money—if you give the man what he wants before he asks. But he already asked, and she doesn't know how to answer.

"Do you," he repeats, "believe in God?"

She frowns, then says, "Do you want to fuck?"

"Look," he says, "I bought you for an hour. If I want you to answer my question, you'll do it. Do you get it?"

"Yes."

"So. . . ."

She remembers that once, long ago, she did believe, and still does enough to wear her mother's cross. But that's in memory of her mother, not Jesus. And it was two years and fifty lifetimes ago that her mother gave it to her, and now both Jesus and her mother are too far away to help. She says, "Yes, I believe—"

He cuts her off. "Oh, I get it. You're afraid I'm some sort of fundy and if you say you don't believe that the Lord Jesus Christ died for you I'll spend the next hour trying to save your soul. Well, I don't believe in souls. I'm a scientist, and so it's against my religion to believe in superstitions." He laughs at his own joke, then says, "It's your body I want."

She doesn't understand his joke. She says, "Should we stop here? We can go down this alley."

He reaches with his right hand into his shirt pocket, pulls out two more bills, and says, "Instead of buying an hour I'm buying two. Let's go somewhere private."

She takes the money. "There's a hotel on North Division, just a few blocks. We can get a room."

"A room? Where other men have fucked you? And even if they didn't fuck you they fucked someone else and left their sperm on the sheets. It doesn't wash out. It leaves traces even after cleaning. Do you think I want some man's DNA all over me?"

She doesn't say anything.

"Do you?"

"Where, then?"

"South of town, a nice little park where we can get out of the car."

Again, she doesn't say anything.

"So like I was saying, I'm a scientist. I look at things from a scientific perspective. That doesn't mean I'm anti-Christian, though. That's a mistake a lot of scientists make. The truth is that science and Christianity are two sides of the same coin."

She tries to look interested. If he wants to spend his money lecturing her, she'll take the money. Maybe he'll buy her something to eat.

He continues, "Both of them are attempts to explain the universe, attempts to explain what is. They're both articulations of systems of power. They both tell us how to live, how to experience the world, how to be in the world. They tell us how to relate to each other. Do you see?"

"Yes," she says, wondering what science and what religion would cause a man to pay to fuck a woman, what science and what religion would cause another man to force a woman to have sex for money and to give that money to him. What sort of science and what sort of religion would cause people to value money over another's freedom or happiness? What sort of science and what sort of religion would cause someone to want to wield such power over another? She says none of this, shows none of this on her face. There are very few men she does not hate.

He says, "There's one line from the Bible I've always especially liked, a line that says everything we need to know about the relationship between men and women. Do you know the Bible?"

"I—" Her great-grandmother used to read the Bible to her.

She no longer remembers much of it.

"I read a lot of books. I want to know everything I can. Because knowledge is power. It really is. The more knowledge you have, the more power you have. Do you see that, too?"

"I understand," she says, but she thinks: no, power is a fist in my face, a knife at my throat, rape after rape after rape until I don't care anymore. You and your books and your science and your religion don't know anything.

He says, "There's a line from the *Malleus Maleficarum* that has always spoken to me. I don't suppose you've ever heard of that? No? Not many people have. It's the Christian response to witchcraft. You could say that's one superstition taking out another, but once again I think that's a mistake. There's a reason they burned those witches . . ."

She has no idea what he's talking about. She hates him. She hates these pompous theories that she knows will somehow—surprise—pretend to prove that men are superior to women and to everything, and that this superiority grants them the right to the lives and bodies of women. She hates all men, except her father and Petya and Osip. Listening to him drone on—no, pretending to listen to him drone—is worse than giving him a blowjob. She wishes he would shut up. It's bad enough that he wants to fuck her for money—to buy her, as he accurately put it—but she wishes he wouldn't try so hard to rationalize it. It is what it is, and he should just be honest about that.

But then he tells her the line from the *Malleus Maleficarum*, "A woman is beautiful to look upon, contaminating to the touch, and deadly to keep."

Nika doesn't understand. The man is starting to scare her. She wishes the car would slow so she could jump out. But he turns onto the on-ramp of the interstate.

He asks, "Are you happy?"

"What?"

"Are you happy?"

"I don't. . . . . That's not what most men ask."

He looks her straight in the eye: "I am not most men." He looks back to the highway. Then he says, light, casual, "Or maybe I am." A pause, then, "You're one beautiful woman, and I'm sure every man wants to have you." Another pause, then, "You have an accent, where are you from?

She hesitates, then says, "Russia."

"What makes you happy?"

"It's my job to make you happy."

"It's your job to do what I say."

She doesn't want to think about happiness. That's back in the box. No one knows about the box. No one gets into the box. She asks, "Do you want to take me in the ass? I won't make you pay extra. I like it. Just. . . ."

"I want to know where you go when a man takes you. Where do you go when you go away?"

She closes her eyes and then opens them. She thinks, *He will not get inside*. She takes a deep breath, but quietly so he can't hear, and tries to force away the answers to his questions.

They turn south off the interstate onto the Pullman Highway.

He says, "I just want to know."

But she knows that's not true. She knows what he wants. He's a liar and a thief. He doesn't want only her body. Him and his words and all his belief that knowledge is power. He wants those deep places inside no one ever touches, not that Lithuanian man Linas who broke her with his lies, beatings, rapes, not Viktor the pimp who now continues where Linas left off, not even the other girls. No one.

He doesn't say anything, and she knows why. He knows that she knows, and she can tell he likes it.

They drive. She tries not to think about the box, tries not to think about anyone back at home, all those who surely by now think she is dead.

"We're here," the man says. He turns right onto a two-lane road, then soon left onto a dirt trail that heads sharply down. He stops next to a small creek, turns off the truck. "Should we do it?"

"Where?"

He points to an opening on her right. She nods, unbuckles her seatbelt, and gets out.

He reaches behind the seat and says, "I brought something for us to put down on the grass." It's a towel, folded tightly and sealed with duct tape. He opens his door and gets out, walks to her side of the truck. He motions for her to walk ahead, then gestures before them, "Beautiful, isn't it?"

"It's nice," she says. She is concerned about being where no one can hear, but the forest just right here, the sound of the stream, reminds her of home. In the opening she sees three young apple trees. She knows apple trees from home. These trees should begin to bear good fruit this year. The trees make her smile. And the smells. They aren't like the city. Kristine was right: *How do we all survive this?*

She begins to walk down the path.

She hears him walking behind her. He says, "Did you know that the word *vagina* is Latin for sheath?"

She doesn't know the English word *sheath*. She keeps walking.

He says, "I never did tell you my favorite line from the Bible. It is from the thirty-first chapter of Numbers, where God instructed his chosen people to kill every woman who has had intercourse with a man, but spare for themselves every woman among them who has not had intercourse."

For just a moment too long she puzzles over the meaning of what he has said, and when she finally begins to understand, the last voice she hears is his, asking, "Nika, have you had intercourse with a man?"

The ground is tilting and she is trying to run but the ground is moving far too quickly. She doesn't know why the ground is tilting but the sound she heard must have been an earthquake that brings the ground up to meet her face. She sees the tan soil, the small stones, the yellow blades of dried grass and the green that lies beneath, and then she falls through all of these and into the dark inside the earth, and she sees her mother and her father and she reaches out to them as she hears her voice say inside her head, "Oh, mother, mother."

five

t h e   m u s e

I wonder if this is what it is like to be dead. I hope not, because I don't want to spend all of eternity this confused. It takes as much effort to think as it does to move my hands, to move my feet. I wonder if this is how it feels to be stupid: maybe this is why people watch sitcoms, why they vote for Democrats or Republicans, why they don't fight back: real thinking is too hard for them, so they simply don't do it. I try to say this to Allison, but it takes too much effort, so I sit. Finally I say, "I'll never be able to write like this."

I wonder if I am insane. I wonder if my brain has somehow become scrambled—and I wonder if I even think with my brain anyway—and if I will spend the rest of my life this way. I think I could do this for a day, maybe two, and then I would kill myself and hope I didn't wake up like this after I was dead.

The forest is beautiful, though, and I am glad it hasn't been clearcut. I stare at the texture of the tree in front of me, the gray and black and green of the trunk, the maze of veins, each a home to tiny spiders and to others most humans never notice. I hear a voice again, "Don't fight it."

I ask Allison if she said anything.

"No."

"Then who did?"

"I don't know, Derrick. Who did?"

I don't actually write what I write. I just write it down, then edit it. It's written by my muse. I use the word *my* not to imply ownership, but relationship, as in my friend, my partner, my lover. She—my muse is a she, though I have no idea if all muses are female—is an actual being. She's not a metaphor, a personification of my unconscious processes, or even some archetypal figure either bubbling up from my organs or the collective unconscious, or, as I've heard some new agers label it, descending from the superconscious. She's a being, like you, like me, like a salmon, like a white pine, like a ghost spider, only different. She doesn't live here, although talking about these things, it's hard sometimes to know what *here* means. So maybe I should say: except in dreams, I've only seen her once, and that, as we'll eventually get to, was because it was absolutely necessary for reasons I still don't quite understand. When I've seen her in dreams her form sometimes changes. In one she had soft features and skin the color of sweet clover honey, and her scent contained the faintest traces of mint. In another she had dark skin that shone like obsidian and had features sharp to match. I've always presumed she takes on these forms because they're easy for me to understand. I sometimes ask in dreams to see her as she is, but the dreams that follow are jumbles that make me feel as though I'm asking the wrong question.

I don't know why she chose me. I know that at the very least I have thumbs and fingers: I have a physical body and can write down what she says. But I suspect there's something more, something in my temperament. Perhaps she saw something in me the same way that even before they begin some sculptors can see their final creations in one piece of stone and not another, like I can sometimes see, with her help, the barest hints of the final shape of a book from its first sentences, or from even before, from the first inchoate ideas and chaotic thoughts and images.

Or maybe it's all so much simpler. Maybe she liked me, loved me, fell in love with me the way I have fallen in love with her, the way any lovers choose each other, fall in love with each other.

I don't know if other people—accountants, for example, or probate attorneys—have muses, although I suspect they do. I don't even know if other writers do. For their sake I hope so, because otherwise writing would be very hard work. Learning how to listen to one's lover is ever so much easier and more fun than trying to do all the work of creation by oneself. It's also less lonely.

I know that Allison has a muse, and that her relationship with her muse is as central to her life as mine is to mine. It's not too much to say that I'm married to my muse, or connected by some bond even tighter and more lasting, and that Allison is married to hers. Neither Allison nor I are jealous of the other's marriage, nor could either of us be in a relationship with anyone who was.

I don't know where these muses live. I sometimes call it the "other side," but that's a shorthand both inaccurate and inadequate in every possible way. This "other side" is both here and there. Where and what is the division? How many sides are there? Do Allison's muse and mine necessarily come from the same place, the same side?

I know my muse has no body, at least here. I know she can go where I go. She may be other places at the same time, or she may not. I don't know, and it's kind of off the point. I know what she does for me, and what I do for her.

The relationship is deeply sexual. It has been from the beginning. It's no coincidence that my sexuality and my writing burgeoned simultaneously. Never mind that my sexuality was at the time almost exclusively solo: not many people read my writing then either. The muse was simply teaching me to listen. Or perhaps helping me to remember how to listen. Or maybe teaching me to trust what I heard and what I already knew.

I don't know, once again, if all relationships with muses are this imbued with sexuality. I once asked Allison if her relationship with her muse was this sexual.

She said, "Oh, yes."

I found this especially interesting since Allison's muse is also female, and Allison is neither lesbian, bisexual, nor even slightly bi-curious. I asked her about this.

"That's because this culture's definitions of sexuality are way too small. Sex isn't just limited to your genitals. How many times have you made love with a tree?"

"Sometimes that's involved genitals."

"And sometimes it hasn't. And what about those times you've made love with the stars?"

"Those all involved—"

"Oh, good point. But you see what I'm saying."

Of course I did.

I think one reason that making love makes me so receptive to the muse is that the muse enjoys making love as much as I do. Sometimes I think that just as the muse uses my fingers to write through me and my voice to give talks through me, that she uses my body to make love through me. It's the same with Allison, so that in a very real way when we make love not only the two of us are present. When Allison is around me, pushing toward me, I sometimes feel not just her, but her muse as well. I feel her muse in the small of her back, and in the places deep inside. I feel her against my fingertips when I hold my hands so close to Allison's chest I feel her warmth but not her skin. And as we get closer and closer, so closer too come our muses.

This is how it has always been with us.

Years ago I had the opportunity to sell out, and didn't do it. I had only a couple of books out, but I had an agent at a prestigious literary agency. I sent her the first seventy pages of the manuscript that eventually became *A Language Older Than Words*. She hated the book, and told me to tone down my anger at the culture to make the book more palatable to fencesitters, and thus to allow me to reach a larger audience and to make more money. She told me that if I took out the family stuff and the social criticism then I would have a book. She would not be comfortable shopping the book, she said, unless I made it less radical, less militant. If I did, she said, she felt sure it would become a bestseller.

I fired her on the spot.

I'm certain that's one reason my muse responds so quickly to me, and gives me so many words. I proved to her in action that the words and books she gives me—what she wants to communicate—are more important to me than fame, money, or any common measure of success. I proved to her that our relationship is more important to me than any of these. I proved to her that *she* is more important to me than any of these.

Another reason my muse works so quickly is that she is

scared of the destructiveness of the dominant culture. That might be why she chose me: I feel the same fear, the same urgency. She knows she can ride me as hard and as fast as she herself can go, and I will do my best, give my life, to keep up.

I know she is scared because she tells me, and she shows me. And who wouldn't be, faced with this culture?

I used to think my relationship with my muse was one-sided, in that she gives me words and I give her little more than gratitude. But now I know that this is not so. The relationship is mutual, like my relationship with the land where I live, like my relationship with Allison, like my relationships with others in my life. I know this because she tells me, and she shows me. She—like all these others—lets me know that non-mutual relationships aren't relationships at all.

I am asleep.

Before sleeping I asked the muse what I do for her, what I give her more than gratitude.

I am asleep.

An indigenous man is teaching me how to pray. Then he turns into a woman who writes poems to me. After she writes these poems we make love again and again.

Soon, though, a homeless man starts attacking other homeless people, and then they all begin attacking people in this village. When villagers are attacked by these homeless ones, they too become homeless, they too begin to attack others. All of these people begin to take drugs.

I am asleep.

The remaining community members begin to look for the homeless person who started all of this. I join them. Many carry weapons. I carry water.

I am asleep.

The woman—my lover, my muse—begins to look for the cause of these troubles. But then she stops and complains to the gods that she no longer has a lover. She wants a lover. She has always had a lover. That is part of life. The gods tell her that they will point one out to her.

I am asleep.

We are all by now wearing prison uniforms. We are all by now using drugs to quench our pain. I find the person who began all this.

I am asleep.

But not for long. My cat jumps on the sill above the bed. Those who write of cats' gracefulness have never had a cat knock books off a windowsill onto their head in the middle of the night. I wake up understanding what I give back to those on the other side. I am a willing student of their prayers. I am a willing intimate partner. I am a part of a community searching for what is destroying our lives. I help to point out the violent homeless person who started it all, which means we have at least the possibility of dropping our addictions and our prison garb, and going back to what we were doing before, back to making love.

The muse gives me the words, but I write them down.

I had a problem. It seemed clear to me from the dream and also from the muse's urgency, that this culture is not only destroying life on this planet, but is also harming life on the "other side," with the caveat as always that I don't know what I mean when I say the "other side." I asked some Indian elders if this culture is as catastrophic for the other side as it is for this one.

They said, "No, the dominant culture is not powerful enough to reach over there. Do not grant it more power than it actually has."

I'm sure you can see my problem. I believed what these elders told me. And I believed my muse. How could I bring together these different truths into one overarching interpretation?

I got the answer from a piece of carved wood on an elder's coffee table: an orca intertwined with a sea lion intertwined with a salmon. Each melded into the others until it wasn't possible to tell where one became the other became the other. It represented, she said, the way none can be defined without the others, the way none can survive without the others.

It came clear to me that the same is true for the other sides as well. Yes, there are places the dominant culture cannot reach—the muse was appealing to the gods for a lover, which implies layers even further than hers from our everyday world of trees and spiders and soil and cats on our laps, and implies as well that these gods are beyond the reach of these homeless, rootless, attackers—but in no way is this geography as simple as here and there, one side and the other. There are layers, and there are spaces, and there are complex intertwinings so complex that sometimes we aren't sure where one ends and another begins. Some places may be affected by this destructive culture, and some may not. And some may be affected in ways we could never predict, even if we were able to begin to understand.

The elder told me that the sculpture is not only about animals but also about time.

I told her I didn't understand.

She didn't say anything, but merely moved her hands in small circles, each around the other.

I want to speak to the director. I want to understand what that dream—that visitation—was about. Who are the vampires, the demons? Where are they from? Are they real, or are they symbols representing something else?

I ask for a dream. One comes. I'm standing in line to use a lavatory. Even while I sleep, even while I dream, this encourages me. I know the landscape of my dreams—the language used between us by those who give me these dreams—well enough to know that for us toilets mean a connection to the unconscious and a connection beyond that to places even deeper. You flush the toilet, and where does everything go? Down through pipes into a whole other world, a world of digestion and decomposition. A world of remaking and re-constitution. A world with dripping, flowing, moving water. A world most of us never see, most of us never think about.

The line is long, and slowly I make my way to the front. Finally I am first. I open the door, step through. I'm inside a bare room: concrete floor, brick walls, dark wood ceiling. There are no toilets. There is no plumbing. There is absolutely nothing in the room. I turn, open the door, and leave.

The message was clear. I do not ask to speak with the director. To do so is to face a brick wall. If the director has something to say, the director will contact me.

Sitting here against this tree I try to not fight it. It's very hard. I feel the slender silver thread that is the only thing that connects me to everything I've known. I feel its delicacy, and I begin to know that if it snaps, I will never return.

"Don't fight it," the voice keeps saying.

I see Allison sitting beside me, looking at me intently. I look beyond her to the forest I know is no longer a forest, to the shadows and to the sunlight who never strike the ground and to the ground who never feels the sunlight, the ground who never wants to feel the sunlight. I see the green leaves, and I see the tan patches of normal disease or fungus: life feeding off life. I see the remains of old trees softening, crumbling. I see someone's scat, and the mold growing on this scat. I see soft mosses at the base of trees. Despite my fear I see the beauty of all of this, and I see the bare movement of needles in a breeze I cannot feel, the scurrying of large-bodied, small-headed beetles with beautiful black backs. I see small brown birds who hop from place to place on two legs. I see tiny plants and fungi. I see ants and spiders going about their days. I see so many lives I would normally never notice.

I hear Allison say, "I'm right here."

I take a deep breath, feel for that silver thread, and let myself fall just a little bit deeper.

six

Wétikos

◉

I don't know about you, but when I catch a cold, I get psychologically down. It sinks into my experience. I get a little bit crabby. I don't deal with that stress very well. The virus infects my spirit as well as my body. I guess what I'm saying is that if my body is sick, my brain changes. So it would make sense that if I have a spiritual sickness, my brain and my body are apt to change as well.

Why are the only epidemics that we recognize physical? I think it's because we take such great pains to keep our physical and spiritual selves apart. It's crazy that people devastated by physical illness receive all kinds of support—or at least some of them do—while those who become desperately sick mentally or emotionally most often do not. In regular hospitals, patients get flowers and people come to visit. Mental hospital inmates are shamed.

Physical illness I can see and measure and diagnose. So because I feel I can understand it, I can respect it. But because we don't know how to understand mental illness we pretend it doesn't exist, and we shut the ill into mental hospitals far away. Even if they're not physically far away, they are far away from our hearts and our minds.

How much moreso, then, do we fail to acknowledge any disease of the soul? There is a cannibal sickness, which is a sickness just like any other plague or epidemic, highly contagious, with physical vectors, spread by contact, by air, by water, by touch, even also by spoken or written word—spread till it now covers the earth and to a greater or lesser degree infects us all. There are no hospitals for this sickness. If we cannot acknowledge it, how can we attempt to cure it?

Of course I'd heard about rabies from when I was a small child: everyone who has ever bawled through the end of Old Yeller knows that any beloved pet who contracts the disease turns into a vicious monster frothing at the mouth and lunging at anyone who comes too near, and everyone who lives in the country knows that the fear of rabies is why you never pick up injured rodents.

But the implications of rabies didn't hit me until my twelfth year, and to this day I remember where I was and what I was doing when the central question of rabies struck me. I was sitting on a wood bench on our deck on a hot summer day, holding an encyclopedia and thinking about the ground squirrel who had gotten stuck in our garage the day before. I'd caught her and put her in a cage, because that's what I'd been taught you do with wild animals unfortunate enough to come in contact with you: you turn them into "pets," whether they want that or not. Fortunately the cage was rickety, and overnight the ground squirrel escaped.

I wasn't thinking about the ground squirrel's bad fortune of encountering me or her good fortune of the cage being old. I wasn't even feeling guilty or bad for caging her in the first place: the understanding that an other has a life of her own, and is not here solely for my use, didn't come to me until a bit later: I'm grateful it's come at all, since the same cannot be said for most people in this culture. Instead I was thinking about the heavy gloves I'd worn to keep her teeth away from my skin, and I was thinking about how gentle ground squirrels seem most of the time, but how she had scratched and bit when I grabbed her. I understood her fighting back, and certainly respected it. But I didn't, once again, yet take that understanding to the next level, that her fighting against being put in a cage was her telling me she didn't want to be caged, and that for that reason alone I should let her be. I didn't, in short, empathize with her. I know we've all been told that children naturally feel a connection to others, and I'm sure that's true, but I know that by the time I was seven, eight, nine, and ten this connection had at the very least been deeply frayed, and it took years of seeing others suffer as a consequence of my actions—or more precisely seeing the external trappings of their suffering, but not actually seeing their suffering at all—before it even occurred to me what I was doing. At that point I began the slow process of reweaving the braided connection between me and others.

The squirrel trying to bite me made me think of animals acting in ways you wouldn't normally expect, and that made me think of *Old Yeller*. That made me suddenly curious about how rabies works and sent me to the encyclopedia, which I brought onto the deck. Rabies, I learned, was a virus passed from creature to creature by saliva (this latter I knew from the book and movie). Creature A has rabies, and bites creature B, or less frequently, slobbers on creature B. The important thing is that viruses in creature A's saliva enter creature B. The viruses move quickly into B's nerves, and from there they inhabit B's spinal column and brain. Creature B will not show symptoms for a few weeks or even a few months. But once the viruses reach the brain, they reproduce rapidly, and soon inhabit the salivary glands. By now creature B will show signs of illness. In humans—and we've no reason to believe anything else for nonhumans—these include headaches, fever, irritability, restlessness, and anxiety. Within days these symptoms progress to cerebral dysfunction, anxiety, confusion, and agitation, leading to delirium, abnormal behavior, hallucinations, and insomnia. All of this is accompanied by muscle pains, salivation, and vomiting. At that point symptoms diverge into two distinct classes. In what's called "dumb rabies," creature B retreats steadily and quietly downhill, with some paralysis, to death. In what's called "furious rabies"—and this is what Old Yeller had—the creature begins to experience extreme excitement and is hit by painful muscle spasms, sometimes triggered by swallowing saliva or water. Because of this the creature drools and learns to fear water—thus the frequent references to rabid creatures being hydrophobic. The creature will also become extremely sensitive to air blown on the face. But there's more. During that final furious phase, the creature may, without provocation, vigorously and viciously bite at anything: sticks, stones, grass, other animals. This stage lasts only a few days before the creature enters a coma and dies. Once infected, death from the disease is almost invariable.

I remember at that point putting down the encyclopedia, leaning against the deck railing, and staring at the light blue sky above the brown and gray and smoky blue and white of the distant Rocky Mountains, and I remember thinking about volition, free will. Of course I didn't use that language—I was precocious, but volition would certainly not yet have been part of my everyday vocabulary—and I couldn't have clearly articulated any of this, but I got it. I understood—or rather asked, which is almost always more important than understanding anyway—"Who's in charge? Who is actually doing the biting? Is it Old Yeller, or is it the virus?"

The virus knows that if it is to survive the death of its host, it needs to find a new host, which means it needs to get Old Yeller to slobber on or bite someone. Thus the painful spasms on swallowing and the excessive salivation, which combine to lead to the drooling. Thus the furious biting.

In some ways central to this discussion is the question of whether you perceive the world as full of intelligence, and so do not hesitate at the possibility of viruses knowing, viruses choosing; or whether you believe viruses act entirely unthinkingly, mechanistically, and so at most you'll allow viruses not to know, but to "know" that they need to find a new host. But in some ways that question doesn't matter at all, because in either case the viruses cause Old Yeller to change his personality, his behavior toward those he loves. Or perhaps loved.

The central point of R.D. Laing's extraordinary book *The Politics of Experience* was that most of us act in ways that make internal sense: we act according to how we experience the world. If, for example, I experience the world as full of wildly varied and exciting intelligences with whom I can enter into relationships I will act one way. If I experience the world as unthinking, mechanistic, and composed of objects for me to use, I will act another.

Clearly the virus changes its host's experience, at the very least by causing pain and hallucinations.

Now here's the question that struck me so hard on that hot summer afternoon: as Old Yeller snarls and snaps at those he so recently protected, what is he thinking? If I could ask in a language he could understand, and if he could answer in a language that I, too, could understand, what would he say? Is he terrified at this awful pain, and is he, because of that pain, lashing out at everyone around him? Is he confused? Is he asking where this pain comes from?

Or does he have his behavior fully rationalized? Has he—or the virus—created belief systems to support this behavior? Is he suddenly furious at the thousand insults large and small he has received from those who call themselves his masters? Certainly throughout the movie the humans—especially his "owner" Travis—have treated him as despicably as we would expect within this culture (where do you think I learned to mistreat animals?). Does he perceive himself as suddenly seeing things clearly, and as hating these others and all they stand for?

Or is he delusional, snapping not at Travis standing in front of him, but instead protecting him as he did before and biting at the rabid wolf who gave him the disease? Is he seeing phantoms dancing before him, just out of reach, so each time he lunges, it is at someone who is not there at all?

Or maybe Old Yeller fights with every bit of his emotional strength to not lash out at the humans who are his whole world, these humans for whom he has already many times offered his life. Maybe he feels like he has picked up some sort of addiction, a compulsion, and he just can't help himself.

Or maybe the virus has insinuated itself into his brain in such a way that Old Yeller now perceives the virus as God.

He hears its commands, and knows he must obey. Maybe this God tells him that he must convert these others to this one true religion, and that in doing so both he and they will achieve everlasting peace and joy—and a release from the torment of this world. Maybe he perceives himself as thus giving these others a gift.

We act according to the way we experience the world. The virus changed Old Yeller's experience of the world. When Old Yeller acts—or when any of us act—who's in charge? Who actually makes the decisions? Why does Old Yeller act as he does? Why do any of us act as we do?

I always thank my muse after she enters me and gives me her words. Sometimes I ask her what she wants. Sometimes she tells me. Sometimes I don't understand. Sometimes I do.

I am asleep. I am dreaming.

I am standing on a lawn holding a heavy mallet. Have you ever seen or played the arcade game Whack-A-Mole? In this game you stand in front of a large grid with holes in it, holding a plastic hammer. Plastic "moles" pop up from random holes, and your goal is to whack them as quickly as you can. As the game progresses they pop up faster and faster. This is what I dream, except that instead of moles popping up, it is men in business suits, it is politicians, it is CEOs, it is scientists. As fast as they pop up I hit them with my mallet, which in the dream is not plastic, but solid wood. I hear my muse's voice, soft, a whisper in my ear, "Keep smashing cannibals. Keep on smashing them."

I wake up laughing. I've had this dream many times before. At first I didn't understand it, but now I do.

The morning after our third night together, Allison introduces me to Jack Forbes.

We're in her bedroom. I wake up laughing from my dream

of smashing cannibals. At this point I've had the dream only a few times, and I don't yet understand it. I tell it to Allison. She doesn't laugh. She doesn't say a word. She holds up one finger, gently taps my hand, and gets out of bed. I look at her long legs beneath the t-shirt she'd worn to sleep. I like what I see. She leaves the room, then returns a few moments later, holding a slender, brightly-colored book. She gets back in bed. Finally she speaks. "Your dream made me think of this." The book is *Columbus and Other Cannibals*, by Jack Forbes. "This book blew apart my world. Forbes really filled in some holes for me."

I move closer. "I like filling in holes for you."

She's on her stomach. She smiles and shifts her weight so her left thigh pushes against me. "I like you filling in holes for me. As often as possible."

I push back. "And?"

"And what?"

"Forbes?"

She rolls to face me. Her knee touches mine. "His take on the dominant culture's destructiveness is different than anything else I've seen. The problem, he says, isn't merely that this culture socially rewards destructive behavior—the acquisition of wealth, for example, at the expense of the community or landbase—or that it creates greedy, traumatized, unrelational people through childrearing practices, schooling, and so on. . . ."

"Although both of those are true."

"Absolutely."

That single word—*absolutely*, and all it implies—makes me move closer still. The skin on the front of her thighs is soft against mine.

She continues, "The problem is a disease that causes people to consume the souls of others, a spiritual illness with a physical vector."

I nod, push in closer still. My hand rests on her hip.

"Reading Forbes made the complete insanity of the dominant culture more comprehensible to me. I mean, saying that people are merely greedy just doesn't cut it. What's the use of retiring rich on a planet being killed?"

"So you're saying the behavior makes more sense when you see it as a symptom of a disease."

"If I have the flu and I cough, and the little germies float through the air and happen to land in your mouth, and if those germs survive and reproduce inside of you. . . ."

"You shouldn't use the word *inside* around me. You'll distract me."

"You shouldn't use the phrase *around me* around me. Besides, you'll be there soon, if I have anything to say about it."

"You do."

"If those germs survive then you might get the flu. You might start coughing, get a fever, chills. Well, if I have the cannibal sickness and I cough and you pick up the germs, you might turn into a cannibal, too. You'll begin to consume the souls of others."

"I'll become a capitalist."

She catches her breath and smiles. She says, "I can't believe. . . ."

"What?"

"You."

"What?"

She puts her lips together for a moment before she says, "Bingo. You become a member of this culture."

Seriously now, is it even remotely possible for life to get better than to be lying next to a beautiful, intelligent woman who's wearing nothing but a t-shirt that reads, "Every time a developer dies an angel gets her wings," with whom you're having a conversation about things that matter?

Evidently it is, because she begins to read to me. She holds the book in her left hand, making certain to never let it come between our faces. "'Many people have examined the subjects of aggression, violence, imperialism, rape, and so on. I propose to do something a little different: first, I propose to examine these things from a Native American perspective; and second, from a perspective as free as possible from assumptions created by the very disease being studied. Finally, I will look at these evils, not simply as "bad" choices that men make, but as a genuine, very real epidemic sickness. Imperialists, rapists, and exploiters are not just people who have strayed down a wrong path. They are insane (unclean) in the true sense of that word. They are mentally ill, and, tragically, the form of soul-sickness that they carry is catching.'"

"So it's not a metaphor."

"Not on your life."

"And it strikes me," I say, "that just like germs grow well in certain physical environments and not so well in others, that certain social environments will make conditions ripe for irruptions of the cannibal sickness, too."

Another sharp breath, another smile.

"What?" I ask again.

She blushes, looks at the book, blinks twice, flips through the pages, and reads again, sometimes pausing to look at me, not for emphasis, but just to look. "'The *wétiko* disease, the sickness of exploitation, has been spreading as a contagion for the past several thousand years. And as a contagion unchecked by most vaccines it tends to become worse rather than better with time. More and more people catch it, in more and more places; they become the true teachers of the young.'"

I look into her eyes. "This is really good."

"Do you want me to keep going?"

"God, yes."

"Do you think I'm overdressed?"

"God, yes."

She removes her shirt. Her breasts are small, perfect. Her skin is pale. I touch small moles and freckles with my fingertips. She shivers, smiles, says, "I'm so happy."

"Me, too."

"Now," she says, "back to the apocalypse: 'It is very sad, but the "heroes" of European historiography, the heroes of the history books, are usually imperialists, butchers, founders of authoritarian regimes, exploiters of the poor, liars, cheats, and torturers. What this means is that the *wétiko* disease has so corrupted European thinking (at least of the ruling groups) that *wétiko* behavior and *wétiko* goals are regarded as the very fabric of European evolution. Thus, those who resist *wétiko* values and imperialism and exploitation . . . are regarded as "quirks," "freaks" . . . who could never exploit enough people to build a St. Peter's Cathedral or a Versailles palace.'"

She's still on her right side. I say, "Do you mind?" and then I gently push on her left shoulder. She follows my lead and lays back. I slide slightly down, and over, to gently kiss the flat space between her breasts.

Her answer is a soft, inarticulate sound. I feel her shift as she puts down the book.

"Oh, don't stop," I say. "More."

As she reads, I focus on what she's saying, and also on the taste and texture of her skin. I feel her belly against my chest, her thigh against my belly. I open my eyes, see the movement of her blood in the soft space just below her sternum. I hear her voice, "'We must keep all this in mind because if we continue to allow the *wétikos* to define reality in their insane way we will never be able to resist or curtail the disease.'"

She stops, takes a deep breath, then continues, "'I believe that this form of insanity originated long ago in several places, but principally in Egypt and Mesopotamia. Subsequently it appeared in India and northern China and much later in Mexico and Peru.'"

I move down, small kisses below her rib cage.

"'To a considerable degree the development of the *wétiko* disease corresponds to the rise of what Europeans choose to call "civilization." This is no coincidence.'"

I turn my face sideways, rest my head on her belly. "No coincidence at all."

"'Over and over again we see European writers ranking as "high civilizations" societies with large slave populations, rigid social class systems, unethical or ruthless rulers, and aggressive imperialistic foreign policies. Conversely, societies with no slaves, no distinct social classes, no rulers, and no imperialism are either regarded as insignificant (not worth mentioning) or primitive and uncivilized.'"

I begin to kiss her again, and again move slightly down, then down farther, then farther still. She rises to meet me.

I hear Allison flipping pages, then I hear her voice again, slower now, as though she's having a hard time concentrating, "'The overriding characteristic of the *wétiko* is that he consumes other human beings, that is, he is a cannibal. This is the central essence of the disease. In other respects, however, the motivation for and forms of the cannibalism may vary. . . .

I pull slightly away, stop what I'm doing. "Yes," I say.

"Yes," she says. "Don't stop."

I start again to softly suck.

Her voice, slower still, "'The *wétiko* psychosis is a very contagious and rapidly-spreading disease. It is spread by the *wétikos* themselves as they recruit or corrupt others. It is spread today by history books, television, military training programs, police training programs, comic books, pornographic magazines, films, right-wing movements, fanatics of various kinds, high-pressure missionary groups, and numerous governments.'" She turns the page. Then, "'Native people have almost always understood that many Europeans were *wétiko*, were insane.'"

I lift up slightly again, say, "Most nonhumans know that, too."

"Yes," she says.

I begin again.

"No," she says.

I stop.

"Look at me."

I do. I like what I see.

She laughs. "No, up here, at my face."

I do. I still like what I see.

"I can't tell you how nice it is not to have to pretend with you."

I shake my head, the barest movement.

"I don't have to pretend I'm not as smart as I am so you won't find me intimidating. I don't have to pretend I don't hate this culture so you won't think me crazy. And I don't have to pretend I want you, because I really do. All of me. I'm not divided: brain here, body there; body here, brain there. I'm all here. No hesitation."

I smile.

She says, "You help me remember I'm an animal."

I keep smiling. I don't say anything.

She doesn't either. We just look at each other. Finally she says, "I didn't mean to interrupt. . . ."

"Interrupt away," I say. "We've got plenty of time."

seven

beauty

I remember the first time I told Allison she was beautiful. She shook her head, and said, "No, no. Don't go there."

I wasn't sure what I'd said. I apologized anyway, to be safe.

"Oh, no. I'm the one who's sorry. Thank you. That's nice. I just have a hard time engaging with the whole concept of beauty. It seems so random, with all the eye of the beholder stuff, and with what's considered good-looking in one era being the next era's horror."

"What does that matter? I think you're beautiful, isn't that enough?"

"It matters because of how much beauty standards hurt women. I know how much they hurt me, and I basically fit, more or less, into acceptable."

"Acceptable? Look in the mirror."

"Thank you, but if I grant a category called 'beautiful' then that means that some of us are left out, and what if it's me who's left out?"

"Well, you're not."

"But what if I were?"

"Look, you're an amazing painter. That leaves some people out. You're really smart. That leaves some people out. You understand that civilization is killing the planet. That leaves some people out. You're attracted to me. That leaves some people out."

"Not many."

"You're sweet, but why do you get to say it and I don't?"

"Because you're a man and you don't have to carry six thousand years of patriarchal pressure on having the overwhelming majority of your worth be determined by whether men deem you fuckable based on how pleasing you are for them to look at. And so far as the painting and intelligence and understanding, those are all things I've worked at, that I've tried to develop in myself. In contrast, I was born with a certain physical appearance and there's only so much I can do about that, for better or worse."

"You were born smarter than other people, too, and more talented. Those were gifts that were given to you."

"But I developed them, and besides, they aren't based on a several thousand year history of abuse that comes from a power relationship of male watcher and female object to be judged. Women's intelligence and artistic abilities have not so often been used against them, but beauty is constantly used as a weapon to render women self-hating and ashamed."

"I'm sorry."

"Here's my experience: you say something nice about my physical appearance and I'm immediately outside my body, imaging it, not being it. And of course I don't measure up. My breasts are too small. . . ."

"They're perfect."

"Thank you. But I've been told they're too small ever since I had breasts."

"Anybody who would say your breasts are too small doesn't deserve to see them."

"It's not just men. It's advertisements. It's movies. It's television programs with large-breasted women looking happy. It's a constant barrage of propaganda telling us what we should look like. We all compare ourselves to these standards reached by one-tenth of one percent of women, and them only after they've had surgery and been airbrushed. And even if you ask *those* women they'll say, 'No, I'm not happy with my body.' Your comments right now get weighed against years of conditioning that go exactly opposite to what you're saying."

"I still think your breasts are perfect."

"Thank you. But then it's this sort of nerve-wracking push-pull of: I want the nice thing to be true, but it's not true, and you're going to realize any second that you were wrong, and then it will be really humiliating. And even if you're right, lots of women are left out by this standard, and their lives are very pained because of it. I don't want what I look like to matter. I want every woman to be loved for who she is, not for what she looks like."

"And what she looks like is *part* of who she is, just as her intelligence is, her politics are, her grace is, her outrage is, and so on. To only care about your mind and not your body is just as patriarchal as to care only about your body and not your mind. It's the same split, only the other half. That's why Christianity and pornography are two sides of the same coin. One wants the soul and not the body; the other wants the body and not the soul."

She thought a moment, then said, "I can see that."

"A desire to be close to beauty is not just a product of patriarchy. Everybody—human and nonhuman alike—has a sense of aesthetics. Why else do you think nature is so beautiful? The problem is not in wanting to be close to beauty, but in wanting to consume it."

"To possess it. To own it. The cannibal sickness."

Another silence, then I said, "I want to tell you a story, about beauty, and about sex."

"Okay," she said, a little hesitant.

"It's a groupie story."

"About you?" Her voice became colder. "Do I want to hear it?"

"Don't worry. It has a happy ending."

"What does that mean?"

"Trust me. It won't make you feel bad."

"Okay."

"I've never done the casual sex thing. It's just never interested me, and frankly I've never understood it. I remember I was at a friend's wedding several years ago, and I didn't know anyone there except my friend. I'm just standing around beforehand and this woman comes up and stands next to me. We introduce ourselves, and then there's this silence. So I ask, 'Who are you?'

"She says, 'What do you mean?'

"I say, 'Who are you? What do you love? What's important to you?'

"She says, 'You don't ask that question.' What she doesn't say, but I can read on her face, is, 'Nobody asks those questions of me. I don't even ask them of me.' Then she shakes her head and stalks off, clearly disgusted. I didn't take any of this personally: it's just that if she and I were going to talk, I wanted to talk about something real; I wanted to know who she was. Anyway, I later learned that that night she got drunk and had sex with—I guess fucked would be the more accurate term—some guy she met that day. The whole thing kind of confused me, because I couldn't understand how someone could find even the most basic conversational intimacy threatening, yet be prepared to take another person into her body."

"That reminds me," Allison said, "of something I read a few years ago. It was an anarchist analysis of sexual behavior of college students. It seemed so true that I've never forgotten it: 'Sexual activity, long repressed, is now tolerated within the context of relationships which could only be described as masturbatory. If it had any meaning, if it opened up new realms of communication, sex would be a force antagonistic to schooling—instead it is a safety valve.'"

"Of course that applies to more than college students."

"And of course it applies to more than schooling. We can just change one word and that last sentence still works: 'If it had any meaning, if it opened up new realms of communication, sex would be a force antagonistic to civilization—instead it is a safety valve.'"

I'm sure you can see why I fell in love with her.

She said, "But you haven't said anything about groupies yet."

"I'd been told before I went on my first book tour that I might encounter groupies. My feelings about casual sex notwithstanding, I didn't want to prejudge. I wanted to remain open to finding out what I really thought about all of this—and once again, Allison, don't worry, it all ends up cool. So the first night on the first tour I end up talking after my gig with this amazing activist who spent a lot of the seventies underground as a violent revolutionary. We have a great conversation that lasted till three or four. It would have been inappropriate for the conversation to turn sexual for any number of reasons, not the least of which is that she's a lesbian. But there were other reasons, too. I go to the next town, do the noon gig, then sleep till evening. That night I had another talk, and then afterwards I am scheduled to do an interview at a pirate radio station. I'd spoken with the people who would be interviewing me, and I knew the conversation would be good. Well, that night at my talk there was a woman sitting in the front row who is one of the most beautiful women I've ever seen. I'd say she's about one five-hundredth as beautiful as you, which should let you know how gorgeous she was. She was as beautiful as a tree or rock or bird. She was just blessed that way, as you are. She spends the whole talk giving me *the look*, and afterwards I announce to the crowd that I am hungry, and ask if anyone would like to go with me to get something to eat. She is the only one who sticks around. But I have the interview, so I call the station to get directions—because it's a pirate station they don't give out directions beforehand. No one answers. We go to dinner, and it takes about ten minutes for the conversation to devolve to, 'What's your favorite movie?' Hers is 'that classic, *Top Gun*.' She is still very interested in me. So I had a stark choice: I could either have sex with a physically beautiful woman with whom I had no interest in having a conversation, or I could have a great conversation about things that matter with the people at the radio station."

"And?"

"I went to the payphone and called the station. They answered and I got directions. I realized that night that the important thing to me is not and has never been sex. The important thing to me is the conversation, and if it's appropriate for our bodies to enter the conversation, as it has been for yours and mine, so much the better. I don't want you because you are beautiful. I want you because of who you are, which includes but is certainly not limited to your beauty."

"I realized long ago," Allison said, "that I could never make love with anyone who didn't understand that the dominant culture is killing the planet, or with someone who couldn't make love with trees, rivers, stars."

Years later, long after I learned about Jack Shoemaker, long after I experienced first-hand what he does, long after what he did to Allison, to me, to others, long after I learned about Nika, I learned also that Jack had said to Nika much the same thing I'd said to the woman at the wedding, and Nika had given him much the same response. For some reason—I think because the horrors I'd seen and experienced were too large, and even years later still too raw, for me to allow myself to fully feel—the parallel behavior shared by Jack and me tore me up inside. My horror at that seeming similarity became a stand-in for those other, stronger feelings. I wanted, for obvious reasons, to have nothing in common with him. I felt dirty, and for a time I couldn't bring myself to ask people who they were, what they loved, or what made them happy. It felt as though there was something wrong in this simple act of communication and inter-est, something intrusive. That feeling lasted maybe a year. Still later, though, I realized that there was something else going on here, some-thing central to the workings of this culture, something central to the workings of the entire cannibal sickness.

The room is barely lit. The woman lies on a metal table. Her hands and feet are cuffed to the table's legs. She feels plastic beneath her. She has been here a long time. She says to the silhouette of the man standing at the foot of the table, "You don't have to do any of this. I will give you sex."

"Do you think this is about sex, Nika? You don't understand anything. It's not about sex at all."

"I love you."

"Say it again."

"I love you."

Silence.

"I want you."

Silence.

"More than I've ever wanted anyone. I've never even *wanted* anyone before. I want you more than life itself."

Silence.

"I am yours, to use however you want."

A warmth in the groin.

"I want you to use me."

Not a pressure yet, but soon. Soon.

"Because you are powerful. Because you are a *man*. Not like other men. A real man."

A swelling.

"I was nothing before you."

More.

"You saved me from myself."

Hard, harder, hard as steel. A steel rod.

"You," she hesitates, then repeats her last sentence, "you saved me from myself. You saved me from the, um, horror that was—"

He slams his hand down on the table. "No! You *never* get that right. It's 'You saved me from the chaos of life, the horror of who I was. You are the only man for me.'"

"I'm sorry, I'm sorry."

Silence.

"Don't," she says.

The warmth, the steel, the pleasure, the calm, everything is gone. "You've ruined everything, Nika."

"Please don't."

Allison says, "I lied to you."

"Okay." Noncommittal.

"Or not so much lied as told only part of the truth."

I wait.

"Because I *am* attractive, and because that has cost me dearly, not only because I want to be noticed—and for some fucked up reason I want to be noticed even by those I don't want to notice me—but far more because of what it has cost me when I *am* noticed. Do you have any idea what it's like to be hired for a job, and then not to know whether you were chosen because of your talent or your looks? And to want so desperately to have someone recognize your talent—because you're a young artist, and still developing, and like any young person needing the strokes of your elders—only to lose that position when there are certain positions—as in legs spread—you won't assume? And to have that happen not once, not twice, but again and again? To have boss after boss after boss presume that his position of authority carries with it rights of sexual access? And to say No, and No, and No, and No, and to have those unheard so many times that you just get tired and your Nos turns into Maybes, which is all the encouragement they need to keep pressing, pressing, pressing? To have a landlord tell you that you can forget about the rent if only you. . . . And so you move, and the next landlord says the same, and the landlord after that. Where do you move to get away from the attention? Maybe that means you shouldn't rent. But when you find some land you want to buy, the realtor suggests that instead of getting a mortgage you find a sugar daddy to take care of it for you. I'm not making this up. 'Use your assets,' he said, looking me up and down. Not that it matters, but I was already an established artist by this time, and taking home more than he did: even by the wretched capitalist valuation system I was 'worth more' than him, not even including my orifices. Can you imagine what it's like to not even be able to stand in line at a grocery store without men telling you they wish they had X-ray glasses? To not go *anywhere* without men looking at you, undressing you, telling you what they want to do to you. I know that men feel entitled to the bodies not only of women they perceive as attractive, but to the bodies of all women—more or less all of my women friends have been sexually assaulted at least once if not more—but there's an added danger to being conspicuous."

"I'm really sorry."

Neither of us says anything for the longest time.

Finally I ask, "What can I do? How can I help?"

More silence. It stretches. Allison doesn't look at me, and I look away, too. At the edge of my vision I see her chest rise and fall with each breath.

She takes air in, holds it, then says in measured syllables, "I'm still lying to you."

I know enough to wait. I still look away. After a time I look at her, at first not at her face, but at the movement of her chest, then up, to her chin, her cheeks, her eyes.

"My sophomore year in college I had a class called *Philosophy of the Enlightenment.* The teacher paid me way too much attention, wanted to conference too often, sat too close during the conferences. It was a night class. One night I was the last student conferencing. We were probably the only people in the building, certainly the only ones on the floor. He shut the door behind me. Usually he left it slightly open, which I believe was department policy. I should have gotten up and re-opened the door. I should have gotten up and walked out of the building. There are many things I should have done. I didn't. I sat down. He sat next to me, too close of course. I remember that several times he brushed his arm against mine as he looked over the paper we were supposed to be talking about. And then he told me I was beautiful. I should have gotten up and walked out, but I didn't. For a long time I hated myself for doing nothing. He said it again. Put his hand on my arm, held it there. I put my paper in my pack and stood up. I took one step and he pushed me against the wall. I told him No. I told him so many times. But I should have screamed. I should have kicked him. I kept telling him No. He held me there with one hand on my throat. I kept saying No. I didn't scream."

I look in her eyes. She's still not looking at me. I don't move. I'm scared to reach to take her hand, scared to do the wrong thing.

"The class was misnamed. It should have been *Gender Relations 101.*"

I don't know what she wants me to do. I don't know what to do.

"I didn't tell the police. I should have screamed. I should have kicked him. I never went back to class. I got an A. I guess I passed *Gender Relations 101* with flying colors."

I close my eyes, take a deep breath. I open them again.

"I was young. And nobody would have believed me. Not the

cops, not the other students. Nobody. They would have thought it was like that horrible movie *Oleana*."

"Which is exactly why Mamet wrote it."

"Do you believe me?"

"Of course."

She nods, sits silent, then says, "After that I started taking self-defense classes. If that happened now I'd slit his fucking throat." She reaches into her pack, pulls out a knife, opens it, shuts it, puts it back.

I think for a long time before I say, "I would help you do that, if that's what you want to do."

"Do you mean that?"

I think some more, then say, "I do."

"Thank you," she says. "He's not worth it now. Or maybe he is. He's probably still doing this to other young women. Someone should do something. I just don't know that he would be worth the risk right now, to me or especially to you."

"You did nothing wrong, by the way."

"I should have screamed."

"Someone once told me that we almost never get mad the first time something bad happens. That first time we're so surprised that we don't know what to do. Then afterwards we stew and reflect, and so the next time we're prepared."

"Some of us don't learn after only one time."

"I don't und—" I stop, then say, "I'm sorry."

"I think the worst part is that all throughout he kept saying over and over how beautiful I am, and how he didn't do this with— can you believe he actually fucking used the word *with*, and not *to*— all of his students, but that I was so beautiful. Beautiful, he said. So so beautiful."

"I'm sorry," I say again. I wish there were more I could say. But finally I know at least one small thing I can do. "I will never again use that word around you, or any other word like that."

"No—"

"I don't want to trigger you. You feeling safe is more important to me than me telling you that you—" I stop myself, then say, "More important to me than me commenting on your looks."

"No."

"I'll do what you want," I say.

"I know I have to do the work myself. I know you can't fix it for me. But I want to have that with you. I want you to say it. Not someone else. I want you to help me make that word clean again. I want you to help me make it mean what it's supposed to."

"He never saw me," says Allison. "Not him, not anyone. They didn't even see my skin. They saw what they wanted, saw what they'd been trained to see. I was nowhere in their view. He was never holding *me* against the wall. I was being held, but in all of this, he never perceived me at all. So far as he was concerned, I didn't even exist."

eight

e n e m y   t e r r i t o r y

◉

Georg Elser was not the only person who tried to kill Hitler, and Hitler's life was saved not only by fog and by the seemingly meaningless choice of when to set a timer. In an odd way, Elser himself not only almost killed Hitler but in that attempt also saved Hitler's life.

In the fall of 1939, as Elser meticulously hollowed out the spot to hold his bomb, others, too, put in place their plans. Chief among the planners were many high-ranking members of the Wehrmacht (German Army) and Abwehr (foreign intelligence), who hated Hitler because they saw, rightly, that he was launching an offensive, illegal, and dishonorable war that could destroy much of Europe and, closer to their hearts, would destroy Germany. But many of these generals, trained in war though they were—which when you get past the abstractions means trained in the art and science of killing en masse—scrupled at assassination. The planners uniformly abhorred Hitler, hated what he was doing, wished he was dead or at least gone, but many—even those who had killed in battle and who commanded campaigns in which hundreds of thousands of lives were lost—could not themselves cross the moral line of killing an individual, especially one who was their leader, that is, one who was higher in their social hierarchy, and most especially one to whom they had sworn personal oaths of loyalty. Many valued their word and their honor more than the lives of those killed by Hitler and his policies.

But some did not.

Abwehr Major General Hans Oster had from the beginning recognized that Hitler must die: Hitler's power over the German people and over the majority of German generals was too great to allow anyone to stop his actions without physically killing him. Oster famously said, "There are those who will say that I am a traitor, but I truly am not. I consider myself a better German than all those who run after Hitler. My plan and my duty is to free Germany, and with it the world, of this pestilence."

Oster's question became: How do we free Germany from this pestilence, when so many refuse to strike? On the first of November, 1939, Oster put the problem succinctly: "We have no one to throw the bomb which will liberate our generals from their scruples."

The man to whom Oster said this, Dr. Erich Kordt, replied, "All I need is the bomb."

Oster responded, "You will have the bomb by 11 November."

Kordt was well-placed to carry off the assassination. His job as a Foreign Ministry spokesperson not only caused him to follow the Foreign Minister "like a shadow," as one writer put it, but made him no longer subject to identity checks and gave him complete access at any time to the Chancellery. He was even allowed to wait in the main anteroom until Hitler appeared.

Having decided to make the attempt, Kordt went to the Chancellery more often than normal so the guards would become additionally desensitized to his presence. He told his cousin and a few others close to him of his plans. I do not know what else he said to them, or what they said to him. I do not know if they spoke of his almost certain death.

Kordt recorded a statement to be delivered after the assassination to the American Chargé d'Affaires and to a member of the Swiss Legation. All that remained was for Oster to provide the explosives.

This was harder than it would seem. Even a Major General was not allowed to requisition explosives without good reason. Oster told co-conspirator Major Lahousen, head of the Abwehr's Section II (Sabotage), that someone was ready to kill Hitler. Lahousen requested a few days to figure out how to remove explosives and a detonator from his section. It would be difficult, but could be done.

Hitler intended to invade France, Belgium, and the Netherlands on November 12 (the invasion was delayed). The plan by the resistance was to get Kordt the bomb, and for him to kill Hitler, on November 11.

Elser's bomb went off at 9:20 p.m. on November 8.

Kordt arrived at Oster's home late in the afternoon of the eleventh to pick up the explosives. Just as I do not know what Kordt said to his cousin, I do not know what he was thinking as he walked up to the house. I do not know if he considered that this might be the last time he would see trees, the last time he would see Oster's face. I don't know if he took in breaths that were extra deep, to taste even the foul city air. I do not know if he was scared, anxious, excited, grim, determined. I do know that he was ready to die. Oster let him in. Perhaps Kordt could see immediately on Oster's face that something was wrong. Perhaps he could not: perhaps years of organizing resistance to Hitler had taught Oster how to mask his feelings. In any case Oster told him the bad news: increased security following Elser's attempt had made it impossible to acquire explosives. Had they made the attempt one week earlier, or had Elser's attempt come one week later, they might have been able to procure the explosives, and Hitler may have been killed. As it was, Hitler survived.

Kordt begged Oster to let him kill Hitler with a revolver. "I can make it through security."

"You are never alone with him, and there are too many aides, orderlies, and visitors. Someone would be able to stop you. We cannot risk it."

Kordt did not make the attempt.

His brother did. Theodor Kordt was also a diplomat. As Ambassador to England, he passed on all information he could to the British. He pleaded with them to not appease Hitler, to stand up to him, to stop him from invading Czechoslovakia. They ignored him.

He, like his brother, volunteered to kill Hitler, knowing it would cost him his life. But he, unlike his brother, often met with Hitler, close-up, where no one could stop him.

A meeting was scheduled. On the appointed day Kordt ate his breakfast, considered it may be his last. He put the gun into his pocket. He went to the Chancellery. He passed one checkpoint, and then another. No sentries searched him. He arrived for the meeting.

He found that Hitler had, for reasons unknown to Kordt, cancelled the meeting. Kordt went home. He did not make another attempt.

⊙

Nika almost never remains on the table. Even when she repeats to him the lines he has made her memorize, even when she groans or screams from the dull or sharp pains he inflicts, she herself is nowhere in the room. She spends more and more time inside her box of memories, with her mother and father and brother and Osip and the land where she grew up. She was, for a time, afraid to bring any of them out, especially Osip, for fear the man would by association contaminate them, but the solution she realized was to not bring out the box for her to hold and open and look at, but instead to leave the box where it was, deep inside, and for her to crawl into it. There she sits surrounded by those she loves as she listens to the distant screams of someone she no longer knows.

This is how she spends her time.

Her bladder brings her back. Her captor—she now knows his name is Jack—has a horror of her bodily fluids, and so periodically uncuffs her, recuffs her hands, and leads her to a toilet in a small room to the side of the basement. He watches out of the corners of his eyes for quick movements as she empties her bladder and bowels and cleans herself. He returns her to the table.

The third time on the toilet, she sees a way out. On the floor, to her left, sticking up behind a canister of bleach and a bottle of vinegar, she sees the handle of a hammer. She pictures herself reaching down—calmly, calmly now—for the roll of toilet paper, then in a flash reaching over the top of the roll and the cleaning supplies to grasp the hammer and in one movement brings it up to smash his face. She sees blood and a broken cheekbone. She sees him stagger, stumble, hit the door jam on his way to the floor. She sees herself on top of him, hitting and hitting and hitting until there is nothing left of him. She pictures this over and over. She figures the distance, the angles. Can she do it?

"Hurry up," she hears him say.

She reaches for the toilet paper. Her hands linger as she makes up her mind. She is scared. She is too scared. If she tries and fails he will hurt her worse that he already has—if that is at all possible. She will only get one chance. So, she decides, she will prepare herself, watch it again and again in her mind, and next time she will do it.

Allison says, "I remember the moment I realized what an amazing experience it would be to walk out into the world as a male and see the other half of the human species as composed of those you actually welcomed and wanted in your life. Not only were they not a threat (well, not physically anyway), they were desirable. Life and the world was like a playground, something good, something you really wanted to participate in. The contrast was so stark, so shocking, I had to stop thinking about it. My anger was so great, I felt so betrayed by life, by the earth, by god, by everything and everyone, I wanted to disappear. I didn't want the rage and the hate, I wanted to love, but all women had been betrayed by the very thing that gives life (I mistakenly thought), and their love had been used against them to destroy them. That feeling remained with me for years. It was and is a terrible, horrible, sickening way to live. I have no words to describe it."

I apologize to her, insofar as you can apologize for nothing you have done personally, but for things done by a group of which you're a member. She knows of my childhood, of my own rapes by my father, of the terror he inflicted, but we both know it isn't the same.

It's different in part because her own father was kind. She often says without a trace of irony that the greatest failing of her childhood was that nothing in it prepared her for the existence of bad men, and for the violence they would later visit upon her. From early on she knew an intimate safety I only discovered after my father left when I was about ten.

On the other hand, I had little to fear from the world at large, which was a far friendlier place than my own home.

Nika realizes there will never be a next time, and she wishes she could go back and do it again, only this time do things differently.

She is not on the table. She is walking along an abandoned road with Osip. It is late at night. The moon is full. It is early spring. Her hand clasps his in the warmth of his coat pocket. She stops and looks down at the shadow of a naked branch as it reaches across the road, sharp, strong, delicate. He stops with her. She can feel his hand. They have never made love. She has never made love with anyone. They walk on. She stops again. It rained earlier, and she can see the moon reflected in a puddle. She looks up through a light haze and sees four stars cradling the moon. "Osip," she says, and he moves closer, kisses her. She presses her body against his. Their kiss ends. It is late.

"I'll take you home," he says.

She nods, does not take her eyes from his face. In the distance she hears the first tentative frogs of spring.

"I'll take you home," he says again.

They walk, her hand holding tight to his, deep in his pocket.

"Ja hochu idti domoy," she says.

Jack looks at her.

"Ja hochu idti domoy."

"Speak English."

"I want to go home."

She'd realized when he'd walked into the basement that he wasn't going to uncuff her, that she would never get that chance to hit him with the hammer. She's not sure how she'd known, but she'd known almost immediately. It might have been the slightly slower pace she'd heard coming down the stairs, or later, when he'd stood over her, the slightly tighter grip he'd held on his knife. His shoulders were more set, and he'd looked at her in a way she did not understand, and at the same time understood too well.

It's all over.

"I want to go home," she says.

"Did you ever have a dream," he says, "where one person kills another, and another, and another? And the killer could be anyone, anyone at all, because everyone is a killer? As the dream wears on you become more and more afraid that you'll be the next to die, because there are fewer and fewer victims left. The victims tell each other to be quiet so they won't be noticed by the killer, but it never seems to do any good, because he finds them, one by one. The numbers keep dwindling until there are only four of you left. You know who the killer must be, because one of them is a woman, and you know she isn't doing it, and the other is crippled, and you know he isn't doing it. So you go to confront the killer, to stop him forever, but when you get there he is dead. So you know it must be the man who is crippled, and you stand over him, accusing him as he cowers, and you get bigger and bigger and he gets smaller and smaller until you're standing over him with a knife in your hand and he tries to crawl away but you stab him with the knife and he keeps crawling and you stab him with the knife and finally he doesn't crawl anymore. And you know he lives with his wife, and you know she lives downstairs, and so you take your knife and you walk downstairs. Did you ever have a dream like that, Nika?

"And so you wake up from the dream, but when you wake up you find you're walking down the stairs and there is a knife in your hand, and so you wake up from *that* dream and you're still walking down those stairs and you're still covered with blood.

"And it's not a dream, Nika. It's all there is. This is the whole world and every other world. This is everything.

"We're not who we are, Nika. That is the central fact of life. We are who we carry. I have a glimpse into whole other worlds. You do, too. And those worlds are filled with so many just like me, so many who stab and slice and cut and chop and pull who don't even know what they're doing. Oh, I know what I'm doing. I know exactly what I'm doing. And I know what I need and I know what I need to do. I know what the problem is.

"Bodies. Bodies. Women. Bodies. We don't live here. Don't you see, Nika? This is not where we live. Even when we dream this isn't where we live. These bodies are filth, Nika. Our bodies. Your body. My body. They're not our bodies. They are filth. Nothing but nothing.

"Did you ever have one of those dreams, Nika, where someone was in your body but when you woke up it wasn't you and it wasn't your body? Whose body? Whose filth? Who are you?

"I know it sounds like I'm still dreaming, Nika. I know you think I'm speaking dream nonsense, but dreams are nonsense, Nika, and I am being very precise. I mean every word I say. Who is dreaming their way into us, and when we dream, who uses our bodies and why do they come here? What do they want and why do they hate us so? Why, Nika? Why do they hate our bodies? But it's not just our bodies. That is the thing we must always keep in mind, that they are in our minds, Nika, which are just as bad as our bodies. It's all filth and I want to be clean and I want for it to all end in one clean bright white light. But it won't and that's what scares me and that's why I have to kill you. They have to kill you for a different reason, because you have a body. If I kill you it will be to find out where you go. Because when I wake up I'm still in this body, and I'm still in this dream, and then another dream and another. I don't know who's in control, Nika, and that's what sets me apart from every other man, every other man who paid to put himself inside of you. I didn't do that, and the reason I'm different than all the others is that I know I don't know who's in control. I know that. Other men don't. That's the difference. Do you see? Don't you see any of it? I don't know who's in control. And I'm scared.

"Doesn't it scare you that we have bodies? They decay. They don't last. They're not firm. Do you get it yet? Do you see what they are saying through me?

"I am scared. I just want to be loved, that's all I ever wanted. And for the love to never end. Never. I want something permanent, something that no matter if our bodies rot—*when* our bodies rot— will still be here. Our bodies are the problem. Our bodies are *one* problem. *They* are another. And I don't know who they are. And I'm scared. Did I tell you I'm scared?

"I'm scared of what comes after. After the dream. The next one. What's on the other side? That's why I'm going to kill you, so you can tell me what's on the other side. But that's me. That's just me. But I'm not in charge. And they're going to kill you because you have a body. Do you finally get it?

"I am a scientist and I am a Christian. I am both. I am being precise. Both of those are who I am. But I am dreaming and I am going to wake up and I will still be in this dream.

"It may seem like I hate you but I don't. They do, but that's because you have a body and they don't. But I don't hate you. I do hate you for being weak, for being passive, for standing by, for not saving me from them and from everyone. I do. You have to understand how much I hate you for that.

"But I don't really hate *you*. We both just think I hate you. But the ones I really hate are the ones who do this. And I hate *them*, of course, but that's not who I'm talking about. Because at least I know who's in charge. I hate the ones in charge and I hate the ones who—no, I can't say it. Not to you. Not to me. I know things. I know things you don't know. But I have to know things I don't know, too, because if I knew them I wouldn't be who I am. And I don't *know* who I am. I am being very precise, Nika, more precise than you know."

"Now, do you love me?"

Nika just looks at him.

"Say it. I need you to love me."

But she can't do it. She can't do any of it anymore. After Vilnius, Amsterdam, New York, Spokane, after Linas, Viktor, Jack, and the thousands of other men, she can't do it. She can't pretend anymore. She has nothing left. "No, Jack, I don't."

He leans over her.

"I used to hate you," she says, "and part of me still does, but I just don't care anymore. I want to go home and I will never get to go home. I should have seen that all along."

He moves his face closer to hers, "You don't love me?" He is trembling, she can tell, with anger.

"No, I don't."

nine

falling through time

We're in the truck, driving home. We never did get any firewood. I don't see the forest anymore. I see clearcuts. I'm glad to be back in my body, but I hate what I see outside.

The return was gradual at first, with me sitting against the cedar, Allison sometimes talking to me and sometimes silent, and me seeing first the forest, and then the forest being overlaid by a blurry, indistinct clearcut that slowly grew sharper while the living forest faded. Then the forest returned the same way—reimposing itself over the clearcut—and I saw animals walking unafraid, as they do when we the civilized aren't around. I watched them, wide-eyed, until they began again to fade, to be replaced by the relative sterility and monotony of the clearcut.

The whole time I couldn't think. The whole time I clung tight to the thread—thread of what?—that connected me back to the world I knew. The whole time I feared this shift in perspective— beautiful as the forest was—would be permanent.

It wasn't. In time the waves where I saw and experienced myself in the clearcut became stronger, longer, until at last they flooded out the forest entirely. And then I slept. When I woke I was back to normal, only a little shaky. Allison helped me to the truck, helped me in.

And now she's driving. I'm looking out the window. I've already told her what I saw, what I experienced.

She asks questions. I expand.

Then a silence, until she says, "I'm glad you're back."

"Me, too."

Another silence.

"But it was beautiful. The forest was beautiful."

It happens again. This time I'm not so scared, since I know that last time I came back. That knowledge, however, doesn't keep me from continuing to cling to the existential thread reaching back to everything I know.

This time I'm sitting next to Hangman Creek. I hear the Pullman Highway not far behind me. Ahead of me, across the stream and across a field, I see a cluster of newly-built luxury houses that abut a golf course. Hangman Creek is maybe fifteen feet wide and eight inches deep. Once it ran strong. No longer.

I'm thinking about what it would take for the stream to recover—the removal of upstream houses, golf courses, and farms would be a good start, as would the removal of downstream dams that impede fish passage—when it begins again. It starts with the highway. The sounds fade. At first I think it's just a lull in traffic, but it goes on long enough that I start to *hear*: insects, birds, some scurrying in the underbrush. I look up, across the stream, and the houses are gone. Pine trees stand in their place. I close my eyes, and when I open them again the houses are back, the trees gone. I'm not so scared this time, only confused.

I close my eyes and as I do I hear a thrashing in the water in front of me. I open my eyes and see that the stream is full of water, a couple of feet deep, and the bottom has turned from the light color of cobbles to a dark gray. Fish. The river is filled with fish. If I stepped into the water I would step on a salmon.

I have read about streams full of salmon—which included essentially all streams in the region before the arrival of civilization, before the arrival of the *wétiko* sickness—but of course I have never seen this.

I don't make a sound. I can't. I don't move. I can't. I notice my cheeks are wet. I don't know what gift I am being given, and I do not know why.

I look up again to the houses near the golf course, but I see only trees. I look beyond, to a steep slope that rises to suddenly flatten at the top: South Hill. I'm used to houses lining the edge of the slope, but they're no longer there. I see forest. I like what I see. I still don't hear the sounds of the highway. I hear fish, birds, insects. I hear the slight wind in the pine trees. I like what I hear. I am not afraid.

That time ended more suddenly than the first. The fish just disappeared, the houses reappeared, and the sounds of the highway came back. As simple as that, all of this other was gone.

I wasn't quite so tired this time as last, and after a short rest I walked on home.

Nika is dead, stabbed through the heart with a knife. Nika is dead, and she is dreaming of rain. She is dreaming of rain coming down so hard she cannot see the trees outside her windows. She is dreaming of rain coming down to pound on the roof. She is dreaming of falling asleep to these sounds. She is dreaming of dreaming about it raining so hard she cannot see the trees outside her windows. She is dreaming of the rain, and she wants to go home.

A few days later, Allison is hanging out at my mom's, a couple of miles away. I'm on my computer, editing what I wrote the night before. I hear Allison's car pull into the driveway, so I get up, walk outside. She opens her door. I say hello. She ignores me, walks to the barn to check that the dogs have food.

"I already fed them," I say.

She looks inside, says absently, "He already fed them."

"That's what I just said."

She starts toward the house.

I say, "Hey, gorgeous. How are you . . ."

She ignores me, walks past, goes inside. Shuts the door behind her.

I wonder what her problem is. I start to follow her, open the door, and hear her say, "Hey, lover, thank you for feeding the dogs." I stand, blink, step inside, and. . . . Well, nothing. I don't see her. I wander room to room, but our place isn't that big, and there aren't many places she could hide, even if she wanted to. I check the closets, under the bed. I go back outside. I see that her car is gone.

I have to admit, I'm a little concerned, not so much about

being existentially stuck in some strange place, but instead that I'm just plain going crazy.

I go inside, sit at the computer, pretend to work.

A little later I hear Allison's car. I'm kind of scared to go outside. I don't know what will happen, and don't really want to find out.

I hear her car door open, then shut. Then I don't hear anything for a while, and when I do, it's Allison opening the front door. I hear her footfalls through the entry, then I hear her putting down her pack. She walks to the door of the room where I'm sitting, and says, "Hey, lover, thank you for feeding the dogs."

I sit a moment, staring at her, or more precisely staring through her at the wall behind. I start to understand something, lose the understanding, and gain it again. I start to stand up, sit back down, then start up again. I do this one more time.

Allison smiles tentatively. I can tell she wants to laugh, but daren't for fear I'm having another of my spells.

I stand up. "No, it's okay," I say. "I got it now."

"No," she says. "You already did."

"What?"

"The dog food. I thanked you."

"No, the spells."

"I'm sorry?"

"The spells. Getting firewood, seeing the forest. Then a few days ago at Hangman Creek."

"Yes?"

"I understand."

"What?"

"Time."

"I don't. . . ."

"I'm falling through time. I know what you did before you came in here. You got out of your car, walked into the barn, looked at the dog dish, said to yourself, 'He already fed them,' and came in.

Right?

"How. . . ."

"I saw you. I was standing right there."

"I didn't see you."

"That's because I wasn't there."

"Where were you? At the window?"

"In the driveway. You walked right past me."

She stops a moment, thinks. That's something else I love about Allison. I've known lots of people—women and men alike—who at this point would have made a joke or taken offense, anything to discharge the energy of the conversation. These are people who are incapable of sitting with any sort of discomfort. This is true of physical discomfort, it's true of emotional discomfort, and it's especially true of cognitive dissonance. It takes a sort of faith to sit with any of these, a faith that your body or heart will heal, a faith that dissonance will synthesize into something comprehensible. Or maybe not. Finally she says, "Tell me."

"When I saw the logging trucks that you didn't see, and when I saw the forest where you saw a clearcut, I was seeing the past. It's the same the other day. I slipped into a time before dams and logging and agriculture killed the salmon. I saw it. Now, this time was the same, except it was the future."

She looks at me, almost getting it.

"Those were in the past. You seeing me in the driveway was in the future."

I move my hands in small circles each around the other, as the Indian elder had done when she'd told me about time.

"But I couldn't see you."

"Neither could the animals in the forest. Do you remember? They were unafraid."

She thinks, then smiles with her whole face. She gets it, grabs me by the shoulders. "Do you think you could go back in time and stop the dams from being built? Or maybe we should move to the East Coast, and you can go back and tell the Indians to kill every white person they see, tell them what will happen to them and to their land if they don't."

I catch her enthusiasm. "I could—"

We both say, "No."

She says, "They wouldn't be able to see you."

"They wouldn't be able to hear me, either. I was talking to you outside, and you ignored me. I thought you had some sort of a problem."

She thinks, asks, "What do you think triggers it? Why do you think it's happening?"

I don't have an answer. We just look at each other.

It's late, but not late enough to bring a chill. We're outside. I'm on my back on a blanket. Allison kneels atop me, straddling me, holding me inside. We don't move, just feel. There's no moon, and I don't see her face, only her black form against the stars. I have never seen anything so beautiful. She settles down tighter. I look at the silhouettes of trees, feathery black against the studded pillow of the sky.

Allison says, soft, her voice throaty and slow, "When we were talking earlier. . . ."

"Yes."

"I think you really got to a primary difference. . . ."

She shifts slightly. I shift in response.

". . . between men and women within a patriarchy."

We don't move. There's the slightest breeze, and I can tell she's feeling it on her back, listening to it in the trees. I ask, slowly as well, "How so?"

"You perceive me as ignoring you, and you immediately wonder what's wrong with me."

"I thought you were mad or something. Maybe you and my mom got into a fight."

She laughs. I feel her laugh all through her body and into mine. She says, "No, we had a delightful time. She wants you to come over and help her weed, by the way."

"If you would have told me that, *I* would have ignored *you*."

She laughs again, says, "If we reverse the situation, so I perceive *you* as ignoring *me*, I don't start wondering what's wrong with you, but rather what's wrong with me. I'm wondering what I did wrong to deserve or at least cause you to ignore me. The masculine focus is that there is something wrong with the other—that others are responsible or to blame for everything that goes wrong—and the feminine focus is that something is wrong with me—that I'm responsible or to blame for everything."

I think a moment. "You're right about that difference."

"Of course I'm right. Women are always right, remember?"

"No, that's men."

"Oh, sorry, I forgot." And then she laughs and laughs, and I feel her laughter all the way through me, and deep into the ground.

Seeing god isn't just a cute name between Allison and me for having sex, like for some people it might be "catching the train" or "docking the ship" or "visiting the thatched cottage." It's literally true. Of course in some ways that's not a big deal: the divine is everywhere, and if you can't see it you're probably trying hard not to look. Naturally it's easier to experience the divine in some circumstances than others. I see it more clearly, for example, in a pond, with the backstriders and tadpoles, the gnats who spiral above the surface and the newts who come up for great gulps of air, than I do in a shopping center, airport, or skyscraper.

The former are encounters, however slight, with some others, while the latter are cathedrals honoring nothing more than ourselves. It's back to that same old masturbatory relationship.

I also don't want to say that all sex leads to an experience of the divine. I've had sex before that is physically or emotionally painful, cold, reserved, half-hearted, distant, boring, ill-advised, sincerely regretted, embarrassing, and even so awful it's hard to keep from laughing. I've had sex that created more distance than closeness, and

I've had sex that didn't engender, but substitute for, communication. I've had sex that blocked, rather than revealed, the divine. I've had sex that removed me from my body rather than bringing me deeper into it.

But that's not how it is with Allison. Have you ever had one of those dreams where the sensations and emotions are especially intense, where everything seems closer, brighter, stronger, more vivid, more meaningful, more alive? And then you wake up and you're disappointed because the world around you now seems so drab, or to step away from my masculine habit of putting all blame on others, you wake up and you're disappointed because you've lost the ability to live in a blaze of reality? If we see a horse in a dream we wonder what it means, what it tells us, where it comes from. It is alight with meaning and drama. Then we wake up, get in our cars, and see a horse in a pasture beside the road, and if we notice the horse at all it's just another goddamn horse.

Entering Allison is like entering that dream. It's like waking up to find I haven't lost that ability to perceive. She says it's the same for her.

ten

the problem is god

The night is dark. It's very late. The headlights of Jack's truck are off. He coasts the truck to a stop in the small parking lot between the golf course and Hangman Creek. The lot is perfect, hidden by trees from all eyes, and paved, making it impossible for police to get tire imprints.

Jack is confident. He's wearing boots two sizes too big, which he'll throw away afterwards. He'll also burn his sweatshirt, sweatpants, and socks.

He gets out—he turned off the domelight before he left his home—and quietly shuts his door, then walks to the back of the truck. He looks one last time for headlights before he opens the canopy and gate, then reaches in for the tarp.

Nika was ultimately a disappointment. She'd made him so angry at the end that he'd killed her quicker than he'd wanted, and hadn't been able to ask her any questions. But she wouldn't have answered anyway. She had become too uncooperative.

He hefts the tarp-wrapped body, then carries it away from the truck, using a maglight held in his mouth. It's a good thing she's slender. Of course had she not been he would have dumped her elsewhere. But her body is perfect for this. He's always wanted to bring someone here.

He carries her toward the creek, through a tangle of wild roses that tear at his sweatshirt. That's why he's going to throw the sweatshirt away. Between the wild roses and the creek is a maze of willows. At this boundary, surrounded on all sides by thick brush, he lays down the tarp, unrolls it. That, too, he'll throw away. He looks at her face, calm now, still beautiful. He looks at the blood on her chest, and at the blood further down.

He's excited about leaving her here, about learning how long it takes anyone to find her, or if anyone even does.

It's time to go. He turns to leave, looks over his shoulder one final time, shines the light on her face, and says, "Good-bye, Nika."

Nika is dreaming of falling. She is dreaming of not being able to find the ground. She is dreaming of ravens flying toward her, then flying away with pieces of her in their beaks. She is dreaming of ants. She is dreaming of being carried away. She is dreaming of being carried home.

She dreams of her mother the last time she saw her, her mother waving and waving until Nika could no longer see her. She dreams of her own body.

She dreams of soil, of touching it with her fingers, her feet, then with the backs of her legs, her back, the back of her head. She dreams of tiny rocks, and she dreams of the sounds of water moving through the night and into the day. She dreams of the stars, and of the sun. She dreams of a cloudless sky she cannot see.

The German victories in Poland and France made more distant the possibilities of victory for any coup attempt, as the regime became more popular and the resistance lost support: then as now, there were many who did not mind a dictator, so long as he was successful. But there were others who persevered in attempted to kill Hitler. Eugen Gersenmaier and Fritz-Dietlof Graf von der Schulenberg were two of these. Together, they assembled a group of officers to arrest Hitler, killing him if, as presumed, resistance was offered. Despite many attempts, they were never able to get close enough to pull it off. The closest they came was in Paris in 1940; they planned to attack Hitler during his victory parade. But at the last moment, Hitler decided against having this parade. Instead he flew into Paris at five o'clock that morning and visited the Champs-Elysées, the Opéra, the Louvre, the Eiffel Tower, and the Invalides (including Napoleon's tomb) before catching an 8:00 a.m. flight back to Prussia.

Evidently—and of course this is true of conquerors in general, on every level from the most intimate to the most global—Hitler could conquer Paris, but he couldn't comfortably visit it. The act of conquest makes any sort of real visitation impossible. This is, once again, as true of those who rape individuals as it is of those who rape countries as it is of those who rape landbases.

I don't think I've told you yet about the bears and the apple trees. A family of bears lives in the neighborhood, and all of us humans have agreed to not call Fish and Game, because we know that Fish and Game would kill them. That's what they do. The cliché is that a fed bear is a dead bear, but it's more accurate to say that a bear who has been ratted out to the state or federal mobile killing units is a dead bear. The humans in our neighborhood who don't like bears make sure to not leave trash where the bears can get at it. Those who do like bears leave offerings of corn or dog food, and are sometimes blessed by seeing a bear or, better, a mother and cub. At the very least we all get to see lots of bear poop.

Allison and I decided to take this one step further. We kept thinking about the old adage about how if you give a man a fish, you feed him for a day, but if you teach him how to fish, you'll feed him for a lifetime (and if you blow up a dam you'll feed his descendants forever). Well, we knew we couldn't teach bears to fish any better than they already do, and besides, the wétikos have killed the streams and rivers (where are the salmon, lampreys, and sturgeon?). And both Allison and I already work on dam removal and anti-logging issues, so we're already helping the fish some, though obviously not enough. We wanted to do something more direct. We couldn't figure out what we should do until bear poop gave us the answer.

We noticed that each year during apple season we often see huge piles of poop that reveal to us all too clearly the inefficiency of bear metabolism. If I can venture perhaps too much detail, the poop looks like filling for apple cobbler. If you had enough patience and really liked three-dimensional puzzles, you could fit the apple pieces back together, glue them, put them on your kitchen counter, and no one would be the wiser.

In any case, we decided that if you give a bear an apple you feed her for a day—or more accurately in a bear's case about five minutes—but if you plant a tree you feed her and her descendants for many generations, maybe even long enough for civilization to crash and for what little wild that remains to begin to recover.

So we planted apple trees. Spokane has hot, dry summers, and we knew the trees wouldn't survive their first few years unattended, so we planted them near water sources. We planted some near Hangman Creek, and some near its tributaries. We planted some in a beautiful little meadow on a tributary that begins near our home, then winds down to cross beneath the Pullman Highway and open into Hangman Creek.

We planted heirlooms. I'm not sure if bears find red delicious apples as bland as I do, but we wanted to give them and all the other critters a variety, and besides, the centralization and standardization of agriculture is destroying diversity of fruit and vegetable varieties just as it is destroying all other forms of diversity, so we bought bunches of different types of apple trees: Ashmead's Kernel, Belle de Boskoop, Black Oxford, Calville Blanc d'Hiver, Cox's Orange Pippin, Kandil Sinap, Pink Pearmain, Scarlet Crofton, and so on.

Someday those trees will hang heavy over the grass and over the water. Sometimes I picture people—including nonhuman people—reaching to pick the apples and wondering at the bouquets of tastes. I picture the apples being eaten by bears, foxes, raccoons, opossums, coyotes, robins, jays, wasps, hornets, ants, flies, worms. I picture some of the apples falling into the streams and flowing down until they're caught against branches, and then I picture those fruits being eaten by those who live in the water as well as those who live on the land or in the air. There is almost nothing that makes me happier than to give something back to the land where I live, something that the land can use for its own ends.

There were others in Paris who wanted to kill Hitler. These included the staff of Field Marshal von Witzleben. Frantic plotters in Berlin often visited Paris to beg the officers to act. The officers assured them that everything was in place. The moment Hitler entered Paris, he would be arrested or killed.

Their best opportunity came in May, 1941, during a planned parade of German divisions down the Champs-Elysées. The troops were assembled, and a saluting base was set up near the Place de la Concorde. Two officers were ready to shoot Hitler at the saluting base, and a third stood by with a bomb should the other two fail in their suicide attacks.

Hitler never showed up.

I say, "I think the problem is God."

Allison opens her eyes wide, says, "Not. . . ."

"No," I say, smiling, "not seeing god, not with you. The problem is God with a capital G."

Allison says, "Do you mean a belief in some distant sky God. . . ."

"No. . . ."

". . . the belief that God isn't of the earth?"

"No."

"That our bodies are shameful and that the earth isn't our real home?"

"No."

"No?"

"Can I say something?"

"Yes."

"I don't think the problem is a virus."

"No?"

"I think viruses get a bad rap. Viruses are necessary, natural. Some are even beneficial to us as individuals: we couldn't survive

96 • Derrick Jensen

without them. We've got long relationships with them. And I think we can say that almost all, if not all, of them are beneficial to their landbases. Even the most predatory of them provide necessary checks, just like any other predator, or for that matter, just like almost any animal. You get too much vegetation, well, some bunnies have to come eat it. Too many bunnies, some lynx have to come eat them. If lynxes aren't around, then maybe a virus will come along to keep the bunnies in check. And the vegetation says, 'Thank you very much.' So do the bunnies. So does the landbase. In fact, the vegetation exists in part for the bunnies, who exist in part for the lynx, who exist in part for the viruses, who exist in part for the plants. We all exist for each other. The point is that viruses aren't malevolent. Whatever is killing the planet is."

Allison nods.

"Which brings us," I say, "to God. Let's pretend that God really exists, and He's just like the Judeo-Christians say. Well, what do we know about this God?"

"That He's one mean motherfucker?"

"He hates women," I say. "He hates sex. He's a God of rape. He's a God of war. He's a God of conquest."

"He's a projection of the patriarchal mindset," she responds. "A bunch of abusers—male abusers—figured out that if they simply went around raping women and children, it wouldn't take long for them to get called out. And maybe some of these abusers even had consciences, and felt bad about what they did. So in order to shut up their consciences and in order to get their victims to stop fighting back, they created this elaborate story of a God who gives them the right to rape and conquer and do all sorts of nasty stuff, who not only gives them the right, but the mandate: who tells them to commit atrocities, who tells them that if they don't they're not good servants of this God, and who tells their victims that they better not fight back, that if they do they will incur the wrath of God and be sent to hell, and tells them that if they are good enough victims, well, the meek shall inherit what's left of the earth."

"No," I say.

"What do you mean, no?"

"No. It means no."

Allison shoots me a look, then says, "This is all Post-Christian Feminism 101."

"But what if God is real?"

"As in. . . ."

"Real."

"I don't know what you mean."

"What if the stories in the Bible are true? Oh, not all of them. God didn't *create* the world. He—and this is so typical of a patriarchal male—just took credit for it. But the smaller miracles, those are true. And the smiting. Lots of smiting."

"So you're saying—"

"Your muse really exists. My muse really exists. So why should we get so skeptical when it comes to the capital G God? Why are the spirits we experience real and the Big Guy is just a projection, a mass hallucination on the part of hundreds of millions of Christians, nothing more than an excuse to commit atrocities on the part of the powerful and a solace for the victimized?"

"Because your muse is good. My muse is good. They haven't told anyone to go forth and conquer. They aren't responsible for the murder of hundreds of millions of human beings. They aren't responsible for the mindset that's killing the planet."

"Why do all of these spirits have to be good? Why do they have to wish us well?"

Allison blinks hard, twice.

I say, "The central questions become: Why does He hate us so much? And, Why does He want to destroy the earth?"

eleven

who's in charge

⊙

I'm thinking about pinworms, *Enterobius vermicularis*. If you accidentally—or I suppose on purpose, although I don't know why you would—ingest pinworm eggs, the eggs pass down to the small intestine, where they hatch. The male and female worms then migrate to the large intestine, and live and breed near your rectum. Early in the mornings females crawl out of your anus and lay eggs, then crawl back into their nice warm home.

Now, you may wake up that morning, and you may have no idea that these pinworms are living inside of you—I mean, how many other creatures live in or on our bodies about whom we know next to nothing?—but here is what you will know: your anus itches. What do you do when your skin itches? You scratch it. If you use your finger to scratch your anus—and I know you're far too sophisticated and health-conscious to do this (and besides, it would be just plain gross), but if you're like me you weren't quite so sophisticated when you were an infant or a young child, but merely knew that when something itched you scratched it with your scratcher—you get infectious eggs on your finger. If you happen to put your finger in your mouth, the eggs are home free. If you happen to touch clothing, kitchen counters, schoolroom desks, the eggs can come to rest there, waiting for someone else to touch that particular cloth, counter, or desk, then put a finger to a mouth.

The question I'm asking right now is this: when a child scratches her itching anus, who is in charge? The pinworm is changing the child's behavior.

Not only that, but if the pinworm changes the child's behavior, is the pinworm now a part of the child? At what point does someone else become a part of you? Is the flora and fauna in your gut part of you? How about the cells of your brain? How about the infection that—who?—makes you sneeze so you can expel aerosols to be picked up by some other host? "I need to sneeze." Who needs to sneeze? You or the infection?

Who is an invader, who is a hitchhiker, and who is a part of you?

But of course, just because someone changes your behavior doesn't mean they're a part of you—otherwise Mrs. Purcell, my fourth grade teacher, would have become a part of me by holding me in during recess. I can change our dogs' behavior by giving them treats, and they can change ours by begging. So there's obviously more to the question of who is part of you than simply affecting your behavior, just as there is more to the question than simply being inside your skin.

I got a pretty bad prostate infection last year. In retrospect, the earliest symptom was that I wanted to have lots of orgasms. Allison was gone, first for a long visit to her parents, and then to oversee the hanging of her works at a gallery in San Francisco, so I was masturbating a lot. I mean a lot. My historical average when I'm on my own is probably three times a week. I was masturbating three or four times a day, not stopping till long after the muscles in my forearm started to burn. I tried switching to my other hand, but that never seemed to work: not only was my right hand out of practice but I felt as though I were cheating on my left. And I knew there was no way I could keep one hand from knowing what the other was doing.

At this point I didn't know I had an infection: I thought it was a temporary obsession. A couple of weeks later, I started to feel pain in the tip of my penis. My first thought was that I had somehow hurt myself. The pain was sharp—not like a strained muscle, but I didn't know what else it could be. Maybe some lubricant or stray bit of fabric had worked its way into my urethra and festered. I was at a loss. The pain kept getting worse. Finally I went to a doctor who, with no tests, insisted I had Chlamydia. Never mind that neither Allison nor I had been with anyone else since well before we met. I had myself tested: he was, after all, an authority figure. Negative. More tests. Negative. I went to a urologist who told me I had a prostate infection. He gave me a prescription for antibiotics, and he also—and here's the interesting part—gave me an informal prescription for orgasms.

He did this because it's very difficult to clear infections from the prostate. The prostate's weak blood supply combines with its shape—it has lots of long skinny tubes that lead to reservoirs of seminal fluid—to render antibiotics relatively ineffective: the antibiotics can't get into these reservoirs. This means that if you don't drain the reservoirs, they become safe havens for the infection. Thus the doctor's orders. Allison was home by then, and very pleased with the prescription.

Now here, for me, is where it gets exciting. I had started compulsively masturbating a couple of weeks before I had any other symptoms, and a couple of months before I got diagnosed. Even had I known I had a prostate infection, the healing properties of ejaculation wouldn't have occurred to me: I'm embarrassed to admit that although I'd been ejaculating for years, I'd been ignorant of how it all works, with no idea the prostate was even involved. But my prostate knew it was infected, and it knew it had to be drained. What I thought was a strange and sudden obsession on my part was instead one part of my body attempting to rid itself of an infection. I asked before, "When you need to sneeze, who needs to sneeze?" I ask now again: Who's in charge?

I asked the urologist why a prostate infection didn't hurt in my prostate, but rather at the tip of my penis (and by then all along its length). He said nerves run past the prostate down the penis. At first this made no sense to me: it would be like pulling my hamstring but feeling the pain in my ankle. I went home and thought about it, and suddenly I understood. If the prostate needs to be stimulated in order for me to ejaculate, and if part of the purpose—at least reproductive purpose—of sexuality is ejaculation, then if the nerves extended no farther than the prostate, sex would be an entirely different and rather more complicated affair (and I don't even want to think about what masturbation would be like from the perspective of a non-contortionist). In order for me to ejaculate, I or someone else would have to stimulate my prostate directly. While this can be done, it's far more handy, if you will, to be able to stimulate the prostate externally. I think I'm stimulating my penis, and in a sense I am, but the real action happens elsewhere, in my prostate, as the prostate is stimulated almost by proxy.

It sometimes seems that every time I learn something new, I become existentially more confused. Not only am I sometimes unclear as to who is in charge—when I do something, who is this action serving?—but now, when I feel something, I begin to wonder whether what I am feeling is what I am feeling. I wonder if where I am feeling it is where I am feeling it. Indeed, I sometimes even begin to wonder if when I feel something there might be others, too, who feel what I feel, only they feel it, like the prostate, by proxy.

Lately I've been thinking about *Dicrocoelium dendriticum*, the lancet liver fluke. It's a parasite with three hosts. The first is a snail, who, in the normal process of eating sheep or cow shit, accidentally eats lancet liver fluke eggs. The eggs hatch, develop into sporocysts and then into cercariae (stages of parasite larval development), then emerge from the snail coated in slime. The second host is an ant, who in the normal process of eating snail slime also eats the larval flukes. The larvae continue their development in the ant's gut, then chew their way out through the ant's exoskeleton. Because the flukes don't yet want the ant dead, once they're out, they patch up the holes in the ant and cling to the ant's outside. That is, all but one of them cling there. One fluke is chosen instead to chew into the ant's brain, where it actually takes over the ant's movement and control of the ant's mandibles. Come sundown, this fluke guides—convinces?—the ant to climb to the top of a piece of grass and to bite down hard, then cling there, waiting for the third host, a sheep or cow. If no ungulate shows up that night, the ant climbs down in the morning to resume its normal life, until the next night, when the fluke once again takes the reins and sends the ant back up a blade of grass. When an ungulate eats the grass to which the ant is clinging, it accidentally eats the ant, and therefore all the liver flukes. The flukes—eventually there can be as many as 50,000 in a mature sheep—make their way to the cow's or sheep's liver by way of the bile ducts, and within a few months begin laying eggs of their own. The eggs are deposited on the ground in the creature's feces, where they are eaten by snails and the story starts all over.

By now you can probably guess the question that I ask as the ant climbs to the top of the grass: who's in charge here?

I've also been thinking about horsehair worms, nematode-like creatures whose name derives from the old belief that they generate from horsehairs that fall into water. They do look kind of like horsehairs, long and slender, and they often do live in water.

Their story begins with eggs laid in water or on damp soil. The eggs hatch, and the young worms enter the body of an insect such as a beetle, cockroach, cricket, or grasshopper, either by being eaten or by simply penetrating the insect's body. For weeks or months the worm develops inside the insect it is slowly killing, until it can often be many times longer than the host in whom it resides. By the end, the worm occupies almost the entire body cavity of the insect except for the head and legs.

But the worm has a problem: if the host dies away from water, the worm will die with it. So what does it do? As it nears the end of this stage of its life, the worm drives the insect away from its home, and when it reaches water the worm causes the insect to jump in, where the worm can emerge, killing the host as it does so. Researchers have found that if you remove a host cricket, for example, from the edge of a pond, it will return and keep returning, until either it is dead or the worm has made its way into the water.

Once again, as the cricket walks slowly toward a pond, what is it thinking? Who's in charge?

And now I'm thinking about a certain solitary wasp. I'm not sure if you know this—I didn't until my mid-twenties—but many species of wasps are not social creatures, but rather live alone. Further, many wasps hunt only one prey species. For example, a particular species of wasp may rely only on a particular species of spider. Typically the wasp paralyzes the spider with a sting, carries the spider to a nest she has prepared, lays an egg on the spider, then closes the nest. The egg hatches and the young wasp consumes the still-paralyzed spider (paralyzed, instead of killed, to keep the flesh from spoiling).

But the wasp I'm thinking of takes things one step further. Instead of preparing the nest for her offspring, she gets the spider to do it for her. It all starts, as it does with these wasps, with a paralyzing sting, in this case on the mouth. The wasp then lays a single egg on the spider's abdomen.

This time, however, the paralysis is not final. The spider soon recovers and goes back to her life of spinning, weaving, waiting, eating. But now a wasp larva clings to her belly, making holes in her abdomen through which she can suck the spider's haemolymph (blood). She injects the spider with an anticoagulant to keep the food flowing. This is how life goes on until the wasp is ready to kill the spider. On the evening of the last day

of the spider's life, the larva injects the spider with another substance. Soon the spider begins to spin a new web, a web that is
different from anything she has ever built before, a web strong
and durable enough to hold the wasp larva as she pupates. When
around midnight the spider finishes this task, the larva injects
the spider with yet another substance, one that kills the spider
outright. The larva feasts until mid-day, then drops the spider's
body to the ground and waits in the web until evening. She spins
her cocoon, where she will turn into an adult.

If you remove the larva from the spider after she has
injected the spider, but before the web is constructed, the spider
will continue to spin this special web, and spin it again, and
again, for several days, until the spell of the larva has worn off,
and the spider can go back to as she was before.

It's not just these particular flukes, horsehair worms,
and wasp larvae who influence or control the behavior of others.
There are flukes and tapeworms who make fish swim near the
surface of the water, so the fish—and thus the flukes or tapeworms—can be eaten by birds. There are barnacles who take
over the bodies of crabs, make the crabs incapable of reproduc-
ing, and get the crabs to take care of the barnacles' offspring.
There are worms who move into the bodies of snails, reproduce,
and whose larvae move into the snails' eyestalks, where they glow
in neon colors as the normally reclusive snails move into the
open, where they can be easy prey for the birds, who are the
worms' next host.

And of course there is the single-celled parasite *Toxoplasma gondii*. These creatures normally cycle back and forth
between rats and cats, as rats eat infected cat feces, and cats eat
infected rats. The parasite doesn't seem to deeply affect cat behavior—after all, the cat merely has to shit to pass on the parasite, and anyone who has ever kept company with cats knows
that they already excel at this—but it does affect the behavior

of rats. This single-celled creature causes infected rats to become less timid, more active, and to have a greater propensity toward exploring novel stimuli in their environment. Infected rats also lose their instinctual fear of cats. I'm sure you can see how all of these changes make it easier for cats to catch rats, and thus to catch *Toxoplasma gondii.*

Cats and rats aren't the only creatures who harbor *Toxoplasma gondii*: they live inside humans too, who also can get them by ingesting infected rats, or far more likely, by ingesting infected cat feces, presumably accidentally through touching feces, then eventually touching fingers to mouth. You can also ingest them by eating undercooked pork, lamb, or venison. Most human carriers show no physical symptoms, but some people suffer severe damage to their brain, eyes, or other organs. Infants in the womb are especially susceptible to damage from infection, which is why pregnant women are cautioned to get someone else to clean the kitty litter. Toxoplasma gondii live inside 60 million Americans. Half the humans in England are hosts to these creatures, and 90 percent of the people in Germany and France.

It may surprise those who believe that humans are fundamentally different than all other animals to learn that rats aren't the only creatures whose behavior is changed by Toxoplasma gondii: the same is true for humans. Studies conducted at universities in Britain, the Czech Republic, and the United States revealed striking personality changes among some infected humans. Changes include an increased likelihood to develop schizophrenia or manic depression, and delayed reaction times that lead to greater risk, for example, of being involved in automobile crashes.

There are more subtle changes, too. Infected men tend to become "more aggressive, scruffy, antisocial and . . . less attractive." They are characterized by researchers as "less well-groomed, undesirable loners" who are "more willing to fight" and "more likely to be suspicious and jealous." Infected women become "less trustworthy, more desirable, fun-loving and possibly more promiscuous." They spend more money on clothes, and are consistently rated as more attractive.

One researcher even stated, "I am French, and I have even wondered if there is an effect on national character."

All from a single-celled creature.

All from a hitchhiker.

Who's in charge?

I tell all this to Allison. We're lying next to each other. We just made love. She came. I didn't. It's the new doctor's orders. The antibiotics didn't work—I'd feel better for a couple of days, then quickly fall back into pain. The pain kept getting worse until it was always there, a needle running the length of my penis on good days, and a screwdriver (flat head) twisting inside my urethra on bad, with metal shavings slipped into my urine for good measure. My ejaculate—and those of you not grossed out by stories of worm-filled crickets and the pulsing eyestalks of snails might yet get pushed over the edge by this one—changed from its normal white to a snotty yellow.

None of this was good.

I tried everything, from expensive herbs on the internet to prostate massage (both by myself and with Allison's help) to groin stretching exercises, to eating several bunches of celery per day, to drinking teas made of local herbs that—who—made my whole body flush in waves, to thinking only good thoughts, to begging the infection to go away, to asking evil spirits to stop harassing me, to almost paying $3,000 for a weeklong quack workshop where they teach that any illness—and the promoters said this was true for social ills as well—will go away if you can just put enough love in your heart.

Yes, I was that desperate, and yes, I'm sometimes that stupid.

Around that time, a friend introduced me to her Chinese

herbalist. He talked to me, asked me questions, genuinely cared about my condition—how strange is that, to have someone in the healing profession who cares about you and your condition?—and prescribed multiple hot baths daily, a series of Chinese herbs, and a temporary reduction in orgasms to one every other day. I asked him what I owed him, and he said I shouldn't be silly, money wasn't as important as my health.

Yes, he really said that, and no, I didn't believe it either.

So here I am a month later, my pain still present but reduced to more or less tolerable—I suppose the needle has been replaced by a thumb tack—my ejaculate back to more or less normal, my life again worth living.

It hardly bears mentioning that a decrease in the frequency of my orgasms hasn't led to a decrease in how often Allison and I make love. But there's also a sense in which it does, since the man's orgasm is seen by many as the point and conclusion of sex. Consider how silly the issue would seem if I were a woman and Allison were a man: of course we'd still make love, even though I wouldn't so often have orgasms.

Of course I still enjoy making love with Allison, whether or not I orgasm. I recall an interview I conduced years ago with Dolores LaChapelle, author of *Sacred Land Sacred Sex: Rapture of the Deep*. We spent almost all our time together talking about what a sacred relationship with the land feels like, and it wasn't until I was standing to leave that it occurred to me to ask, "What is sacred sex?"

She answered with a dismissive wave of her hand, "Sex without orgasm."

I sat back down, looked at her, said, "I don't. . . ."

She said, "You will."

I did. When I got home I asked Allison.

She said, "Process."

"What?"

"It's all about process."

"What process?"

She took my finger, put it in her mouth, curved her tongue

to make a suction against the tip, took my finger back out, and said, "That process."

"I like this conversation," I said, "but I have no idea what you're talking about."

"What is the essence of industrialism?"

I thought a moment. "I don't know."

"How many books," she asked, "have you written on this subject?"

"But what's the relationship between industrialism and sexuality?"

"Forget sex," she said, unbuttoning her shirt. "What's the essence of industrialism?"

"Help me out."

She wasn't wearing a bra. She rarely does. She said, "Okay then, what's the essence of science?"

"Objectification. Quantification. If it can't be counted, it doesn't count."

"Bingo," she said. "And orgasms. . . ."

"Are quantifiable."

"Attraction, affection, emotion, feeling, sensation, communication. . . ."

"Aren't. Thus they don't count."

"Now, what's the point of industrial production?"

"I. . . ."

"Come on, you know this." A button, a zipper.

"Production?"

"Very good. And what gets short-shrift in this emphasis on production?" She slipped off her shoes, slid her pants around her thighs, sat, lifted her feet off the ground, said, "Pull, please."

I did. "Life. Production is more important than life."

She removed her socks, stood, dropped her panties. "And where does process fit in?"

"I'm having a hard time breathing."

"Production values product over process."

"Product over process," I said distractedly.

"Yes, orgasms—"

I understood. "An emphasis on orgasms is a valuing of product over process. It devalues the actual process of sexuality, just as industrial production devalues the processes of creation. An overemphasis on orgasms desacralizes. . . ."

"Sexuality. The sacred is always about process." She sat.

"What do you want me to do now?" I asked.

"What do you think?"

I sat next to her. "I like this."

She nodded.

"But I don't think I entirely agree."

She waited.

"I don't think sex without orgasm is necessarily any more sacred or sustainable than sex with. I think sex without orgasm can be just as product-oriented, just as dishonest."

She still waited.

"We've all heard of men using sex only to get off, or men using sex as conquest."

"Yes."

"What about women who use sex to 'catch' a man? Isn't that just as profane, whether or not she has an orgasm? I think orgasms are beside the point. The point is presence, and the point is honesty."

"It's like in your dream."

A few years before, I'd asked for a dream that would reveal my biggest fear in relationships. That night, I dreamt I walked into a tackle shop and asked if they had any worms. The man behind the counter said, "We don't have any worms, but we have some lips." He reached underneath, pulled out a styrofoam container, opened it. Inside were disarticulated lips squirming in some base material. He picked up a pair and put it on the counter, where it continued to wriggle. I woke up. The dream was clear. My biggest fear in relationships was lip service, was that someone would use her lips to deceive me, to hook me, to reel me in, whether through talking, kissing, or anything else. That someone would present herself one way to catch me, and then I would find out she was not what she seemed. The worm was no worm: it was a lure, with a hook attached. The lips were not lips: they were a lure, with hook attached. That's something I've always loved about Allison: she acts the same now as she did on our first date, only better.

"Those are all just different ways," I said to Allison, "of valuing product over process."

"It's even more complex," she responded. "I've had a few female friends who said they've never had an orgasm with a partner. I've always thought that was sad. But what appalled me was that all of these women said none of their partners ever knew."

"Which means. . . ."

"Exactly."

"Not a single one of those fuckers. . . ." I stopped, raised my eyebrows.

"By definition," she said.

"Ever bothered to ask."

"Or if they did they believed the lie."

"The point isn't orgasms. The point is mutuality." I delicately pressed the skin on her shoulder with my forefinger. I love to look at the slight incurvation of her skin under this pressure, and its return when I release. I said, "It's no wonder passion dies."

But that conversation was long ago, and now I'm lying next to Allison, still sexually hungry, but with an aching prostate, talking with her about who's in charge.

"Bacteria," she says.

"What?"

"Bacteria create cities."

I shake my head.

"Bacteria get into people's minds and they change people's behavior. They make people build cities, gather in large groups. All so the bacteria can feed. Cities are giant factory farms to provide food for bacteria, and in addition, the bacteria are slave drivers. It's like the spider who's been taken over by the wasp larva. She builds the structure in which she'll soon die. Humans construct their own mausoleums, too, only they call them cities." She pauses, then says, "We should just acknowledge that bacteria are the main beneficiaries of cities."

I start to say, "I don't—"

But she interrupts me, says, "Or maybe chickens are in charge. Chickens used to have a fairly small range in Southeast Asian jungles, and now they're all over the world. I think the deal they made with humans is that we could eat some of them if we increased their range. That deal has worked out well for both of us, except that now factory farms are an abrogation of the deal.

"Or it could be various plants. I've read that the plants we say we've domesticated have actually domesticated us, so they could increase *their* range."

"What do you mean?"

"Grains contain opioids, specifically exorphins. This has led some researchers to suggest that addiction is the genesis of agriculture. Really, no other explanation makes sense. Backbreaking labor for piss-poor nutrition? Why? Why did people ever start doing it? But in most places that the right plants (and animals) have existed, humans have done it. Why? Because we get a little happy hit."

"You serious?"

"Dead. The effects of exorphins are qualitatively the same as those produced by other opioid drugs: reward, motivation, reduction of anxiety, a sense of well-being, and perhaps even addiction. Perhaps nothing. For some people, their brain chemistry is already so good that they don't feel it, but others take one bite and fall in headfirst."

"What you're saying is. . . ."

"Yes. Maybe the plants produced substances that got us hooked, and humans have basically conquered the world on behalf of those plants, doing the plants' will, by which I mean spreading their genes, in exchange for that happy little hit. Maybe that's the basis of civilization. Human culture was completely transformed, and not in a good way: we got hierarchy, militarism, slavery, starvation, disease. And, so the theory goes, annual grains are in charge."

I stare at her, stunned.

She says, "If you don't like that theory, I've got another. Maybe cats are in charge. I know that's true in this household."

"I don't. . . ." I sort of expect her to keep talking, but she doesn't. I continue, "I don't think it's any of those, for the same reason it isn't viruses."

She looks at me for a moment, then says, "Tell me."

twelve

necrophilia

◉

The health of the landbase is everything. I'm thinking about the roles parasites play in maintaining that health. I'm thinking about parasites who take over the bodies of marine snails, and of the snails living full lives—fifteen years—but over that time, fostering more parasites instead of creating more snails. I'm thinking of the grasses those overpopulated snails would otherwise have eaten. And I'm thinking of parasites leaving the snails and moving into fish, and causing those fish to swim near the surface and flash their shiny underbellies to be seen by birds who eat those fish. Catching infected fish is ten to thirty times easier for those birds. If fish did not get infected, birds would starve to death. I'm thinking of birds becoming infected with parasites who lay eggs to be dropped off by birds in feces, and I'm thinking of the cycle beginning again. I'm thinking of how parasites help all these species—though not always individuals—and I'm thinking of how they help entire communities. I'm thinking they are absolutely crucial to their landbases, that their landbases would die without them. I'm thinking of the words of one former professor of parasitology and invertebrate zoology, "The irony is that to support healthy bird populations, maybe [the birds] need to be infected with parasites."

I'm thinking about a world far more complicated than any of us may dream.

I'm thinking about hitchhikers.

I'm thinking about a conversation I had with the writer and activist Aric McBay in which he said, "I have a friend who lives in an intentional community. All of her kids have gotten pinworms at some point, probably from hanging out in the garden and eating dirt, although pinworm eggs are also in the air. When she compared her kids with the kids who hadn't had pinworms, she found that hers had almost no allergies, but the kids who didn't have pinworms had many allergies. She figured pinworms probably stimulated their immune systems in a good way."

I said, "I've heard about that. I always wondered if the pinworms weren't lying, though: maybe something else cures the kids' allergies, and the pinworms just hitchhike, and maybe they even con the parents into thinking the pinworms are doing the kids good when all they're doing is living in their intestines, being parasites."

He ignored me, which was probably a good thing. He continued, "I wonder if civilization could be the direct result of one or more behavior-altering parasites. Perhaps a parasite that benefits from the dense, concentrated populations of cities with immuno-suppressed hosts. Reading from the very good book *Parasite Rex* that the 'gruesome trypanosomes that cause sleeping sickness had nearly been routed from Sudan when the country's civil war began: now they're back,' I can't help but wonder if those same parasites that benefit from the conditions of war might actually cause those conditions as well: they would certainly benefit from a large, growing, sick population which invades adjacent lands and expands the range of the parasite."

He continued, "Perhaps civilization is, in a literal and pathological sense, a disease. It would explain a lot."

I nodded.

He kept going, "On the flipside, I wonder if land-based cultures are inhabited by subtler microorganisms that, instead, nudge them to work with the land and each other. Certainly such subtle relationships exist; I interviewed Diana Beresford-Kroeger, a renegade scientist who told me that scientists are now beginning to realize that trees produce certain hormones in their leaves, and that these hormones run off into streams and rivers. The hormones seem to moderate the metabolism of fish in those streams. In autumn trees produce dormancy hormones that slow fish growth down, and in spring they produce stimulant hormones that wake fish up and help them grow. There are many examples of this.

"Helpful behavior-altering microorganisms might have similar effects on humans and other creatures living on their landbases, giving them feelings and urges appropriate to survival and to the encouragement of life there. Perhaps each landbase would have its own set of such microorganisms, so that when you move from one place to another, you become imbued with the 'spirit' of that landbase at least partly through the microorganisms. It would make a lot of sense: the most long-lived parasites are those who don't kill their hosts—or more precisely don't harm their landbases—but encourage their landbases, and sometimes their hosts, to live and be healthy, so that the parasites are healthy too. In that sense they are symbiotic.

"And if such helpful behavior modifiers exist, they would surely be wiped out by a physical separation from the land in cities, and especially by modern medicine and antibiotics. I wonder if civilization is not the *C. difficile* of the behaviour-modifying parasites, wiping out helpful organisms and carrying out this awful work."

"*C. difficile?*"

"Recently someone in my family was prescribed heavy doses of antibiotics, which killed off the natural microorganisms in her digestive tract. With those helpful microorganisms gone, she got pretty sick when she contracted an infection of a pathogenic, antibiotic resistant 'superbug' called *C. difficile*, a bacteria that has been giving hospitals a lot of trouble lately, because it slips in once antibiotics have killed off the natural microorganisms."

I'm thinking about civilization as *C. difficile*. And now I'm thinking about parasites. And now I'm thinking about hitchhikers, and I'm thinking about spirits of places. I'm thinking about my muse, about how she hitchhikes in my body, about how she enjoys physicality, enjoys sex, orgasm, eating, walking, breathing, enjoys feeling wind in my hair, and how much she enjoys giving me feelings, words, ideas. I'm thinking about the ways we work together. And I'm thinking that hitchhikers aren't generally the problem. Parasites aren't the problem. Bacteria aren't the problem. Viruses aren't the problem.

Maybe there are many problems, and maybe one of the problems is God. Maybe God really exists. I'm thinking He has no body. Imagine forever having no body, feeling no physical embodied pleasure, feeling no physical embodied pain. Imagine never knowing the joys of gesture, touch, caress, as winds caress the leaves of trees and as ants tickle the surfaces of stones. Never. Imagine being too frightened, too arrogant, too distant, to allow yourself to then hitchhike as does my muse and as do so many others, to feel these things through others with whom you join, and unjoin, and join again. Imagine the resentment and hatred this would cause, festering age after age after age, as these others experience embodied life in all its myriad forms and you remain distant, unchanged, disembodied. What if God does not respond to being disembodied by hitchhiking and enjoying embodiedness through us, with us, but instead resents our embodiedness? What if He—and how arrogant it is that He demands to always be capitalized—has forever been disembodied, has never breathed fresh air, drank cold water, felt sun on skin, felt skin on skin, never been inside another or had another inside, body in body? He has lived a very long time and has never experienced physical intercourse—as trees do with wind, and as the wind does with trees, as flowers do with beetles and with the soil, and as beetles and soil do with flowers, as clouds do with mountains and mountains do with clouds, as wolves do with snow, as we all do with each other in ways great and small, every moment of every day. God does not join us in our bodies, but has become deeply envious of anybody who gets to experience the beauty (and pain) of living in a physical world. Maybe God hitchhikes into us, not so He can experience with us, but so He can destroy our experience and get us to destroy our own, can cause us to hate our own bodies as He hates our bodies, to fear our own bodies as He fears all bodies. God infects people with this hatred and this fear, and then causes them to infect others, through trauma, through teaching, through the creation of many religions that, in fine spoiled-grapes fashion, attempt to convince us we've been condemned—not privileged—to live on this planet, attempt to convince us that this life is not good enough, that we will achieve the bliss of heaven or nirvana if only we turn away from this life. When none of this quells God's emptiness which, by now, we have even come to accept as our own—when none of this makes Him finally forget that He does not have a body and that others do, He moves beyond the creation of these religions, moves beyond traumatizing us, moves beyond causing us to hate and fear our bodies, moves even beyond causing us to hate and fear embodied life, and causes us to destroy our own bodies and the bodies of those around us. Even more than that, He is trying to get us to kill embodied life, to kill the planet, all so we will not remind Him of what He is missing, the beauty of being in a body.

And He's succeeding.

What if the stories in the Bible are true? What if they are not merely the ravings of half-mad men in a wholly mad culture? What if they really are the voice of God? What does that mean for our present? What does it mean for our future?

I read in Revelation, "And I heard a great voice out of the temple saying to the seven angels, Go your ways, and pour out the vials of the wrath of God upon the earth. And the first went, and poured out his vial upon the earth; and there fell a noisome and grievous sore upon the men which had the mark of the beast, and upon them which worshipped his image. And the second angel poured out his vial upon the sea; and it became as the blood of a dead man: and every living soul died in the sea. And the third angel poured out his vial upon the rivers and fountains of waters; and they became blood. And I heard the angel of the waters say, Thou art righteous, O Lord, which art, and wast, and shalt be, because thou hast judged thus."

And then I read, "And the fourth angel poured out his vial upon the sun; and power was given unto him to scorch men with fire. And men were scorched with great heat, and blasphemed the name of God, which hath power over these plagues: and they repented not to give him glory."

And then I read in Genesis: "The Lord was grieved that he had made man on the Earth, and his heart was filled with pain. So the Lord said, "I will wipe mankind, whom I have created, from the face of the Earth—men and animals, and creatures that move along the ground, and birds of the air—for I am grieved that I have made them."

And then I read the words of St. Augustine, from his seminal *City of God*, "But any space of time which starts from a beginning and is brought to an end, however vast its extent, must be reckoned when compared with that which has no beginning, as minimal, or rather as nothing at all." The point is that "without motion and change there is no time, while in eternity there is no change." Changelessness is the essence of God. But life is change. Death is change. The only thing that is not change is stasis: the absolute absence of life, and death. Life, which means change, is, in this perspective, "nothing at all" compared to stasis: an utter lack of life.

And then I read the words of Mary Daly, "Patriarchy is itself the prevailing religion of the entire planet, and its essential message is necrophilia. All of the so-called religions legitimating patriarchy are mere sects subsumed under its vast umbrella/

canopy."

And then I read a definition of necrophilia by H. von Hentig, from his *Der Nekrotope Mensch*, which is that it is the passionate attraction to all that is dead, decayed, putrid, sickly; it is the passion to transform that which is alive into something unalive; to destroy for the sake of destruction; the exclusive interest in all that is purely mechanical. It is the passion to tear apart living structures.

And then I read the words of the American Indian Aunt Queen James, "Why doesn't the white man accept things as they are and leave the world alone?"

And then I read in the *New England Journal of Medicine*, "To be men, we must be in control. That is the first and the last ethical word."

And then I read in Erich Fromm's T*he Anatomy of Human Destructiveness*, "I propose that the core of sadism, common to all its manifestations, is the passion to have absolute control over a living being, whether an animal, a child, a man, or a woman."

And then I read in Genesis: "The fear and dread of you will fall upon all the beasts of the earth and all the birds of the air, upon every creature that moves along the ground, and upon all the fish of the sea; they are given into your hands."

And then I read this account from a Vietnam veteran: "I had a sense of power. A sense of destruction. . . . In the Nam you realized you had the power to take a life. You had the power to rape a woman and nobody could say nothing to you. That godlike feeling you had was in the field. It was like I was God. I could take a life. I could screw a woman."

And then I read this account from a veteran of the most recent invasion of Iraq: "In Iraq we can do whatever. You think they put all that shit on the news? Man, ask anybody, we rape those bitches over there and we take their men and blow their brains out just like that and nobody ever knows."

And then I read in Numbers: "Now therefore kill every male among the little ones, and kill every woman that hath known man by lying with him. But all the women children, that have not known a man by lying with him, keep alive for yourselves."

And then I read in the *Journal of Police Science and Administration*, "The [sexual sociopath] individual is not psychotic, is not neurotic, is not mentally retarded, and frequently appears not only normal but hypernormal."

And then I read the words of the researcher Allan Griswold Johnson, who after stating that twelve-year-old girls stand a 20 to 30 percent chance of being violently sexually attacked in their lifetimes (and of course a much higher chance of routine sexual assault), "It is difficult to believe that such widespread violence is the responsibility of a small lunatic fringe of psychopathic men. That sexual violence is so pervasive supports the view that the locus of violence against women rests squarely in the middle of what our culture defines as 'normal' interactions between men and women."

And then I read the words of serial sex murderer Kenneth Bianchi, "When you fuck a broad, you take full charge. . . . You gotta treat em rough. . . . It wasn't fucking wrong. Why is it wrong to get rid of some fuckin' cunts?"

And then I read the words of two criminologists: "In every neighborhood there are men who choke their wives or are choked by them, men who cut their wives slightly with a razor in order to see blood at the moment of ejaculation or are cut by them, men who stab a pillow alongside their partner's head with a butcher knife in order to stimulate the climax."

Every neighborhood.

And then I remember that recently I saw a poster at a university proudly proclaiming that 83 percent of males respect their partners' sexual wishes. Which means 17 percent don't.

And then I remember a conversation in which a man told me that the word *fuck* comes from Middle Dutch *fokken* meaning to thrust, to copulate with; dialectical Norwegian *fukka* meaning to copulate; and dialectical Swedish *focka* meaning to strike, push, copulate. And I remember saying, "That's one reason I would never use that word to describe making love." And I remember him saying, "Why not?" And I remember saying, "Strike?" And I remember him saying, "Yes, your hips slam together sometimes when you fuck." And I remember saying, "That sounds really violent." And I remember him saying, "Sometimes sex is really violent." And I remember being very sad.

And I remember reading the words of Ted Bundy, "He should have recognized that what really fascinated him was . . . to a degree, possessing them physically as one would possess a potted plant. . . . Owning, as it were, this individual."

And I remember reading the line by the Canadian lumberman: "When I look at trees, I see dollar bills."

And I remember reading the murder of runs of salmon described as the loss of fisheries resources. I remember reading deforestation described as the wise use of timber resources. I remember reading the damming of rivers described as the capturing of wasted hydroelectric resources.

And I remember reading the words of serial sex killer Edward Kemper, "If I killed them, you know, they couldn't reject me as a man. It was more or less making a doll out of a human being . . . and carrying out my fantasies with a doll, a living human doll."

I remember also more words from Ted Bundy: "With respect to the idea of possession, I think that with this kind of person, control and mastery is what we see here. . . . In other words, I think we could read about . . . people who take their victims in one form or another out of a desire to possess and would torture, humiliate, and terrorize them elaborately—something that would give them a more powerful impression that they were in control."

I think again about God, and I wonder what He is so afraid of. I wonder, like Queen Aunt James wondered about the *wétikos*, his servants, "Why doesn't God accept things as they are and leave the world alone?"

And then I read the words of Mark Twain: "The portrait of the Almighty Father revealed in the books of the Old Testament is substantially that of a man—if one can imagine a man charged and overcharged with evil impulses far beyond the human limit—a personage whom no one, perhaps would desire to associate with now that Nero and Caligula are dead. In the Old Testament his acts expose his vindictive nature constantly. He is always punishing, punishing trifling misdeeds with thousandfold severity, punishing innocent children for the misdeeds of their parents, punishing unoffending populations for the misdeeds of their rulers, even descending to wreak bloody vengeance upon harmless calves and lambs and sheep and bullocks as punishment for inconsequential trespasses committed by their proprietors. It is perhaps the most damnatory biography that exists in print anywhere."

And finally, I think again about Erich Fromm, and his fundamental question: "Is necrophilia really characteristic for man in the second half of the twentieth century in the United States and in other highly developed capitalist or state capitalist societies?"

And I think about his answer: "This new type of man, after all, is not interested in feces or corpses; in fact he is so phobic toward corpses that he makes them look more alive than the person was when living. (This does not seem to be a reaction formation, but rather a part of the whole orientation that denies natural, not man-made life.) But he does something much more drastic. He turns his interest away from life, persons, nature, ideas—in short from everything that is alive; he transforms all life into things, including himself and the manifestations of his human faculties of reason, seeing, hearing, tasting, loving. Sexuality becomes a technical skill (the 'love machine'); feelings are flattened and sometimes substituted for by sentimentality; joy, the expression of intense aliveness, is replaced by 'fun' or excitement; and whatever love and tenderness man has is directed toward machines or gadgets. The world becomes a sum of lifeless artifacts; from synthetic food to synthetic organs, the whole man becomes part of the total machinery that he controls and is simultaneously controlled by. He has no plan, no goal for life, except doing what the logic of technique determines him to do. He aspires to make robots as one of the greatest achievements of his technical mind, and some specialists assure us that the robot will hardly be distinguished from living men. This achievement will not seem so astonishing when man himself is hardly distinguishable from robot.

"The world of life has become a world of 'no-life'; persons have become 'nonpersons,' a world of death. Death is no longer symbolically expressed by unpleasant-smelling feces or corpses. Its symbols are now clean, shining machines; men are not attracted to smelly toilets, but to structures of aluminum and glass. But the reality behind this antiseptic façade becomes increasingly visible. Man, in the name of progress, is transforming the world into a stinking and poisonous place (and this is not symbolic). He pollutes the air, the water, the soil, the animals— and himself. He is doing this to a degree that has made it doubtful whether the earth will still be livable within a hundred years from now. He knows the facts, but in spite of many protesters, those in charge go on in the pursuit of technical 'progress' and are willing to sacrifice all life in the worship of their idol. In earlier times men also sacrificed their children or war prisoners, but never before in history has man been willing to sacrifice all life to the Moloch—his own and that of all his descendants. It makes little difference whether he does it intentionally or not. If he had no knowledge of the possible danger, he might be acquitted from responsibility. But it is the necrophilous element in his character that prevents him from making use of the knowledge he has."

Earlier I asked who is in charge. I ask now, What is God so afraid of, that he must through his servants destroy all life on earth?

◉

thirteen

confusion

I'm at Wal-Mart. I'm supposed to buy something. I don't remember what. I'm confused. Wal-Mart doesn't normally confuse me so much as it infuriates and demoralizes me, but today I'm confused. Time is shifting quickly, jumping, not like before.

I see a small man with dark hair, walking alone, wearing a red shirt with the slogan "Butt man." The shirt has a five-by-five grid of stencils of people in different positions having anal intercourse. He's carrying a case of diapers, a case of Sam's cola, and a bag of Doritos.

I see a woman wearing sweats, a "Jesus Saves" t-shirt, and a gold ring with a large diamond. The skin on her face is stretched. She has too few wrinkles for her age. Her hair is blond, her eyebrows dark.

I see fantail guppies swimming back and forth in tiny tanks.

I hear two different pop songs piped in to different parts of the store.

And then I don't see or hear any of this. I'm standing in an open ponderosa pine forest. The grass is sparse, dry, brittle. There are few bushes, lots of large orange-bellied pine trees. I smell vanilla. I hear a flicker call, then a woodpecker drum. I see a blue lizard on a rock.

And then I don't. I see an overweight father and mother and their three overweight children standing next to a cart filled with electronic equipment, dvds, peanut clusters, potato chips, more Sam's cola, two rolled-up posters, and a handful of slender white paper bags of prescription medicines.

And then I don't. I see empty shelves, broken aquariums, pieces of paper and plastic, old feces, and the disarticulated skeleton of a rat.

And then I don't. I see a man, rail thin, speed thin, with long greasy hair, teeth rotted by crank. I see him carrying 2-cycle oil, the sort used in lawnmowers.

And then I don't. I see rubble. The sun is bright. The wall where moments ago I saw tanks of tropical fish has collapsed. Beyond, I see other buildings, some fallen in, some still standing, all with broken windows.

And then I don't. I see a forest. I see a man—obviously an Indian—walking quietly by. Of course he doesn't see me. It's cloudy, and the air is cold. I feel the first stinging spits of freezing rain.

And then I don't. I can't move. I don't know where or how to step. I don't know if I'm perceived by the butt man or the woman without wrinkles. I'm guessing they didn't notice me. I'm guessing they saw me no more than did the Indian or the meth addict or the red-shafted flicker.

I continue to flip through time. Backward and forward. I see Indians making love. I see whites building houses. I see deer and elk and bears. I see stars at night, more stars than I've seen in my life. I see forests, I see fires, and then I see forests. And then I see the aisles of Wal-Mart, and I see people, and I see people, and I see people. I know I'm back where I started. I walk, at first carefully, and then with more confidence, out of the store and into the day.

I don't know what causes these dislocations, or what triggers them. I've tried to find patterns, but there are too many variables. I don't know if *I* cause the dislocations or someone else does, or many someones, or no one at all. Does fatigue, hunger, restedness have anything to do with it? How about location? Do some places call me more strongly to fall through time? And if I do fall, what determines how far forward or back I see? Is it all chance? Or are there those beings who want me to see certain things?

Not all of the dislocations are unpleasant. Some are beautiful. The salmon I see in Hangman—Latah—Creek. Of course the salmon make me cry, not only at their beauty, but at the sorrow of them no longer being there. I see the region as it was long before it was destroyed by our culture. And sometimes the dislocations are pleasant for other reasons. Several times over a few day period I walked into the bedroom and saw Allison and me making love. The first time felt slightly intrusive, but that night I asked Allison if she minded me watching, and she said of course not: she just wished she could get dislocated, too, and we could watch ourselves together. So the next couple of days I watched. Over the next few weeks I popped into the bedroom far more often than usual (I'd say fifteen or twenty times an afternoon is more than usual, wouldn't you?) but it hasn't happened again since.

Damn.

The dislocations don't happen at regular intervals. Sometimes they happen many times in one day—for shorter or longer periods—and sometimes they don't happen for weeks. I also can't tell if they happen in clusters. I began graphing the occurrences, but I ran into the problem we run into with any set of even slightly complex relationships: how do you separate signal from noise?

I realized, though, that I was facing an even deeper problem, which has to do with my reasons for wanting to separate signal from noise. In this case it was because I wanted to control these dislocations, when and where and how they occurred. I realized that instead of trying to figure this all out, maybe I should just experience it, and see what these experiences could or would teach me. Saying it like this, it seems so obvious to me, but the truth is that allowing myself to fall into experience—allowing myself to learn—is often much harder than I would like to think.

Allison and I go for a picnic. For once, our story doesn't include sex. We're going to a public place, and though we make jokes—hinting in a restaurant, for example, that we're going to sweep the dishes onto the floor so we can make better use of the table—the truth is that we're both quite shy and modest, and would be mortified if someone else saw too much of our skin, and even moreso if someone else saw us *doing* anything. It's one thing for me to watch us, and quite another for someone else.

We're going to where Latah Creek runs into the Spokane

River, beneath the Interstate. In retrospect, it was stupid of me to suggest we go there. I should have known what I might see, what I might hear. But I—and I suspect this is true for many of us—have paid so little attention to the land where I live, and to the scars it carries, that I actually thought I could go and have a nice picnic with Allison. I did not mean to see a man die, and I certainly did not mean to see a people lose their land.

We arrive. We park. We get out of the car. I hear a gunshot. I turn to Allison. She doesn't stop reaching into the back seat for the paper bag of sandwiches.

I hear another shot, and another. She doesn't flinch at any of these.

"It's starting," I say.

"Do you want to sit?"

"I'm okay."

And then I hear the boom of cannon. I've never heard cannon before, but I know this is the sound they make. I think I see smoke, but I'm not sure.

And then nothing. Back to normal. I grab the water from the car, and begin to walk away from the road, down a small road that has undergrowth on either side.

I stop.

Allison: "What?"

"Nothing," I say. And we walk.

We get to a small ledge overlooking the river, perhaps ten feet up. The road ends here. We continue down a path to the river. I hope to see salmon, but I do not. For a few moments I don't see anything unexpected.

Then suddenly it begins. I see men running for the river, men riding horses painted with brown and red figures of animals. I see men with feathers in their hair and blood on their skin. I hear gunshots. I hear cannon-fire. I hear whoops, and I see men in blue uniforms riding horses, chasing these others. I see men jumping into the river, trying to cross. I see other men stopping on the banks to shoot at them. I see many of the fleeing men fall.

"Allison," I say.

I want to go back to the car, but I can't turn away. I hear bullets fly past. I wonder, *Can these bullets hit me? If one hits me, will I die?* I wonder, *Can they hit Allison, even though she doesn't see them?*

But then I stop thinking, because I see a man running toward me. He's an Indian. He wears a white buckskin shirt and a tanned skin hat. He comes closer, and closer still. He doesn't see me. I hear a shot, see a red rose appear on the breast of his shirt. He stumbles, rights himself, keeps running. Closer and closer he comes. The rose expands. He slows, sways, stands not a foot from me. He looks me in the eye. I cannot move.

I say, "I—"

The rose gets larger. He reaches with both hands, grabs my shoulders, says something to me in a language I don't understand.

I want to help him, but I don't know what to do. I search his eyes as he searches mine. He falls. I watch him die at my feet.

And then he's gone.

Finally I take a step back, turn to face Allison. There are no more gunshots, only the sounds of cars on the interstate. Without a word she comes to hold me. I start to cry.

But I don't learn my lesson. We try again, another picnic, another day. This time we drive east of Spokane, to the Idaho border. We stop, get out of the car. I don't fall through time. We walk away from the road, find a nice spot near the river, put down a blanket, lay out the food: fried chicken, biscuits, and jojos. We bought the jojos, and Allison cooked the chicken and biscuits. They're good. Had I cooked them, the chicken would have been dry, the biscuits tasteless and hard.

After lunch we sit, Allison cross-legged watching ants in the grass, me leaning slightly back, legs extended. I'm looking far away, at nothing in particular.

This time it begins with a smell.

Have you ever smelled fear? I don't mean anxiety or tension.

I don't even mean dread. I certainly don't mean resignation, a smell too familiar to too many of us. I mean animal terror. That is what I smell.

I hear gunshots. Many of them. The same sort of gun I heard at the mouth of Latah Creek. I stand. Out of the corners of my eyes I see Allison look up at me. I shake my head, begin to walk. She stands, follows.

The smell gets stronger, mixing now with gunpowder, sweat, and the smell of horses. The sounds get stronger too: rifles, laughter, the whinnying of horses, and in my chest—not my ears—I hear the rumble of thousands of horse hooves pawing the ground.

I walk toward the sound, around a bend in the river, Allison a couple of steps behind me and off to the side.

And then I see before me a sea of horses, contained on one side by the river, on two sides by steep banks, and on the final side by a rope fence. They're the Indians' horses. Or they were. Men in blue surround the horses. Men in blue stand beyond the rope fence. Men in blue shout orders. Men in blue throw back their heads and laugh. Men in blue wade into the sea, clubbing the smaller horses and shooting the larger horses once in the head, just behind the ear. I look at one horse among the many hundreds, and I see the whites of her eyes as her child is killed, and then I see her fall, too. I hear another shot, and see another horse fall. And another. And another.

I stop, stand, stagger, say, "I can't. . . ."

The dust below turns to mud, mixing soil, blood, piss, and shit. The slaughter continues. The men in blue laugh and laugh and laugh.

Allison stands next to me, takes my hand.

"What," I say, 'is wrong with these people?"

I knew what I saw and I knew of course the larger cultural context in which what I'd seen took place—takes place—but I went to the library to learn the specifics. That first day I'd seen the end of what's called the Battle of the Spokane Plains, where in September,

1858, a combined force of Spokane, Palouse, Yakima, and Coeur d'Alene Indians attempted to drive a column of U.S. soldiers commanded by a Colonel George Wright from the Indians' land. It's a story we've heard tens of thousands of times, in tens of thousands of places at the frontiers of this culture. It's the story that the *wétikos* never seem to tire of realizing. It's the story of *wétikos* encountering a people who've lived on a land—with a land—for as long as that people can remember, who've become a part of that land as it has become a part of them. Or maybe that's not the story, since the non-*wétikos* do not exist, but are merely a barrier to the *wétikos* getting what they—we—want: a barrier to resource extraction, a barrier to the destruction of a piece of land, no different than thorns on a blackberry bush, no different than a snake who strikes at you before you cut off its head and sell its skin. It's the story of the *wétikos*, the civilized, those suffering from—or, from their perspective, blessed with—the cannibal sickness, those driven to conquer, to fulfill their manifest destiny. And it's the story of resistance by some members of the noninfected group, flight by others, the death of others, and the conversion or infection of still others.

In this case, as in so many, the Indians won a few battles, but the *wétikos* kept coming, wave after wave, until, finally, in the Battle of the Spokane Plains, the Indians were routed.

Soon, Indians came to speak with Colonel Wright, to tell him they wanted to fight no more. Colonel Wright responded, in words perfectly capturing the *wétiko* mentality of this entire culture, "I did not come into this country to ask you to make peace; I came here to fight. Now, when you are tired of the war, and ask for peace, I will tell you what you must do: You must come to me with your arms, and your women and children, and everything you have, and lay them at my feet; you must put your faith in me and trust to my mercy." Sounds like God, doesn't it? Maybe that's because it is.

Wright held one of the chiefs who had come to speak with him as his prisoner, and a few days later hanged him at sunset.

Colonel Wright and his *wétiko* soldiers also captured—*stole* would be the less polite term—most of the Spokane Indians' horses.

Of course, from the beginning of civilization the *wétikos* have insti-
tuted scorched earth policies everywhere they've gone—and I mean
scorched earth in its most literal as well as figurative senses—systematically ruining all foods, fouling all waters, wrecking everything they
cannot carry off to sell, enslave, or destroy elsewhere. Wright called
a meeting of his officers to determine what to do with the horses.
One officer later wrote, "I told him I should not sleep so long as
they remained alive, as I regarded them the main dependence and
most prized of all the possessions of the Indians." Wright and the
rest of the officers evidently agreed with this logic, because they allowed themselves and other favored officers to "select a certain number" of horses, and they gave one or two to each of the "friendly
Indians"—in other words, those already infected—who had fought
beside them. The other horses they ordered killed. The same officer
who would not sleep so long as these horses lived later wrote, "They
were all sleek, glossy, and fat, and as I love a horse, I fancied I saw in
their beautiful faces an appeal for mercy. Towards the last the soldiers
appeared to exult in their bloody task; such is the ferocious character
of men."

Or maybe such is the ferocious character of *wétikos*. The
Indians had a different response. As I read in one book I found in
the library, "Indians who heard of these latest developments now had
very good reason to keep a great distance away from Wright. Entering Wright's camp clearly resulted in death."

This is the story we have heard so many times: encountering
the *wétikos* clearly results in death.

What are we going to do about the fact that civilization—the dominant culture, the cannibals, the *wétikos*, whatever—is killing the planet? I've written book after book describing
this culture's destructiveness—and certainly I've read hundreds
more—and I still don't understand it. I don't understand the
motivations for the destruction—as we already talked about,

what's the use of retiring rich on a planet being murdered, or more to the point, being rendered uninhabitable?—and I don't understand its wantonness. I don't understand the hatefulness on any level, from the most personal to the most global.

Today I learned that a friend of a friend was recently raped by an acquaintance of hers, in the presence of others of their social group. Although she actively tried to fight the man off, other members of this group later tried to convince her she had brought it on, and she had enjoyed it. She told them she was going to press charges, and every one of these people suddenly changed stories: far from her precipitating the rape, it never happened at all. One called her home and left a message threatening her with (more) physical harm if she pursued this case. The man's girlfriend has threatened her. Most of her friends are telling her not to ruin this man's life. Her bosses—a couple who live next door to the rapist's girlfriend—told her that if she pressed charges they would fire her.

I don't understand.

Salmon, bison, ivory-billed woodpeckers, Eskimo curlews, Carolina parakeets, Siberian tigers, Javan rhinos, swordfish, great white sharks, blue whales, gray whales, Steller's sea cows. Every stream in the continental United States is contaminated with carcinogens. There's dioxin and flame retardant in every mother's breast milk. There are more than 2 million dams just in the United States. It is entirely possible that global warming could enter a runaway phase that could effectively end life on this planet. We are told we must balance the "needs" of the economic system against the needs of "the environment." And did I mention that deforestation of the Amazon is accelerating?

I don't understand.

The good news, I suppose, is that the point is not and has never been simply to understand the hatefulness, the destructiveness, as though describing it well enough, writing enough books about it, will somehow make the hatefulness go away and the destruction stop. The point is to stop the destructiveness, stop this malignant form of hatred. Ultimately our attempts at understanding the destructiveness are only helpful insofar as they help to stop that destructiveness. Otherwise they're a waste of time.

If the destructiveness is caused by some cultural sickness or by some hitchhiker, then the magical hope of many mainstream activists for some spiritual transformation leading to peace, justice, and sustainability becomes even more absurd than it already is. Sure, we've all heard of people facing death from some horrible disease who undergo a miraculous spiritual rebirth that leads to remission of the disease and a long healthy life for the initiate, but we've also heard of those who undergo this rebirth and then die anyway. Sometimes diseases might be teachers for us, but sometimes cancer, Crohn's, diabetes, leprosy, AIDS, tuberculosis, Ebola, smallpox, and polio aren't teachers so much as they're simply diseases that kill us. Similarly, how many psychopaths have suddenly become warm and loving individuals? I know that the recidivism rate among perpetrators of domestic violence approaches 100 percent. To be clear: could words stop a rabid dog? Could waves of loving kindness stop an infected cricket from reaching water? Could impassioned pleas and precise articulations stop a spider from spinning her own scaffold for the wasp who will soon kill her? Will entreaties and moral pronouncements stop the wétikos from turning this entire planet into a death camp—which of course from the perspective of the indigenous and of nonhumans they already have—and even worse, from killing the whole planet?

These are questions with answers I understand.

Yet another day, yet another picnic. You'd think I'd have learned. This day we're going to visit some of the apple trees we planted. Planting trees for bears hasn't worked like we'd hoped. The damn bears keep snapping off limbs, sometimes trunks. Don't they realize we're planting these trees for them?

I have to admit, though, that when I think about it even for a moment, I realize that the bears don't break all the trees, and in fact destroy a lot fewer trees in general than do *wétikos*.

We drive toward Latah Creek, then turn right onto a dirt trail that heads sharply down. We stop next to one of Latah's small tributaries. Allison turns off the truck.

We get out, follow a path to our right. We see that bears haven't damaged the three young trees we planted in a small clearing by the water. The trees are growing nicely. They should bear good fruit this year. We walk back a ways toward the truck, out of the sun, still by the stream.

It's a hot day, not a dry heat like you'd normally expect in Spokane, but beneath this covering of leaves and branches, a sort of green heat. In the clearing, or by the road, or above the trees, or in the city, the world is dry, crumbly, radiating a wilting, scorching, searing, killing heat that sucks the water—the life—out of your lungs. Here, under this canopy, the air, the ground, your skin, is nearly as hot, but the heat is heavier, wetter. It makes plants grow tall and slender in the shade. The plants sway in the slight breezes that always promise to cool you off but you so rarely seem to feel, and even when you do they just seem to make you hotter with their damp.

We sit by the stream, shoes off, feet in. The water soon makes us cool all over.

I'm a bit traumatized from our last two picnics, afraid to look up for what I might see, afraid to take a deep breath for what I might smell. I'm like the cat who's been hit and who now panics with every sound or sudden movement. Every strange noise, every unexpected sight makes me wonder whether it's beginning again. And I somehow know that if it does begin again it won't be salmon or elk or a healthy forest that I'll see, but something I'd rather not, something from which I would turn away if I had the choice.

Allison tells me about some new galleries interested in her work. I nod. She trails off. We sit a moment. She tells me about her friend Deborah, who's been calling several times a day to complain about her newest boyfriend, who never calls when he says he will, but then when he comes over she gets tired of him anyway (and he *is* going bald, and she never has liked the shape of his penis anyway) but do you think, Deborah asks every day, that he might be the one?

I look at Allison out of the corners of my eyes.

She says, "You're bored."

"Deborah bores you. What makes you think. . . ."

"Sorry."

We sit. I know something's coming. I don't know how I know. I just do.

She starts to describe an argument with her sister. I don't know what it's about. I'm not listening.

I hear the sound of duct tape being removed from cloth. It's a very soft sound, but it fills my head. I don't know how I know what it is. I just do.

I look around. Nothing.

Allison is still talking about her sister. I'm still not listening to her.

Then I hear footfalls on the path from the truck. Two sets. One slow. The other faster. I turn again.

Allison: "Why do I waste my breath?"

"I'm sorry."

"Don't blame Deborah for you not listening. You're not listening to me now."

"I—"

I hear a soft grunt as a man—definitely a man—exerts some effort: pushes, pulls, lifts, or strikes. I look again at the path.

"And you weren't listening when I was talking about the galleries."

"Allison. . . ."

The thud of something hitting bone. A soft exhalation.

"How would you feel if I got distracted when you tried to read me your work?"

A quick glimpse of a young woman, falling.

"You're still not listening."

She hits the ground.

I say, "Someone's dying."

Silence.

I say, "Someone's being killed."

The woman lies unmoving. A man stands over her. He leans down. Sticks a needle in her skin. The scene freezes, skips, backs up. I see him walking behind her. I hear him softly say something. I cannot make it out. He raises his arm. He holds a blackjack. I stand, walk toward the spot.

Again the scene freezes. Again it skips, backs up. Some things I can see clearly. Some I cannot. I see the woman. Young, long blonde hair, pretty face, squarish jaw, small nose, tired eyes. Sorrow. Tension. The man I do not see as well. But this time I hear him. Not sentences. Just words. Clipped, lost, torn out of their context. His voice. Vagina. Sheath. Kill. Intercourse. Intercourse. Sheath. Vagina. Kill. I see the blackjack rise. Vagina. Sheath. That slight hesitation as the arm finishes cocking. Intercourse. Kill.

It begins its descent, at first almost imperceptibly. I'm standing by the path now. I try to step between, to block the blackjack with my arm, with my body, but the whole scene explodes. The blackjack moves faster than anything I've ever seen. A pain shoots from the back of my brain to the front. I see this woman—this girl—standing with a boy on a moonlit country road. I see clouds behind black silhouettes of trees. I hear her call her mother.

The scene freezes, skips, backs up. The blackjack rises, falls, the pain shoots through my head. Again. Again. Again. I cannot make it stop. A body falls. The blackjack rises, hesitates, explodes, rises, hesitates, explodes. Vagina, sheath, kill, intercourse.

My face is flat against the ground.

The blackjack rises. Pain. It falls. Vagina. The girl and boy. The moon. Mother. Pain.

The world goes black. Nothing.

I hear a man's voice, saying again and again, "Nika."

"Who was this woman?"

I'm sitting with Allison in a room in a police station, talking to a cop. I'm thinking about what I've come to call the 90 percent rule, which is that 90 percent of all people are incompetent. This is as true for cops as it is for writers as it is for doctors as it is for killers as it is for auto mechanics as it is for psychotherapists as it is for poker players as it is for politicians as it is for grave robbers. Some of that incompetence is inherent no matter how much effort a person makes (see me, for example, when I bet on sporting) and some of the incompetence comes from people not caring about what they're doing (see me, for example, when it comes to organic chemistry, car repair, and cooking). In this cop's case I have my suspicions about the former, but I can vouch for the latter. He doesn't give a shit—about me, about Nika, about his job, about anything other than the clock on the wall to one side of the room.

I tell the cop again that I know only her name and what she looks like. He's asked me four times. Not because he's searching for an answer, but because he's not listening to mine. He looks again at the clock. Ten minutes till shift change.

He asks, "And when did she die?"

I say again, "I don't know that either. I'm not even sure she's dead. I don't think she was."

"Did she moan?"

I'm starting to wonder if I'm falling through time. He asked me this before. I say, "She was thinking about her mother, and about a boy, and a moonlit night."

"She told you this."

I wouldn't have minded if he didn't believe me. I fully expected him not to believe me. I wouldn't have believed me. I get notes all the time from people who want to tell me how we can dematerialize toxic waste vibrationally, or how space aliens give messages to us through a complex code where letters translate into numbers which you must add up and then break down into other letters, or how if we can only bring JFK's real killers to trial, the United States will become a democracy, or a thousand other theories. They all want attention. I can't give it. There aren't enough hours in the day, and all of the attention in the world wouldn't suffice to make these people feel heard. I've tried, and it only encourages them to keep sucking at my energy until I'm as empty as they are. I was prepared for the cop to be dubious, if not downright cold, but not incompetent and distracted. I'd hoped that if I was clear and precise and honest the cop might at least listen. Perhaps these other people feel the same when they write to me.

I think for a moment about keeping my mouth shut, but then I just go ahead and tell the truth. I say, "I could see her thoughts."

He glances at the clock.

I know it doesn't matter what I say. The only thing that would have mattered would have been if I had brought Nika in here with me. Then he would have cursed me for making him work overtime. I've noticed that he hasn't written down anything I've said, not even before it started getting weird.

He asks, "Like in the funnies?"

I blink.

He says, "You saw her thoughts, in a bubble like in a comic strip."

"No, I saw her thoughts like I see my own. How do you see your own memories?"

"And this happens all the time?"

"Sometimes."

"Do you see dead people, too, like in the movie?"

I start to get up. "I'm sorry I've wasted your time."

Again a glance at the clock. "What do you want me to do?"

"Find her. Save her."

"Who is she?"

"I've told you, I don't know. Nika. That's all I know."

"Let me get this straight. You want me to find a woman named Nika who may have been kidnapped at any point in the past, or who may not yet have been kidnapped, but who may get kidnapped at some point in the future. Right? You want me to protect this woman who may very well not yet have been born. Right?"

"You don't even want me to look at pictures of missing women?"

He shifts uncomfortably, looks at the clock.

"Maybe I would recognize her."

Silence. He stands. "I'm off duty now. You find a body, and we'll talk."

fourteen

t h u n d e r

Nika is dreaming. She's dreaming of nights and days and the sounds of a stream. In her dream she feels the breath of willows on her cheeks and inside her bones. She feels ponderosa pine roots pulsing beneath the ground, and she feels the ground itself breathing its way into her. She no longer cares or even notices how long these breaths last. She merely takes each one in and lets it back out.

She feels herself settling deeper into the spot where she lies, like a cat on a lap, like a river in a canyon, like being in bed after a hard day of playing when she was young.

Nika is dreaming, and sometimes she sees other people, people she doesn't recognize. They walk like ghosts, and sometimes notice her. Most often they don't.

Nika is dreaming, and sometimes her dreams are filled with yearning, yearning for her mother and father, and yearning also for other things she has never known, yearning for things she cannot yet name, and does not know if she ever will.

Nika is dreaming, and she's filled with yearning. She's dreaming of fish longer than her arm and bigger than her thighs, and they're swimming shoulder to shoulder in a stream. She's dreaming of grizzly bears walking humpbacked along the bank. She's dreaming of the weight of ancient trees pressing down on her chest, and she's dreaming of fire and rain and snow and willows and more birds singing than she ever imagined existed. The songs fill her rib cage and leak out of her throat, and sometimes she cannot hear her own voice over the songs of the birds, the bears, the salmon, and the trees.

Nika is dreaming.

I'm lying in bed. Allison says, "I'm sorry."

"I'm sorry, too. I'm not much fun this way."

"That's okay." She smiles, says, "What do you think is happening?"

I shake my head, say, "I'm scared, for Nika, for myself."

"What do you want to do about her?"

"What can I do? Wait. Maybe I'll learn more."

"And what about you?"

"And us," I say.

"We're fine," she responds.

"You're losing patience. The other day wasn't the first time. I'm a mess. I can't drive. You have to run all the errands. I can't always attend to what you're saying. I feel like I can't do *anything*. I'm falling apart, and I don't want to bring you down with me."

"You're not."

"I can't control this. If I could turn it on and off at will—if there was some button I could push or incantation I could speak—this would be a good thing. But I've lost control of my life because of this."

"Have you?"

"I have no continuity. I could fall through time at any moment. Do you know how scary that is?"

"My cousin has MS. Your mom had a car wreck. I have a friend who gained a hundred and fifty pounds and hasn't had sex in a decade since she got raped."

"That doesn't help."

"None of our lives are in control."

"That still doesn't help. I don't want to hear other people's stories, and I don't want to hear theory, and I don't want to hear that the belief that we have control is the problem, and I don't want to hear that the notion of personal control is meaningless when the culture is killing the planet. When I had the prostate infection you didn't tell me that other people have pain, too. I don't want that."

"What do you want?"

"I want it to stop."

"Do you?"

"Yes."

"You do?"

"Yes." A pause. "No. I don't know."

"What do you want?"

◉

In 2003, researchers set up remote cameras in the Lan-jak-Entimau Wildlife Sanctuary in East Malaysia. In August that year, one of the cameras snapped a single picture of a Borneo bay cat, a wild animal the size of a large domestic cat with an extremely long tail. The sighting was significant in part because the Borneo bay cat had not been observed by humans since 1992, and had been thought to be extinct.

In 2005, in swampy forests in Arkansas, scientists videotaped an ivory-billed woodpecker, the largest woodpecker in the United States. On seeing the woodpecker, one of the scientists put his head in his hands and began to sob: although there had been many rumored sightings of the bird over the last seventy years, this was the first undeniable proof that the ivory-billed woodpecker lived.

Also in 2005, a botany graduate student at UC Berkeley found a dozen Mount Diablo buckwheat plants blooming on the side of that mountain. This was the first time a human being had seen this plant since 1936. No human knows where the plants have been in the meantime, or why they chose to bloom right then.

And yet again in 2005, an ecologist found a species of grass—california dissanthelium—who hadn't been seen by humans in more than ninety years on Santa Catalina Island. The grass used to grow on three different islands, but had not been seen since 1912.

All over the world, in jungles, in mountain lairs, in swamps and desert caves, in other places, too, places they are safe, plants and animals are lying low, ghost dancing, waiting for their time to return. Perhaps the cannibal sickness—perhaps God—isn't so powerful as we fear, isn't so powerful as it wants us to think.

Or perhaps it is.

Have you ever considered how extraordinarily lucky the Europeans were—how lucky they had to be—in order to conquer the Americas? Have you ever considered the delicate thread of circumstance—of which the fraying and snapping of any part could have doomed the whole endeavor—that led to these stunning European victories? European civilization was at the time of Columbus on its last legs, having already hyper-exploited much of that continent's resource base well past the breaking point. Without a massive influx of resources—in other words, without the discovery, conquest, and exploitation of new continents—European cities and cultures would soon have begun to collapse.

What would have happened to European civilization—to this whole wétiko culture—if, for example, Columbus had turned back on his first voyage, as many of his men wanted? The trip was far longer than anyone—including Columbus—had anticipated. To keep his crew from mutinying, Columbus kept two logs: one known only to him, showing the accurate distance traveled each day; and one grossly underreporting to his crew the distance they'd traveled from Europe. What if his deception hadn't worked? It almost didn't. By October 10, the only way Columbus could keep his crew from mutinying was by promising that if they didn't sight land within two days they'd turn back. Well, we all know what happened October 12, and we all know why October 12 is a day of celebration for wétikos and a day of mourning for everyone else. How would the world look today had the crew made their demands one day sooner? What if the currents on which the ships rode had been one day slower, the land one day farther away? What if the crew had known that Columbus would steal not only from those whose land they "discovered," but from them as well?

Or what if Columbus hadn't landed at what is now called Hispaniola, had not first encountered the Arawaks, of whom he wrote, "They do not bear arms, and do not know them, for I showed them a sword, they took it by the edge and cut themselves out of ignorance. They have no iron. Their spears are made of cane. . . . They would make fine servants. . . . With fifty men we could subjugate them all and make them do whatever we want"? What if instead the wétikos would have first encountered a more warlike group of people, a group of people ready to defend themselves, ready to kill Columbus and crew to the last man? What if Columbus had never returned to Europe? How long would it have been before any crown repeated the folly of spending so much money to send someone to sail so far to the west? Would it have happened before Europe entered an irreversible and hopefully terminal decline?

When Hernando Cortés invaded what is now Mexico with only six hundred men, twenty horses, and ten small cannons, what would have happened had the inhabitants of the region not had long-held myths that told them of fair-skinned gods coming from the east in sailing ships? Who gave them those myths? Who taught them those lessons, lessons which would destroy them? What would have happened had Cortés not found Indian nations with whom he could ally against the Aztecs (only to subjugate these others once their usefulness had passed)? What if these Indians had slaughtered him on the beaches, as he later slaughtered them in their homes and streets, in mines, in forests, plains, deserts, hills?

The Europeans could not have conquered the Americas without the assistance of smallpox and other diseases, introduced both intentionally and accidentally. How different would the world look today if the Indians would not have been wiped out by these diseases? Would we be experiencing worldwide ecological collapse had the Europeans not given but received smallpox, carried it back home with them, had the civilized and not the indigenous suffered from its effects, and thus had the Europeans not been able to steal the resources and the land of those in the western hemisphere?

Something as insubstantial as fog saved Hitler's life. Something as short as a single day, something as small as a virus, saved European civilization from crashing.

Not only had those in Germany and on the Western Front tried to kill Hitler. Many assassination attempts originated in Army Group Center, which formed the hub for resistance on the Eastern Front. Key to this resistance was senior operations officer Lieutenant-Colonel Henning von Tresckow. Unable to abide meanness or injustice, his opposition to Hitler and the Nazi regime was both deep and consistent. In 1939 he told a fellow conspirator that "both duty and honour demand from us that we should do our best to bring about the downfall of Hitler and National-Socialism."

He worked tirelessly. He organized, cajoled, delegated, he gathered and experimented with explosives, he recruited people for attacks on Hitler.

Not all of the attacks went anywhere. Sometimes Hitler was saved, not because of luck or the help of some God, but because of scruples. In early 1943, Georg Freiherr von Boeselager, known as one of the Army's best pentathletes, joined the opposition. Tresckow asked Boeselager if he could kill Hitler with a single pistol shot. Boeselager responded he had the technical skill, but wasn't sure he had the nerves. It's one thing, he said, to kill an anonymous enemy on the field of battle, and quite another to kill someone you can recognize. This is often true, it seems, even if you recognize that killing the one person will save millions of others. He did not carry out an attack.

Later that year a group of twelve officers determined that together they would kill Hitler during a briefing on the horrendous military situation on the Eastern Front. This attempt had to be abandoned because one of those present would have been Field Marshall von Kluge. It was necessary to inform Kluge so he could stay out of the way. Kluge disallowed the attempt because of the risk to senior officers (including himself) and because, he said, it was not seemly to shoot a man at lunch.

About this same time, General Hubert Lanz and Colonel Graf von Strachwitz made plans to use Strachwitz's Grossdeutschland Panzer Regiment to arrest Hitler the next time he came to the Eastern Front to speak with Field Marshall von Weichs. Lanz and Strachwitz were fully prepared to kill Hitler if, as expected, his police, SS, and army bodyguards resisted. By the time Hitler came east for a conference, however, circumstances had forced Weichs to move his headquarters away from Poltava, where Strachwitz's regiment was billeted, to Saporozhe, too far away for Strachwitz to be able to move without raising alarms. Thus that plan came to nothing.

Hitler's life was saved on that trip not only by the movement of Weichs's headquarters, but by another providential occurrence. While Hitler was in Saporozhe, Russian tanks made a sudden—and coincidental—thrust toward the town. The tanks were only two hours away when Hitler's driver became aware of the threat, and drove from the airport into town to get Hitler. They returned to the airport as quickly as they could and boarded their planes. As they took off they saw Russian tanks just sitting at the end of the airfield. The only reason the tanks had not attacked, trapping Hitler deep inside Russia, is that they'd run out of fuel.

◉

"What do I want?"

"That's what *I* asked."

"I want to stop the *wétikos*."

"It's what I want, too." Silence. Then, "But in the meantime. . . ."

"I want to not be so scared."

"Is there someone you could talk to?"

"Like a shrink? They'd look at me like the fucking cop, presume I'm delusional, and try to resolve whatever childhood trauma led to this disorder. Or even worse, they'd believe me: would you want to trust your psyche to the sort of psychologist who'd believe a story like this?"

"No, someone else."

"Who?"

"That's the problem. I have no idea. I don't even know what you want from *me*. I'm glad to just hold you when you get scared if that's what you want. Or. . . ."

"Or what?"

"I don't know. I just know that what you want will help determine whom you should talk to. If you want the dislocations to stop there's probably someone who can help. If you want to learn to cope with them, maybe you talk to someone else. If you want to learn how to ride them—if possible—then maybe it's someone else again."

Images from the dislocations rise up in my mind. I ask myself exactly what about them terrifies me. "It's not being out of control," I say. "When I fell through time and saw us making love, I was delighted. It makes me happy to see the salmon, at least for the time I'm there. Now that I know—or at least feel confident—that I'll come back, the dislocations themselves don't terrify me. Inconvenience me, sure. But terrify, no."

"What terrifies you?"

I see Nika. I see the rose blooming on the man's chest. I see the look on the horse's face as her child is killed. I hear men laughing. I see the hammer rise and fall. I hear the man say *vagina*. I hear the man say *kill*.

But then I also see glaciers melting. I see driftnets. I see longline trawlers. I see clearcuts. I see chainsaws. I see vivisection labs and factory farms. I see plastics. I remember why Allison did not like to be told she is beautiful. I think of the other women I know who've been raped. None of these require I fall through time. They merely require I not look away.

"I want," I say, "to stop the wétiko culture."

"Then that means," she responds without hesitation, "you need to talk to someone else entirely."

It's late that night. The room is dark. The last thing I see before I close my eyes is a flash of lightning joining cloud to cloud. I sleep, then awaken to thunder so loud and so insistent I think someone is knocking on the window. I look without rising, and there's no one there but more lightning, and more, and more thunder, and more. I do not go back to sleep, but sit partway up to watch and listen and to let the lightning and thunder fill me as I wait alone in the room with Allison asleep next to me.

fifteen

miracles

⊙

I go to the library. One of my favorite parts of being a writer is getting to be in a library and calling it work. The library is at Gonzaga University. It's beautiful, except there is a sculpture of Bing Crosby—abuser of wife and children—that I walk past to get here.

I fall through time once or twice as I walk through the stacks. Or maybe stumble is better, since I see only flashes before coming back to the present. I see myself. I'm sitting on the floor in the stacks, surrounded by books, holding an open book in my lap, crying. The book—I see as well as remember—has photos of children as young as three and four and five forced to work in textile mills, coal mines, brickmaking factories.

And now I'm back, almost walking into a coed who's wearing too-tight blue jeans and a too-tight white t-shirt. I step around her and stumble again, this time seeing myself in a different row, reading different books, these on the European conquest of North America.

Today I'm hoping to read an account of the systematic genocide perpetrated against the indigenous of Europe by the civilized between, say, the beginning of the current era and 1500, sort of an earlier European version of *American Holocaust* or B*ury My Heart at Wounded Knee.* Maybe something called *Bury My Heart in Saxony.* Of course it's the same story I mentioned earlier, the modus operandi of the dominant culture. It was true two hundred years ago, it was true two thousand years ago, and it's true today. Just yesterday I read, "Deep in the Amazon rainforest a small tribe of uncontacted Indians is on the run, fleeing chainsaws and bulldozers as logging companies penetrate their forest home. They shun all contact with outsiders. They are fighting for their very survival. If urgent measures are not taken to protect them and their land from this invasion, they will disappear forever. That this is genocide is indisputable. Very little is known about the tribe, commonly referred to as the Rio Pardo Indians, who live on the border of Mato Grosso and Amazonas states. They may be the last survivors of their people, or they could be related to one of several neighbouring tribes who nickname them 'Baixinhos' (the tiny people) or 'Cabeças vermelhas' (the red heads). Since the 1980s, sightings and rumours have abounded. Arara Indians, who live in the area, report hearing them at night near their villages, mimicking the sounds of animals. Settlers and miners in the area have come across their abandoned houses. The government's Indian Affairs Department FUNAI has disturbing evidence that the heavily armed loggers are hunting down the Indians. One field worker told Survival, 'The loggers are going to clean out the Indians. They will just shoot them to kill them.'" The day before, I read an article about the destruction of different Indians that had the pull quote: "'They killed my mother, my brothers and my sisters, and my wife.' Karapiru Awá, survivor of a massacre." The article: "Unless the Brazilian government, the World Bank and the mining company CVRD take urgent action, uncontacted Awá Indians in Brazil could soon be wiped out." A couple hundred years ago the Shawnee Chiksika pretty much summed up this pattern when he said, "The white man seeks to conquer nature, to bend it to his will and to use it wastefully until it is all gone and then he simply moves on, leaving the waste behind him and looking for new places to take. The whole white race is a monster who is always hungry and what he eats is land."

I want to find a book that will help me understand how the Europeans became subsumed into the cannibal culture. Walking down a row I see one that looks slightly promising: *The Barbarian Conversion From Paganism to Christianity*, by Richard Fletcher. At least it's the right subject. I know I'm in trouble, however, as soon as I open it: the author dedicates the book to his late mother, thanking her, for among other things, encouraging him to be a regular church-goer. At least he doesn't try to hide his prejudices.

I spend the afternoon there in the stacks reading the book. I'm simultaneously disappointed and blown away.

My disappointment is the same one I used to feel when I'd watch cowboy and Indian movies, the same one I feel today when I read newspaper accounts of U.S. invasions: the authors' heroes are so often my villains, and their villains are my heroes.

In this book, the Catholics—the civilized—are the heroes, not the committers of genocide. One of the results of this is that the role of the sword in the "barbarian" "conversion" gets de-emphasized, and the g-word—genocide—doesn't get mentioned at all. The author can't, of course, avoid all mention of the sword, but he allows his language only to hint at the impact, as when he calls without much elucidation the Christian conquest of Saxony a "precedent" for "ugly episodes" in sixteenth-century Mexico.

I stand, return to the row where I once sat reading about the conquest of the Americas, and see myself again through the years. I look closely at myself, sitting in corduroys and flannel shirt, clean but disheveled hair down to my collar, face unshaven. The me on the floor glances up, looks right through me, and I wonder how many of us ever get to see ourselves unselfconsciously. I hold that moment, treasure it, look at myself as I would look at anyone else I love. And then the vision fades. I step to where I was sitting, and pick up one of the books I read before.

I shake my head to clear it, to return fully to the present, and think again about that author's language. I think about ugly episodes; an argument with Allison where she and I both fought unfair; yelling at the cat because she peed on my handwritten notes for the next section I was writing; snapping at my mom over an entirely imagined slight. Those are the real ugly episodes.

I open the book in front of me, flip through it, find examples of what this apologist for genocide calls "ugly episodes" from sixteenth-century Mexico. Ugly episodes. Cortés sent a "peace" delegation to the Aztecs, who welcomed them with songs. In the midst of the celebration, according to the sixteenth-century historian Bernardino de Sahagún, "The first Spaniards to start fighting suddenly attacked those who were playing the music for the singers and dancers. They chopped off their hands and their heads so that they fell down dead. Then all the other Spaniards began to cut off heads, arms, and legs and to disembowel the Indians. Some had their heads cut off, others were cut in half, and others had their bellies slit open, immediately to fall dead. Others dragged their entrails along until they collapsed. Those who reached the exits were slain by the Spaniards guarding them; and others jumped over the walls of the courtyard; while yet others climbed up the temple; and still others, seeing no escape, threw themselves down among the slaughtered and escaped by feigning death. So great was the bloodshed that rivulets ran through the courtyard like water in a heavy rain. So great was the slime of blood and entrails in the courtyard and so great was the stench that it was both terrifying and heartrending. Now that nearly all were fallen and dead, the Spaniards went searching for those who had climbed up the temple, and those who had hidden among the dead, killing all those they found alive."

Ugly episodes. Cortés: "I resolved to enter the next morning shortly before dawn and do all the harm we could . . . and we fell upon a huge number of people. As these were some of the most wretched people and had come in search of food, they were nearly all unarmed, and women and children in the main. We did them so much harm through all the streets in the city that we could reach. . . ."

Ugly episodes. Cortés and other Spaniards enslaved Indians and sent them to work on plantations and in mines. They killed them faster than they could be replaced, even at a cost of seven pesos each.

Ugly episodes. In about a century the Spaniards reduced

the population of the Tepehuán people by 90 percent, the Irritilla by 93 percent, the Acaxee by 95 percent, the Mayo peoples by 94 percent.

Ugly episodes. I see Indians chained together at the neck, being led to mines. I see Spaniards decapitating them if they slow. I see Spaniards cutting off women's breasts. I see Indian babies being killed and used as roadside markers. I see Spaniards cutting off Indians' hands and noses, then stringing these dismembered parts around their necks and sending them home. I see Spaniards throwing "pregnant and confined women, children, old men, as many as they could capture," into pits packed with spikes, so that the Indians are "left stuck on the stakes, until the pits were filled." I see that, in the words of one contemporary, "The Spaniards cut off the arm of one, the leg or hip of another, and some their heads at one stroke, like butchers cutting up beef and mutton for market. . . . Vasco ordered forty of them to be torn to pieces by dogs." I see Spaniards testing the sharpness of their swords on the bodies of Indian children, and I see them tearing infants from their mothers' arms to feed to their dogs.

I think, for that matter, about the "ugly episode" that gave Hangman Valley its name. Before Colonel Wright arrived in Spokane, Hangman Valley and the creek that runs through it were known as Latah, which means in the native tongue stream where little fish are caught. Soon after the battle near the Spokane River, soon after Colonel Wright and his men hanged a chief who had come under a flag of truce, soon after Colonel Wright and his men slaughtered the horses, Colonel Wright sent a note to the Yakima warrior Qualchan, saying once again he wanted to talk about peace. Qualchan's father Owhi responded. He was, of course, put in chains. Qualchan came in after his father. Still believing that a flag of truce might mean something, he brought along his wife. Qualchan was immediately put in chains and taken to a tent. His wife describes what happened next: "We were waiting for developments when in a moment, two soldiers entered the tent from behind where we were sitting, grasped my husband about the head and shoulders, threw him on his back and bound him with cords. I tried to cut one soldier with my knife, but another one kicked the knife out of my hand and then a great number of soldiers crowded in, overpowered us, and we were at their mercy. I thought then that the worst that could happen would be a few months' imprisonment, and you may imagine my consternation when I saw that they were making preparations to hang my husband. I first thought it was a huge joke, but when I saw the deliberateness of their preparations, the fullness of their treachery and cowardice became apparent." Qualchan first tried to go for a revolver he had hidden under a blanket, but did not succeed. Then he tried to bite the hand of the man who put a noose around his neck. In that, too, he did not succeed. After that Qualchan called upon the spirits of the mist, and twice the rope by which he was to be hanged broke. The third time he was killed. Qualchan's brother Lo-kout was also there. He was also tied. He was also to be hanged. He heard a voice say in his native language: "Jump on your horse and flee or you are a dead man." Another Indian cut the ropes that bound him, and he jumped on Qualchan's horse and rode for the mountains.

As Wright noted in his report to headquarters: "Qualchew came to me at 9 o'clock this morning, and at 9 1/4 a.m. he was hung." The next day Wright similarly hanged six Palouse Indians. He was a hero.

A few years ago the city of Spokane decided to put a golf course in Hangman Valley. The golf course is named Qualchan.

I know why the author of *The Barbarian Conversion* didn't provide examples of such "ugly episodes": to do so would undercut his thesis of the "conversion" of the indigenous of Europe, just as today similar presentations of "ugly episodes" (perhaps those including cluster bombs, napalm, nerve gas, machine guns, imprisonment, sensory deprivation, torture, dispossession with consequent mass starvation, and so on) would undercut the thesis of the "conversion" of people everywhere to capitalism, the most recent name of the God of civilization, the cannibal God.

That's why I'm disappointed.

At this point—given our near-total inability to face who we are and what we have become—my disappointment more likely stems from stupidity than optimism. Come to think of it, at this point—given that this culture is killing the planet—any sort of eternal optimism is probably inseparable from stupidity.

I return to the other book, read more, and despite the author's prejudices, I start to get more and more excited. I start to get blown away. Why? Miracles. The book is full of descriptions of miracles. And I understand: just as Hitler and through him the Nazi government experienced numerous miraculous escapes from death and dissolution, and just as the conquest of the Americas (and the consequent founding of the United States) required such good fortune that even George Washington noted in his first inaugural address, "No people can be bound to acknowledge and adore the Invisible Hand, which conducts the Affairs of men more than the People of the United States. Every step, by which they have advanced to the character of an independent nation, seems to have been distinguished by some token of providential agency," so, too, the conquest of Europe—the conversion of the barbarians—required countless miracles.

What if these miracles were real?

They're everywhere. Martin, bishop of Tours, had demolished a pagan temple and was getting ready to cut down a sacred tree. The people to whom the tree was sacred challenged him to stand directly where the tree would fall. He did. The tree screamed the scream of dying trees—you can hear it if you listen, and sometimes even if you don't—and began its arc toward him. He made the sign of the cross, and the tree fell to one side. The hagiographer Sulpicius related what happened next: "Then indeed a shout went up to heaven as the pagans gasped at the miracle, and all with one accord acclaimed the name of Christ; you may be sure that on that day salvation came to that region.

Indeed, there was hardly anyone in that vast multitude of pagans who did not ask for the imposition of hands, abandoning his heathenish ways and making profession of faith in the Lord Jesus." That was from only one miracle. Another: A young man named Aquilinus was hunting with his father when he suffered a seizure and fell into a coma. His relatives recognized immediately that he had been put under a spell by some enemy. They called a local healer, who was able to do nothing. The boy's grief-stricken parents brought him to the shrine of St. Martin, where he recovered. There was the hermit Caluppa, who, cornered by a brace of dragons, put them to flight by making the sign of the cross (although one dragon did fart defiantly before leaving). Amandus raised a hanged man from the dead, and "when this miracle was diffused far and wide, the inhabitants of the region rushed to Amandus and humbly begged that he would make them Christians." Emilian cured the blindness of the slave-girl of a senator, exorcised demons from the slave of a count, cured the paralysis of a woman who had traveled great distances to see him, and through the sign of the cross cured the swollen belly of the monk Armentarius. Miracles were almost as important as the sword in "converting" the indigenous of Europe. As Fletcher put it, "Like it or not, this is what our sources tell us over and over again. Demonstrations of the power of the Christian God meant conversion. Miracles, wonders, exorcisms, temple-torching and shrine-smashing were in themselves acts of evangelization."

Now, I know that history is written by the victors. I know how easy it is to scoff at farting dragons and the exorcism of demons. But I also know that there exists something called audience consideration. If your audience expects miracles to take the form of dragons, the curing of swollen bellies, and safety from falling trees, then this is the sort of miracle you—as God—should and probably would provide. If your audience expects miracles to take the form of fog or smallpox or moonlight reflecting white off sandy beaches on the very last night possible (what if it had been cloudy or had there been no moon on October 12, 1492?), then this is the sort you should provide. And I know as well that the most powerful dictator is the one who need not show himself openly, one whose omnipotence is assumed and internalized, metabolized into the very being of the subjects until they no longer recognize the dictator's existence at all. A dictator on the way up may need to wow by turning away dragons. One already ensconced has the luxury of using fog.

○

Over the next few weeks I returned many times to where Nika was struck, but only fell through time once. I did not fall back, but slightly forward, and saw to my delight that at least in the short term neither bears nor *wétikos* had knocked down the apple trees. The trees were tall, perhaps twenty years old, and beautiful pink apples hung plump from branches dangling low over the ground and over the stream. As I watched, an apple fell into the water and bobbed its way past.

I'm sitting by Latah Creek with Allison. The salmon are running. I cannot see the bottom of the stream for the fish. Even this little stream roars with the slapping of their tails against the water. I am happy, and of course sad.

"This," I say, "is a miracle."

I fall through time, see something not so miraculous, unless perhaps from the perspective of God. I'm sitting by Latah Creek. There is no life. No trees. No grasses. No shrubs. No fish. No flies. No gnats. No insects at all. The water still flows, though over rocks free of algae. The sun still shines. I cannot believe it is the same sun. I cannot believe it is the same water. Maybe it is not. The stream is as dead as everything else, though its body still flows.

I know what I'm seeing. I'm seeing the future. I'm seeing the end point of this culture. I'm seeing the final victory of God.

The director comes to me in a dream. I do not see him. I see the demons. I see millions of them. They are not feeding. They are standing. They are talking among themselves. They are waiting. And mainly they are watching. I do not know what they are watching. I do know the intensity on their faces as they look from where they are to where they will soon be.

I know what they are waiting for. They are waiting for the director to let them move forward, to let them cross over to where they will feed, to let them loose upon the humans of this world.

I don't know whom to ask for help. But I keep thinking about a line I read in *The Barbarian Conversion*, that one of the church's necessary tasks was to cause people to stop relying on the assistance of their dead ancestors and to rely instead on God. That shift, I think, is everything. For a place-based people the dead and the land become increasingly intermingled. That this is true physically should be obvious. But it is just as true spiritually, emotionally, and experientially, insofar as there is a difference. A reliance on the dead thus means a reliance on the land. No people who rely on the dead—who rely on the land—could destroy the land, could disrespect both the land and the dead the way we do.

In order for God to enlist people to help Him destroy the life that terrifies Him—to help Him create stasis—it is imperative for Him to get them to transfer their loyalty from the dead and the soil over to Him and His timeless, placeless, changeless heaven.

It became clear to me, then, that I would need to reverse the process my more recent ancestors had undergone when they converted from land-based religions to Christianity. I would try to speak to my ancestors. But it would have to be my long-dead ancestors, not the more recent ones. The more recent ones were, after all, wétikos themselves, and thus wouldn't be able to tell me anything about deep relationships to land, time, or much of anything.

Years ago, long before I'd written any books, I got this strange idea that I could gain some wisdom by interviewing my elders. So I went to old folks homes. The project didn't last long, because I realized quickly that for the elders to be able to impart wisdom to me they had to have some in the first place. The gaining of wisdom, I realized, is no accident, nor is it something that comes inevitably with age.

Years later, I asked American Indian writer Vine Deloria what, in the Indian perspective, is the ultimate goal of life.

He said, "Maturity . . ."

"By which you mean. . ."

"The ability to reflect on the ordinary things of life and discover both their real meaning and the proper way to understand them when they appear in our lives.

"Now, I know this sounds as abstract as anything ever said by a Western scientist or philosopher, but within the context of Indian experience, it isn't abstract at all. Maturity in this context is a reflective situation that suggests a lifetime of experience, as a person travels from information to knowledge to wisdom. A person gathers information, and as it accumulates and achieves a sort of critical mass, patterns of interpretation and explanation begin to appear. This is where Western science aborts the process to derive its 'laws,' and assumes that the products of its own mind are inherent to the structure of the universe. But American Indians allow the process to continue, because premature analysis gives incomplete understanding. When we reach a very old age, or have the capacity to reflect and meditate on our experiences, or more often have the goal revealed to us in visions, we begin to understand how the intensity of experience, the particularity of individuality, and the rationality of the cycles of nature all relate to each other. That state is maturity, and seems to produce wisdom."

I didn't know any of this back when I was visiting old

folks' homes. All I knew was that I was interviewing elders who, to be honest, didn't have much wisdom to offer me, probably because they themselves had never made the effort to gain it.

So I wanted to contact my ancestors who lived before their conversion to Christianity, with its consequent destruction of their relationship to the land and to their ancestors.

I faced a problem: I had absolutely no idea how to talk to my ancestors. Do I light two candles and stare into a mirror until my eyes blur and I see the faces of those who came before? Do I hire a medium? Do I ask for dreams?

I asked for dreams. Nothing. I looked at the stars and asked. Nothing. I sat beneath trees and asked. Nothing. I held soil in my hands and asked. Nothing. My only hint of anything, and I'm sure this was simply a projection on my part, was a faint voice saying, "I can't hear you very well. You're too far away."

Projection or not, what the voice said was true. My ancestors, the ones whose blood mingled for generations with the same soil, are a half a world away, in Europe, too far away to be able—at least with my inexperience—to help me.

For several weeks I saw snakes everywhere I went. Live ones. Dead ones. Big ones. Under my feet. Lying stretched across a path. A tiny one who crawled into the track of a sliding glass door. Everywhere. I didn't know what to make of it.

And then I saw mice. Just as often. I saw them clinging to tall grasses with their back legs, reaching out with front legs to eat the seeds from other stalks. I saw them dead on the ground. I saw them scampering. Everywhere. Live ones. Dead ones. Big ones. Tiny ones. I didn't know what to make of that either.

I accidentally killed a snake. I was writing, and I got a strong urge to go plant some potatoes. There was no reason. It was August, meaning they wouldn't be ready before winter. But the potatoes were soft and sprouting beneath the kitchen sink, and I didn't want to just throw them away. I may as well let them feel the soil, feel the sun, before they die. And if I planted them deep enough, they might survive to come up next spring.

So I took them outside, picked up the shovel, walked to a semi-random place. I was about to dig when I got the urge to move a few feet over. Then I got the urge to move again. Then I got the urge to turn ninety degrees. I stopped, waited. This was the place. I waited again. This was definitely the place. I pushed the point of the shovel through the tall grass, touched it to the ground, stepped on it, pushed hard, and suddenly the grass erupted in a frenzy of movement: a thin thrashing cord of brown and yellow with a red and fleshy end. I had cut a garter snake in half. I looked more closely. The cut was high enough he would surely die. I crushed his head to stop his suffering.

The next day I saved a snake. Allison was driving. I was in the passenger seat. I saw two crows trying to kill a snake on the sidewalk in front of a hospital. They lunged. He struck at them. They flew a few feet in the air. He moved away from them. They lunged again. He struck again. They flew again. He moved away again. I realized they were driving him into traffic. They were going to have a car kill him, then pick up his body.

I don't normally interfere with predator/prey interactions. The crows need to eat as surely as does the snake. But the timing seemed too significant. I asked Allison to pull over. She did. I whipped off my shirt, threw it over the snake, bundled it back up, and got in the car. We drove home. I let the snake loose.

That night Allison said, "You know what that was, right?"
"A snake," I said. "replacing the one I killed."
"Two snakes."

"I only killed one."

"But there were two," she said. "And what else?"

"Birds."

"Where did we find the snake?"

"On the road."

"In front of what?"

"A hospital."

I rubbed my face.

She said, "We have snakes, we have wings. All we need's a rod."

"I killed him with a shovel."

"There's your rod. That completes it."

I shook my head.

"A caduceus," she said.

I shook my head again.

"Two snakes twining around a rod, with wings at the top."

"I've seen those," I say.

"It's the rod of Hermes. He's the messenger for the gods, creator of magical incantations, and conductor of the dead."

At one point I might have stared at her open-mouthed, both because she knows this stuff, and because it happened at all. But I've long ceased being amazed at what she knows, and so far as the latter, well, the rose on the man's chest, the demons, the dead horses, and Nika have all combined to make me at least slightly less susceptible to shock at such things.

She smiled, and even she would have to admit she was the tiniest bit smug at having put this together.

To temper the smugness I said, "But where does the hospital fit in? You made a point of that, and Hermes has nothing to do with hospitals."

She smiled the smile of someone doing a check raise in poker, and said, "At least in this country, the rod of Hermes is commonly mistaken for the rod of Asclepius, the Greek god of healing and medicine (and of healing dreams). Asclepius's wand isn't winged, and has only one serpent, but most people don't know that. It's entered our consciousness enough, I think, for it to become a symbol."

What she said made sense.

She continued, "In the Hermetic tradition, the caduceus is a symbol of spiritual awakening. It's also a symbol in Egypt, Mesopotamia, and India, where it's *always* a symbol of harmony and balance."

"So what does all this mean?"

"Don't ask me," she said. "Ask the snakes."

I did. I still didn't get anything. Maybe I just don't yet know how to listen.

sixteen

c o l l e e n

Jack Shoemaker has a wife. Her name is Colleen. She often visits her parents, the Mondors, in Boise. Jack never brings home women unless Colleen is away. And she is away, so Jack is bringing one home. Her name, she said, is Missy. She has hair all the way down her back. Jack hit her too hard. She is bleeding too much. Not enough to kill her, but enough to make Jack uncomfortable.

That's not all Jack has to worry about. He's been wondering if Colleen has a boyfriend. What would this be: the twenty-five year itch? His suspicions are based on nothing dramatic, but instead an accretion of many subtle things: a look away at the dinner table; her habit of carrying packages or her purse on the side closest to him as they walk, as though she were trying to keep a barrier between them. While it used to be that on the nights they scheduled sex she would come to bed without any clothes, she now keeps on her nightgown until he asks her to remove it. And when he does enter her, she no longer opens her legs. She says it's because it feels better this way, but he knows that's not it.

He's never told Colleen about the women. He doesn't think she would understand. If he thought she would understand he would tell her. He's not ashamed of it. He's not ashamed of anything. It's just there are many things she wouldn't understand, and this is one of them.

Jack stops at a light. He glances at the interior rearview mirror just to make sure Missy hasn't awakened, struggled free, and sat up. Not likely, but better safe than sorry. He sees nothing unexpected.

The light turns green. He accelerates.

He's still thinking about Colleen as he hits the garage door opener and turns into his driveway. He waits for the door to come to a stop, then pulls inside. He pictures her with someone else, pictures her talking, laughing, holding him, and has to hit the brakes hard when he notices he drifted too far into the garage. He considers backing up, but doesn't, since this just means he has to carry Missy's body that much less. He hits the opener again, waits for the door to close. He gets out, walks to the back, opens the shell and tailgate. Missy still sleeps. She still seeps blood. Her long hair hangs outside the tarp.

Jack hesitates. He wonders how Colleen met this man, wonders who he is. He wonders what the man does for a living. He mostly wonders what he—Jack—would do, and how he would survive, if Colleen left him. He doesn't like to think about how very much he needs her, how much he relies on her.

He reaches in, slides the tarp toward himself, picks up its contents to carry inside.

He doesn't know why Colleen would want someone else. Jack gives her everything she needs. Security, stability. When she asks, "Will you be with me forever?" he always answers, "Till the day I die." And he means it. He will never leave. He could never leave.

Jack prides himself on his reliability, his solidity. He prides himself on being supportive. He bought this house for her. He buys her a new car every other year. He never makes her account for the money he gives her. She has no reason to leave.

Jack approaches the door between the garage and the house. It's shut. Normally he leaves this door slightly open when he goes on these trips—odd language, but what else should he call them: hunting? gathering? collecting? He likes *collecting* best: collecting data. But this time he forgot to keep the door open. He shakes his head. All this worry about Colleen has made him sloppy. No matter, though. He shifts the woman's weight higher on his forearms, slides his left hand out to the doorknob, twists, and pushes open the door. As he passes through the doorway, Missy stirs and her head slides out of the tarp. He shifts her weight again. Her long hair sways.

Jack wonders what it will take to keep Colleen from leaving. He's not sure what more he can give, what more she could want.

The door to the basement is already open. The light over the stairs is on. He takes her down, unrolls the tarp, uncuffs her wrists and removes the duct tape holding her ankles, puts her on the table. He cuffs her. Then he picks up the scraps of tape, meticulously folds the tarp, pulls a chair up close to the table, sits, folds his arms across his chest, and waits for Missy to awaken from the tap on the head and from the ketamine.

Jack always likes to be there when the woman wakes up. It's only partly to see the look on her face as she realizes what has happened to her—and what will happen to her—to see her unmasked, then unmasked again and again as successive waves of understanding pass through her. It's more because he is so interested—literally captivated—by those moments of transition, by boundaries. Wakefulness and sleep. Consciousness and unconsciousness. Life and death. And certainly in this case, the transition from free to caged, at least slightly saved to almost certainly doomed. There is tremendous power in all those moments.

Less personal transitions captivate him as well. The transitions, for example, from day to night and night to day. Dusk and dawn are times of great spiritual meaning. Or the moment when water freezes, or when it thaws. If you look under a microscope, you can actually watch water crystallize. Even though these liquids and solids are very near in temperature, they are worlds apart in form. Yet there is that moment—that precise moment—when those worlds join. That's the moment that captivates him. The same is true for combustion. One moment at one temperature the paper is white and smooth, but increase the temperature slightly and the paper browns and curls. Increase it again and flames appear as if from nowhere—or not *as if*, but actually *from* nowhere, unless of course the flames *were* somewhere else waiting for conditions to appear here that would call them into this world. But it doesn't really matter whether the flames are formed in that moment or whether they seize that moment to push their way past boundaries keeping them out of this world: the point is that those moments of initial conflagration are always times of unimaginable import.

And there are the boundaries between a person and the world. So sharp. So clearly defined. Skin here, air there. Person here, no person there. Life here, no life there. That's one reason he stabs the women, one reason he often stabs them slowly: so he can see that point where the knife just begins to penetrate the skin, so he can clearly observe the breaking—the passing, the violation—of that boundary. There is great power in that moment—and at that physical junction—as well.

The boundary is what's important, and even more important is the breaching of that boundary. The *moment* of the breaching of that boundary. The *moment* of transition, from one state to another.

And so Jack will wait here to share—no, not share, but see—that moment of transition when Missy awakens not only from sleep, but to the knowledge that she will never leave this room. To see that realization enter her body—enter her body as surely as the knife that will, too, eventually find its way inside—is to witness—to cause, in this case—a breaking of a boundary that though emotional is just as real, just as detectable, just as penetrable, as skin.

Colleen is beginning the long drive home from her parents. She's on I-84. She left several days earlier than anticipated. Not because of her parents—she was actually having a decent time—but because of Jack. She wants to surprise him, to show him that she really does appreciate him, that she really does want him.

It's hard, mainly because she doesn't want him.

She doesn't know what's wrong with her, what has been wrong with her for a very long time, maybe forever.

She wouldn't say precisely that she has lost interest in Jack—by which she doesn't just mean sexually, although that was gone even long before they got married—but more that she has lost interest in everything. Even that, though, might not be precise: doesn't losing interest imply that you had it to begin with?

She remembers a conversation with her mother when she was about fifteen. She asked if it would be better to marry for love or money. Her mother said, "Security, because love doesn't last." At the time she took that as an authoritative statement, rather than a comment on the relationship between her parents.

Colleen never had that choice. She doesn't think she's ever felt the depth of love she was taught—through books, movies, songs—was out there, the sort of love that would complete her, the sort of love that would transform her and her life into whatever it was that she and her life were supposed to be. Or perhaps she met the man and didn't know it. Or perhaps she'd just been lied to.

She followed her mother's advice. Jack was very secure. He was never rich, but rich enough. She has never wanted for things. But she soon learned—though she learned too late—that things don't fill gaping holes inside any better than do phantom—nonexistent—lovers. She has long suspected that there are no lovers who would suffice to fill those holes. She discovered far too late that if the path of true love completing her was a fairy tale, then the path of security was a waste of time.

She doesn't know when she first realized she was hollow. Was it in second grade, when she caught herself pretending not to know answers on tests so she wouldn't show up boys sitting next to her, or was it in fourth grade when she no longer noticed she was doing that? Was it in sixth grade, when she couldn't have outscored them if she tried? Maybe it was in high school, when a counselor asked her what she wanted in her life, and Colleen froze. The counselor said, "Look within," but when she tried she found all those doors locked. She pried one open and peered inside. What she saw horrified her. She saw . . . nothing. She slammed the door, locked it, nailed it, and never looked back. Or tried not to.

Colleen no longer knows what it means to lie. If you have nothing inside, can anything you say really be considered a lie? By the same token, can anything you say really be considered the truth?

She still resents the fact that before they were married, Jack used to take her dancing. It ends up he never liked it. She didn't find that out till they were married. That's okay, though, because she never liked science, and never liked sex. She tried in both cases, but the passion never developed.

She loves her mother, but she resents her for the bad advice she gave, and she resents her mother and her father for not teaching her by example how to be anything but hollow. She doesn't think their own emptiness bothers them at all. Of course she can't remember the last time she saw her father smile—and his grins at football scores and jumps in the Dow Jones don't count.

A few years ago Colleen found an old photograph that perfectly portrays her mother. Colleen is maybe six years old in the photo. She is sitting on the floor wearing pajamas. It is Christmas. Her mother—auburn hair, slender, beautiful—is handing Colleen a gift, and smiling. But the smile is not just a smile. It is a desperate plea for her daughter to love her. And the gift is a prayer: if I give you this thing, will you love me? My prayer is that this thing is good enough to *make* you love me. The smile is a wide open window into nothingness.

Colleen is glad she is on the interstate. Sometimes on two-lane roads she has to fight hard not to steer into oncoming traffic. Sometimes she wants to drive over a cliff. Sometimes she thinks she already did, and she just doesn't know it yet.

She drives. She tries not to think. She wishes the question had never occurred to her, as she presumes it has never occurred to either Jack or her parents: "How did life turn out so bare?" It's almost as though she found the pot of gold at the end of the rainbow and it turned out to be empty. Or maybe it was full, but she found you can't eat gold. Or maybe there had never been a pot, never even been a rainbow. Maybe all there ever was, was her and Jack and all their emptiness.

She knows what the problem is. She has never felt loved. Not by Jack. He tries. But she doesn't think he knows how. And she has never been able to teach him because she doesn't know how either.

Lately he's gotten into his head the idea that she's having an affair. If he thought clearly about it even for a second he would realize how silly that is. It's not just that she doesn't like sex with him.

She doesn't like sex. And why would she want to try to start any sort of relationship—sexual or otherwise—with someone else? The thing Jack absolutely cannot understand is: she doesn't know how.

Colleen won't be back for several days. Jack is going to drag this out. Or he will if Missy ever wakes up. It's getting late, and he has sat here for hours. He's touched her a few times, poked at her, but she hasn't come to. Perhaps she is extra sensitive to the ketamine. That's one reason he prefers to stun the women and then drug them instead of merely knocking them out with the blackjack. One time he did hit a woman too hard, and she never woke.

Jack sits. He waits. He sits. He gets tired. He gets bored. Still he sits. His eyes start to lose focus. His face gets heavy. To wake himself he goes upstairs, into the garage, and shuts the truck's shell and tailgate. He comes back inside, closes the door to the garage, goes back downstairs to check on Missy one more time. Still out. He's going to bed. She'll still be here in the morning.

Jack is dreaming about boundaries. He is dreaming about God. He is dreaming about God telling Israelites—His Chosen People—to kill women who have had intercourse with men. He is dreaming about intercourse. He is dreaming about men having intercourse with women. He is dreaming about Israelites killing women who've had intercourse. He is dreaming about God telling Jack—one of His Chosen People—that he must do the same.

Jack knows why. Even in this dream he knows why. He has always known why. It all comes down to boundaries. Who has them, and who does not. Virgins have intact boundaries. Those boundaries must be broken. And when those boundaries are broken, the women must be killed. Why? Because their boundaries have been broken. Because the women have been contaminated.

So many people think God hates women. But Jack is dreaming of God, and God is dreaming through Jack, and Jack knows the truth. God hates women, all right, but God especially hates men. Why else do you think God wants men to kill women who have had sex with men? Isn't it obvious? The women have been contaminated. By who? By men.

Jack stirs, wakes up enough to check whether Missy is making any sounds, then falls back into his dreams, of God, of women, of men, of hatred, of boundaries breaking like glass.

Colleen is thinking about the old Jesuit saying: if you put yourself in a position of prayer long enough, you might start feeling like praying. She has tried. She has tried that so many times. And she is going to try it again tonight. That's why she's driving these long hours. She wishes she would have left earlier, so she would have arrived before Jack went to bed. She would have walked into the house, not said a word, and led him into the bedroom. She would have taken off his clothes, and then hers. She would have pulled him on top of her, and she would have opened wide.

That is exactly why she didn't leave earlier in the day. That's why she dawdled. That's why she took her mother grocery shopping, and that's why she filled up her parents' car with gas. All so that through no fault of her own she would get there too late to do any of this. Jack will be asleep, and she will wake him with this offer. With any luck he will be too tired to take her up on it.

She knows she shouldn't think that way, but she does.

Colleen pulls into the driveway, opens the garage door, drives in. She parks, takes out her keys, picks up her purse, and opens her car door. She'll bring in the rest of her things in the morning. She gets out, walks around the front of Jack's truck, then hesitates when she notices dark droppings on the concrete floor. She continues to the door, opens it, sees a feathery stain of what looks like blood on the jamb. She looks more closely. It is blood.

Jack must have cut himself.

She steps inside. Jack left the door to the basement open, left the light on over the stairs. She calls softly to him, waits, listens carefully. She thinks she hears breathing. Maybe he fell asleep down there. She's going to go check. She takes one step, then hears his familiar slight snoring from their bedroom. She moves back up, turns off the light. The stairs don't go completely dark, though, as he also evidently left on the light in the basement. She wonders for a moment if someone is downstairs. But then she hears her husband again, and knows it must have been the wind.

She stands at the top of the stairs thinking about going to turn off the light and to check if there is anyone there, when suddenly the full weight of the night comes down on her. She's too tired. She'll do it in the morning.

Jack hears a woman say his name. "Jack," she says. "Jack."

He opens his eyes, sees a woman silhouetted against the light now on in the hallway. He recoils. "You!" he says.

"Jack," she says.

How does Missy know my name? He slides across the bed away from her. Finally his eyes focus. It's Colleen. She's naked. He says, "What are you doing here?"

"I wanted to surprise you." She runs her hands down her body. He presumes she presumes this is sexy.

"Why?"

"I've missed you so much."

"You should have called."

She stops. "What's wrong?"

"Nothing."

"You don't seem happy to see me." She steps slightly away, changes the subject: "You left the light on in the basement."

"No, I didn't."

"Yes."

"No. Maybe. I don't remember."

"Do you want me to turn it off?"

"No!" he exclaims.

"What?"

"Leave it till morning."

"What's wrong?" she asks again.

"Nothing."

She scratches the end of her nose, says, "How's your cut?"

"What?"

Her voice softens, and he can tell she's trying to recapture a mood: "I'll kiss your cut, make it better."

Now Jack frowns. "Kiss my cut?"

"Did you cut yourself?"

"No." He thinks. "Yes."

"Where?"

This isn't happening, he thinks. But it is, and every answer is making it worse. He reaches out, takes her hand, squeezes, holds it tight. He thinks. Finally he says, "You frightened me."

"I'm sorry."

"I was dreaming." He thinks as quickly as he can. He says, "I was dreaming you were gone. I've missed you so much. I was dreaming you were . . . you were kidnapped." *Dumb*, he thinks. *Why did he say that?*

"I was? By who?"

Be smart, Jack. "It's horrible. You were kidnapped and you were happy because you didn't want to come back to me. You wanted to stay with the other man, the man who took you away." He searches her face, thinks he sees a flicker of recognition, realizes he's succeeded in shifting the focus off himself.

She leans toward him, puts her free hand around his shoulders, hugs him. "I don't want anyone else."

He hugs her back. She kisses his cheek, his chin, his lips. She pulls slightly away, starts to unbutton his pajamas. He helps her remove his clothes, helps her into bed, and rolls on top of her, the whole time glad his wife is no longer asking questions, and the whole time hoping Missy doesn't make a sound.

Afterwards, and after Colleen has fallen asleep, Jack gets up. The whole time he thought not of his wife, of course, but of Missy, wondering what he would say and what he would do if she woke up and moaned. Twice he thought she did, but each time he was wrong. He made sure things with Colleen were loud and they were quick. He was glad Colleen was tired and fell asleep almost instantly.

He goes downstairs. Missy still breathes. He dare not wake her. He dare not leave her. When he was inside his wife he figured out what he would do. He puts a tarp down in the bathroom. Then he quickly kills Missy and carries her to the tarp, wraps her up. He picks up the plastic he'd laid down to protect against bloodstains, urine, and feces, folds it, puts it in with the body. He shuts the door. He can't come up with a reason to barricade the door, so he'll just have to get up when Colleen does and steer her away. He goes up-stairs, into the garage, looks at the floor, sees the spots. He goes back into the kitchen, picks a steak knife from a drawer, holds it in his right hand, and touches it to the third finger of his left. He goes to cut himself, but just can't do it. No matter how he tries he can't force himself. He doesn't want the pain. Thinking about his own blood he almost passes out. So instead he puts away the knife, puts water and a little bleach on a rag, and cleans the spots on the floor. Finally done, he goes back to bed. He tells himself to awaken if he hears Colleen stir, then like Colleen, falls asleep almost immediately.

Jack awakens with a start. It's still dark. He can't keep the body in the house. He wouldn't be able to survive the morning making small talk with Colleen, each moment fearing she might go downstairs, go into the bathroom. What would she do? Would she scream? Would she look at Jack with disgust? Would she call the po-lice? Jack knows he couldn't kill her. Or at least he doesn't think he could kill her. What would he do if she picked up the phone? He'd rip it from the wall. Then what? He'd cuff her down, hold her till she calmed, and then he would explain it to her. He would explain it to her fifty times if he had to, explain it to her till she understood. And he knows she would understand. Maybe it would even draw them closer.

He stops. He thinks about it. Maybe he should leave the body there, let her find it. That would force the issue. No more hiding. He could explain it to her and she would understand.

No. It's not worth the chance. What if she doesn't understand? He would lose her. The risk is too great.

He slowly lifts off the covers, slides his feet out and onto the floor, sits upright, stands, waits, listens. There's no change in Colleen's breathing. He makes his way to a dresser, soundlessly opens a drawer, pulls out a pair of sweats. Then to the closet, where on the left side he finds an old t-shirt. He carries them from the room, shuts the bedroom door without latching it, turns on the hall light, changes, and takes his pajamas to the laundry room to put into a partially full basket. He listens again.

Nothing.

He goes to the front door, puts on an old pair of shoes. He's not wearing socks or underwear, but there's nothing he can do about that. Then to the garage, where he opens the rear of the truck. He goes to the kitchen, grabs his keys, puts them in his pocket. After that it's down the stairs and into the bathroom. He lifts her. Now's the hard part. He walks back up the stairs, listens carefully, goes back down, picks up the body and carries it step by slow, heavy step up the stairs. By the top, his arms and lower back ache. He carries her to the garage, puts her in the back of the truck, softly closes the rear. He unhitches the automatic garage door opener, opens the door manually, gets partway in the truck, puts it in neutral, and rolls the truck down the driveway and into the street, where finally he starts it.

He doesn't know where to take her. He can't take her to the quarry, to where he grabbed Nika, or to any of the places he dumped the others who came before: they're all too far away. He needs to get back home as quickly as possible: he has no idea how to explain his absence should Colleen awaken.

He decides to drive to the park near the river beneath the interstate. He twists through paved roads to get there, never rolling through stop signs, never speeding. He finds the park, turns in.

From here on the roads are dirt. If he sees anyone, he'll obviously go elsewhere. Nothing. He finds a secluded spot, stops, turns off the domelight, grabs the maglight from the glovebox, gets out, walks to the back. He can't leave her here: the dirt holds perfect impressions of his tires and footprints. He looks around, sees a very small road off to the side.

Not knowing what else to do he gets back in, starts the truck, turns it into the road. Thick underbrush fills in either side. He wonders if there's a turnaround.

And then the road ends. Jack laughs out loud. Perfect. He's on a ledge over the river. He couldn't have planned this better, so long as the water is deep enough to carry her away. No one will know where she was dumped, which means no one will know where to search for tire tracks. He gets out, walks to the overlook, shines the light down. It's about ten feet. He can't tell how deep the water is, but it will have to do.

Back to the truck. He pulls out the tarp, carries the load to the edge, sets it on the ground, stands on one end of the tarp, and pushes the body over. The tarp unwinds as the body rolls down the steep slope until the body spins free and into the water with a splash.

God is good. Already the body drifts into the main current, floating feet first, hair trailing behind, spread like a fan.

This was the perfect place, Jack thinks as he drives back home. *I'll have to use this place again and again.*

He turns off the engine, coasts up the driveway and into the garage, stops, puts the truck in gear, and engages the emergency brake. He gets out, shuts the garage door, reconnects it. Then he goes to the door to the house, opens it, listens. Nothing. Back at the rear of the truck, he takes off his shoes and clothes, puts them in the back with the bloody tarp that had been Missy's shroud. He'll get rid of them soon. He covers them with another tarp to keep Colleen from casually observing them.

Naked, he goes in to the house, into the laundry room. He quietly washes his hands, puts on his pajamas, and heads to the bedroom. The door is still shut, still not latched. He turns off all the lights, softly opens the door, and creeps inside.

Colleen still breathes heavily. He makes it to the bed, starts to get in.

She stirs, says sleepily, "Where'd you go?"

He keeps his voice from showing fear: "I used the toilet."

She gives a moan of sleepy understanding.

"You were right," he says.

"Yes?" Still very sleepy.

"I left the basement light on. I turned it off. It's all taken care of now."

"That's nice."

He crawls in, spoons behind her, and soon she is back asleep.

The next morning, over breakfast, Colleen asks Jack about him leaving on the lights overnight, something she's never known him to do. He says he was tired. She understands. She can see this inside her head. She sees Jack sitting downstairs—doing what, it never occurs to her to wonder—growing more tired by the moment until he staggers upstairs under the weight, not of a dead woman—for why would this possibly occur to her?—but of fatigue, and simply forgets to turn off the lights.

Sheepishly she mentions hearing someone downstairs, hearing someone breathing. He responds by telling her how grateful and happy he is that she drove all the way late at night just to be with him. He's sure that's what caused her to hear that: it was fatigue and the lingering echo inside her head of tires on asphalt, of the engine's hum. It's an interesting and common phenomenon, he says, almost like hearing the wind or the ocean in a seashell, or your ears ringing after a loud noise: if you drive long enough, your ears play tricks on you. Mentally she puts herself again in that position, and the sound she hears no longer resembles human breathing at all, no longer resembles anything but tires, a car, her own fatigue. Jack's right, as he so often is.

She almost doesn't want to ask him about the blood in the garage, but her curiosity is up, and he has been so very wonderful and so very wise about the other two, explaining them in ways that make so much sense, that she goes ahead and asks.

He says, "I'm not sure what you mean. Will you show me?"

They go to the garage, where after a few moments she says, pointing, "I would have sworn they were there, and there, and there."

He looks at her lovingly. "You were so tired."

"And your truck," she says. "I remember it being about a foot farther forward. I had to walk around it."

He shakes his head. "I've been with you all morning, and I don't think the truck drove itself." He pauses, then says, "Maybe the bleeding, breathing ghost took the truck out for a spin."

"Maybe," she says, laughing with him at her own silliness.

She sees herself the night before, getting out of her car, sees herself walking across a pristine floor, sees herself not stepping around the truck. Everything Jack says feels so right. She almost makes a joke about the truck being driven not by a ghost, but by Jack's secret lover, but at the last moment she doesn't, because she wants to be sensitive to his unfounded suspicions about her. She doesn't want to make him feel bad.

They go back inside, finish breakfast.

It isn't until hours later that she remembers the feathery stain on the doorjamb. She goes to look. When she sees it's still there, she does not question everything Jack said that morning—which, after all, had made so much sense—but instead begins to remember that she has seen this stain for days, for weeks, for months, and for the longest time she has been meaning to clean it up.

She does. For as old as that stain is, she's surprised at how easily it comes off.

seven
teen

more   miracles

☉

In March, 1943, Hitler made another visit to the Eastern Front, this to discuss the Kursk offensive. Security was extremely tight. Men with submachine guns were everywhere. Some of the security squads, however, were under the command of Georg Freiherr von Boeselager, the pentathlete who had joined the resistance. The squad chosen to line the path where Hitler was to walk to and from the meeting place was made up of members of the resistance. They were to shoot Hitler as he walked back to his car.

Hitler took a different route to his vehicle.

Another assassination attempt took place that same day. During lunch Lieutenant-Colonel Henning von Tresckow, center of the resistance on the Eastern Front, asked Lieutenant-Colonel Heinz Brandt, who was going to be on the same plane as Hitler, to take a package to Colonel Stief. This sort of favor was routine. This sort of package was not: unbeknownst to Brandt, it contained a live bomb.

The bomb consisted of two pairs of British "clams": adhesive explosives the size of very small books, yet powerful enough to penetrate a one inch steel plate or twist a railway line.

Shortly before the plane took off, Tresckow's assistant, Lieutenant Fabian von Schlabrendorff, surreptitiously used a key to press through the wrapping and break the acid capsule, which began the timer. He then handed the package to Brandt, who got on the plane.

The fuse was set to detonate in thirty minutes.

Several hours later Hitler landed in Prussia.

The conspirators faced a problem: they needed to retrieve the package before its delivery to Stief, who knew nothing of the plot. Tresckow called Brandt and told him to hold on to the package: the wrong one had been sent. Schlabrendorff then flew to Prussia and exchanged the package for one containing a gift for Stief. When he was alone, Schlabrendorff opened the package. The fuse had functioned perfectly, eating through the wire and releasing the striker onto the detonator. The striker had struck precisely as it was supposed to. The detonator had gone off: it was burnt and black. But the explosive had not ignited.

Another attempt was made eight days later. Each year during March, the Nazis held a "Heroes Memorial Day" in a large hall, during which Hitler would give a speech (in which he could state that victory was now assured over bolshevism, capitalism, Asiatic barbarians, criminal warmongers, Churchill, and the Jews), watch a guard battalion parade by, listen to the national anthem, speak very briefly with war-wounded, and inspect captured materials.

The potential assassin this time was Colonel Freiherr von Gersdorff, chief of the Intelligence section organizing the materials captured from the Russians. When Tresckow asked him to make a bomb attack on Hitler, the recently-widowed Gersdorff assented after being reassured that if the attempt succeeded, the plotters would not stop at Hitler, but overthrow the entire Nazi government.

Gersdorff's first option was to plant a bomb to go off during Hitler's speech, much as had Georg Elser. He rejected this option because he only had access to small bombs (and couldn't hide a big bomb, anyway), and the venue was very large, meaning the shock of the explosion would dissipate too much to guarantee a kill. Further, he had only a vague notion of Hitler's timetable, which would make setting a fuse impossible.

This meant the attack would have to be made during Hitler's inspection of Gersdorff's exhibit. It also meant the attack would of necessity involve Gersdorff's suicide.

Gersdorff and Tresckow faced more difficulties. At this point they had access to plenty of explosives, but not to appropriate fuses. Most of the fuses had delays of up to thirty minutes, and of course it would not be possible to set the fuse, then try to chat up Hitler for a half an hour. They had access to a fair number of German pioneer explosives with very short fuses, but these fuses had to be activated by an extremely conspicuous pulling motion. Even a hint of this movement and Gersdorff would be shot, Hitler whisked away. Another possibility would be for Gersdorff to use a German hand grenade, with its four-and-a-half second fuse, but this fuse made a distinctive hissing sound which would similarly get Gersdorff shot to no avail.

He decided on ten-minute fuses attached to clams, one in each pocket of his greatcoat. He was able to smuggle them in on the day of the speech. Because he did not know how long Hitler would talk, he kept his hands in his pockets, but didn't start the fuses until Hitler approached his exhibit. Then, Gersdorff gave the Hitler salute with his right arm, and with his left hand still in his pocket set off that fuse. The explosion would, he thought, set off the clam in his other pocket as well.

They entered the exhibit. There were a few other people with Hitler—Göring, Keitel, Dönitz, Himmler, aides, and bodyguards—all of whom were fair game to be blown up. But at the last moment Hitler asked Field Marshall von Bock to come along with them. This concerned Gersdorff, because Bock was a member of the resistance, yet did not know about this assassination attempt.

Gersdorff decided to go ahead with it. Now, he merely had to stay next to Hitler for the final ten minutes of their lives. This would not be a problem, since this was precisely his duty: to explain the various pieces of equipment.

In contrast to all previous years, Hitler literally ran through the exhibit hall. He would not listen to a word Gersdorff said. Not even Göring—acting innocently—was able to get Hitler to slow down. Hitler was out of the room in less than three minutes, surprising even the radio announcers, who were unprepared for his quick return.

All that Gersdorff could do was excuse himself into the lavatory and remove the fuse. He never made another attempt on Hitler's life.

eighteen

the land

I wake up. Allison lies next to me. A cat presses against my other side.

Allison says, "Did you have any dreams?"

I smile. "I did, as I drifted awake. A wonderful half dream, half memory."

"What about?"

"You."

"That's nice." She presses toward me, tighter even than the cat. "Tell me."

"Do you remember that time we made love next to a cemetery?"

She says, "I. . . ."

"That's what the dream was about. It was so beautiful. That was one of my favorite times ever."

Part of me feels her slightly stiffen, but the rest of me doesn't quite notice.

I continue, "Remember, we found that mossy space at the edge of some trees? Do you remember how soft that moss was?"

"Derrick."

"And it was a little bit cold and windy and we put down our coats so we could lie on them?"

"Derrick."

"The dream was so wonderful. I wish I could fall back in it. Or maybe we can just make something similar happen now.

"Stop. Please stop."

I do. "What's wrong?"

"That wasn't me."

"What do you mean, it wasn't you?"

"That was someone else."

"No, I see you so clearly. I can see your face and your breasts and the goosebumps on your belly and on your hips, and I can see where we join together. . . ."

"Why are you giving me those images? I don't want them. I

tell you it wasn't me."

"You really don't remember this?"

"You're confusing me with someone else. Please stop." She pauses. "What's the name of the cemetery? I've probably never even been there."

I hesitate. I don't remember. That's odd. Everything else is so clear.

She says, "Don't tell me. I don't want to know the name. I don't want to make the connection."

"I understand. I'm sorry."

Memories live in places. They live in trees, stones, soil, water, birds, mice, insects, air. They live in us.

When I put my face to the ground, and when I keep it there long enough, I can feel the memories moving from my bones to the soil's, and from the soil's bones into mine.

When I put my face into the wind, I can feel the memories move back and forth between us, too, only this time the memories are different.

Memories are living beings, like salamanders, like snakes, like stones, like storms, like flowers, like flames, like breaths of wind, like mice, only different.

Memories are spiderwebs, shining, delicate, translucent, sticky, binding grass to grass. They are stones, solid, buried or exposed, worn away by water and wind. They are water, and they are wind. They are droplets. They are hurricanes.

They are as alive as you or me. Put your face to the ground. Leave it there. Feel the memories move bone to bone, yours to theirs, theirs to yours.

I lie face down in a small patch of forest behind our home. A fire swept through maybe a dozen years before we moved in, and the new trees have grown tall in the time since. I smell small plants, and soil, and the calming brown smell of duff. I feel plants on my face, and a small stone against my cheek. I shift slightly so it doesn't poke me.

Almost immediately—literally within two or three seconds—I have to fight an almost frantic boredom. For all I've written about a relationship with the land, and for all I've tried to live in relationship with the land where I live, I still feel an overwhelming urge to get away, to do *anything* but stay where I am, to do anything but touch the ground. I want to go back to the house, play some poker online, check my e-mail, call a friend. I think about the sound of distant cars on the interstate. I think about the phone bill I need to pay. I think about the celery I need to buy (my prostate is pretty much fine by now, thanks to Doctor Lu, the miracle-working Chinese herbalist, and part of the maintenance program is that I'm supposed to drink a fair amount of celery tea and eat lots of watermelon).

I am anywhere but where I am.

It shouldn't be so hard to stay where I am, but it is. What am I afraid of?

I try to bring myself back. I'm not trying to meditate: I've never really liked meditation as such. People ask me if I meditate, if I sit silently with my breath and try to still my mind, and I always tell them I live with trees and butterflies, and I like to sit with *them*.

That's true enough, so far as it goes, but all of my time touching trees now seems superficial to me, as though I was looking at them and even seeing them as well as I could, but still not seeing them at all.

Lying here, I realize how very scared I am. My frantic boredom is not really boredom, but fear. Of what?

I hear a voice. Not Allison's, but the voice I heard in the forest when I first fell through time. The voice says the same thing it said then: "Don't fight it."

I want to feel Allison's belly against my back, her warmth and wetness against my hip. She doesn't have to move. I just want to feel that skin to skin contact.

The voice says, "Come closer."

I want to feel my face tight against her skin, buried anywhere she can wrap around me, between her neck and shoulders, her arm and chest, her breasts, her thighs. I want to feel my cheek against her belly.

"Come."

I know what's wrong. I don't know what's right, only what's wrong. I remove my clothes, lie flat on my stomach. I hold my arms and legs tight to keep my weight from fully pressing on the rough surface of the ground and the sharp pine needles.

"Come closer."

I do. I open my arms and open my legs. I press down my hips, no differently, no less gently, no less intimately, no less invitingly, than I would with Allison.

If I am expecting some miracle, it doesn't come. I merely feel myself flat against the ground.

But I do begin to relax, starting with my shoulders, then my arms, then my back, hips, belly. I'm less stiff, more smooth.

I smell the soil, I smell the old needles, I smell the plants. And now mixed with all that are the intimate smells from between my legs, front, back.

And then? Nothing. Not yet.

I see the sun glinting off the torn leaf of some plant whose name I don't know, and hovering near my face I see a tiny gnat whose name I also don't know. I see a fly crawling on a rotting log not far away, and farther off I see a chipmunk take three lightning steps, then stop, tail flicking, then take three more, then stop.

I relax more. My face falls into the ground. I open my legs further.

It's quiet. I hear a blue jay calling as it flies overhead. In the far distance a hawk. In the small slice of sky I can see without moving my head, I see two crows dancing with each other.

I close my eyes. I don't know if I sleep.

When I open them I see a snake. It is maybe five feet from me. It is a garter snake. It doesn't move.

I watch it for a while, then close my eyes again. When I open them the snake is gone.

Finally I know what I need to say to the land. I say, softly, yet out loud, "Tell me."

It doesn't. I know it doesn't yet trust me that much.
I don't blame it.

I go back every day. Every day I see more, every day I presume more sees me. Every day I lie body pressed flat against the earth, and every day I say, "Tell me. Tell me who you are."

Why should the land trust any of us?

To be honest, anytime I walk through a forest, or walk anywhere, really, I feel like a Nazi. All I need are the jackboots. And when I lie down naked here in this copse, I feel what I'd imagine I'd feel if I were a Nazi visiting a concentration camp rape factory (sometimes called a brothel). I know myself well enough to know that if I were a Nazi, I'd be a really *nice* Nazi. But that wouldn't alter the fact that I'd be a Nazi.

Think about it.

We hear lots of talk about the Nazi belief in a master race, but who perceives themselves to be the master culture of the master species? Who perceives this so deeply that we don't even need to discuss it?

The Holocaust of the Jews was conceptually, numerically, and in many other ways a small undertaking compared to the destruction of the indigenous of Europe, Africa, the Americas, Oceania, Asia. The destruction of the indigenous is small scale compared to the destruction of life on this planet. Just yesterday I read that there is essentially *no* phytoplankton off the coast of California or Oregon this year, in great measure because the ocean there is eleven—*elev-*

en—degrees warmer than normal. Say hello to anthropogenic global warming. Say good-bye to the oceans.

If you were wild, would you trust a civilized human?

Pretend for a moment you're a tree. Would you trust members of a society that is systematically cutting down all your relations? Pretend you're a river. Would you trust members of a society that is entombing you and all your relations in concrete?

What is the fundamental relationship between members of the dominant culture and the wild? If you are wild, what would it take for you to start to trust?

Pretend aliens invaded from outer space. Pretend they began killing or enslaving everyone you knew. Pretend they perpetrated atrocity after atrocity, holocaust after holocaust. Pretend they were insatiable in their appetite for atrocity. Pretend their destructive behavior was so deeply rationalized that most of them utterly failed to perceive it as anything other than entirely normal and entirely desirable behavior. How much would you fear and hate these invaders? And pretend one of these aliens approached you, told you how much she or he hates the other aliens, tells you she or he will do whatever it takes to stop them. What would it take for you to begin to believe this other?

I finally have a chance to do something tangible to help the land. It would be more dramatic and far more interesting for this story if I rushed in with a sword and singlehandedly saved the land from timber barons, or if I took matches from madmen who were going to light fires for reasons only they understood, but the truth is much less dramatic, with far less danger to me and far more to the land.

I walk to the corner to get the mail, and the carrier happens to be there. She says I'm a lucky guy. I ask why. She says she heard the gravel road that goes to my house is going to be paved. I ask why. She says they're going to put in a subdivision just beyond my place, which, though she doesn't know it, is the forest where I walk. I ask why. She looks at me like I don't speak English.

I get home, call a friend who happens to be a realtor and also a local politician. I ask him if this is true. I wait while he looks on his computer. He says it just sold. He says he has even worse news.

"I can't imagine what that would be," I say.

"The realtor handling it is Mike Stremburg. He sold it to his developer buddy."

"Stremburg doesn't mean anything to me."

"The guy is a sleaze. He's a liar and a cheat. I won't have anything to do with him."

I thank my friend, get off the phone. I go to my two closest neighbors. They are as appalled as I am. They're the only neighbors I know. I've never spoken with the ones beyond. I write a lot about community, but the truth is that I'm not very social. I'd like to say that my community consists of the nonhumans who live near me, but while I know them better than I know most humans, I fear I don't know them all that well either. I go to visit the third neighbor. His name's Marvin. I tell him they're going to put in a subdivision behind us.

He says, "Good."

I don't say anything for a moment. Finally, "You don't mind?"

"Why should I?"

"It will kill the forest."

He asks, "How long have you been here?"

"Twelve years."

"I grew up here. Mine was the first house in this area. When I was a kid I used to see thousands of quail. Used to hunt them. I used to hunt bear here, too, and cougars. Now they're all gone, except a few bears and coyotes. It used to be paradise."

I don't see his point. "If it was paradise, why won't you fight for it? That's exactly why we need to protect this forest. We can help those animals come back."

He says, "The city has to grow or die."

I suddenly understand the reason I didn't see his point: he

didn't have one. He's not thinking. To make sure, I ask, "What does that mean?"

He just looks at me. I can tell he has no idea what my question means. I can tell he has no idea what his last statement means. I can tell he is repeating something he heard on the radio. I can tell he doesn't much like me. That's okay, I don't like him either.

"If a city grows," I say, "by destroying the land on which it depends, how long will it last?"

"I'll be dead by then," he says. "It doesn't matter."

A ridiculous politeness prevents me from saying or doing what I want.

He says, "If you don't like the city growing, move back where you came from. You're a part of the growth."

"I moved from the last place because there were too many people."

"There's too many people everywhere, but what are you going to do about it? I'm a realist. You can't fight progress. And also, I'm not selfish. I have no right to keep others from pursuing their dream of moving into a new home. And you don't have that right either."

I tell him that one third of all new homes are either second homes or built for investment. I tell him that the homes to be built here are all in the latter category. He tells me again that if I don't like it, I should go back where I came from.

Now you know why I don't talk to my neighbors.

"So," I say, "you don't oppose the subdivision?"

"Not only that," he responds, "if you oppose the subdivision, I will oppose you."

I go to the next neighbor, and the neighbor after that, and after that. With the exception of Marvin, we're unanimous.

Now this is where the timber baron or madman scenarios would be more exciting. They would involve bravery, cunning, drama, danger, lots of fighting, and probably some sex in order to garner the coveted R rating. Instead, I take a bunch of remarkably dull trips to the planning department, hold meetings with the neighbors (crisis works wonders for creating community), and comment at public hearings.

It ends up that Mike Stremburg, years before, had "slimed"— to use their word—several members of the planning commission in separate financial transactions. The members of the planning commission are only too eager to find any reason to turn Stremburg down flat.

In this case the (very small) forest is saved, for now, because we spoke up. And we persevered. In this case, that was all it took.

It's the day after the planning commission's decision. I walk into the forest. A small bird suddenly flies from the nearby underbrush directly toward me, only turning at the last moment. It flies so close that I feel its wing brush my chest.

It's the day after that. Walking through the forest I see a toad the size of a small dinner plate. It doesn't move.

It's one more day later. Today I see the biggest pile of bear poop I have ever seen.

I know what this is: it is the forest saying thank you.

I'm lying on my back in the forest. I'm naked. My knees are bent, my feet are flat on the ground. I'm looking at the tops of trees, and beyond them clouds, and beyond them the pale blue sky.

By now I'm no longer afraid to feel the ground on my skin. I like it. It feels good.

But I guess I should be explicit. Although we've shared much skin to soil contact, we haven't made love in any more active sense. I turn over, rest my cheek against the duff.

The day is warm, almost hot. I close my eyes. I say, "Tell me about yourself."

If I'm expecting the land to miraculously open up to me, give me some marvelous vision simply because I took some trips to the planning department, I'm disappointed. Not much happens.

I think about the fact that often when I'm stuck writing, it's because I'm asking the wrong question. The same is often true with Allison: if we're stuck in some argument, we sometimes step back and see if the problem is that we're asking ourselves and each other the wrong questions. More often than not, new questions appear, and we find that asking the right questions resolves the conflict, or at least opens it—and us—to more meaningful communication.

I wonder if that's part of my problem (presuming I even have a problem: it seems ungracious to consider myself as having any problems when I'm lying naked in a forest on a sunny summer afternoon). I search for a different question, and one strikes me almost immediately with the power of a fist. It's a question I've never before asked anyone, nor has anyone ever asked me. I've never even asked Allison. It is immediately clear to me that it is *the* fundamental question to be asked by anyone who wants to be in any sort of relationship with anyone else. The question is very simple, and the desire to have someone ask it of me almost brings tears to my eyes. I ask the forest, "What is it like to be you?"

Still, no miracle comes. No bolts of lightning cross the palest blue sky I've ever seen. No trees fall, then swerve at the last moment. No dragons fly away farting.

But I do see a bumblebee walking floret to floret on a sweet clover. The stalk hangs heavy under her weight. I see small solitary bees buzzing the tops of yellow flowers, and I see the flowers themselves moving ever-so-slightly in a breeze they feel far better than I. I see a long-legged spider walking leg over leg across air between two plants. I feel a tickling on my arm, and look over to see a tiny inchworm—maybe a quarterinchworm—making his way across my forearm. I lean up close to the long, slender stalk of some grass, and the worm quarterinches his way from me to a plant.

What is it like to be a forest? It is to be alive. It is to be filled with aliveness, to be ablaze with aliveness. It is to be rooted in place, like a tree, and it is to move, like bees, like bears, like spiders who throw out webs as sails and travel around the world. It is to be connected one to the others in spiderwebs of memories, parasites, nutrients, hitchhikers, neighborly and nonneighborly relationships, time, joys, sorrows, regrets, anticipations, deaths, births, hatchings, germinations, eatings, sex, dreams. It is to be living the same blazing, burning, comforting, joyful, exhilarating, calming dream. It is to carry all these lives and all these deaths and all this sun and soil and decomposition and growth and disease and all these memories in one's bones, and in the marrow of one's bones, and in the woody fiber of one's bones, and in the nectar of one's bones, and in the breath of wind of one's bones, and in the dragonfly-red pigment of one's bones. It is the marriage of hitchhiker and hitchhiker and bone and blood and memory and wood and soil.

That's the barest start.

I see a white crab spider sit motionless on a white flower, waiting to bring death to some bee who lands here, waiting to feed. I see two ants carry a dead grub presumably toward their home. I see a leaf fall from a bush, and I see another bush bright and bulbous with galls. I see wood dust from boring beetles, and somewhere in the distance I hear the rapid rapping of a woodpecker searching for a meal.

I'm as surrounded by death as I am by life, and suddenly I'm having trouble seeing where one begins and the other ends. I even start to think that one may not be so different from the other, but then I reach to scratch a tickling on my leg and accidentally come away with a dead spider on my hand. This brings me right back to knowing that there *is* a stark difference between life and death: moments before, the spider was alive, and now she is irrevocably dead.

To be a forest, I think—or feel, or am told—is to realize, to be, that contradiction: of life and death melting together on one hand, and separated by a chasm on the other. And of course it's not just life and death that are both miscible and immiscible. The same is true for everything: where does the bee start and the wind end? Where does the tree start and the boring beetle end? Where do the bush, the gall wasp, and the gall each begin and end? To be a bee, or spider, or tree, or woodpecker, or wild human being, is to have entirely different relationships with life and death and each other than all of those relationships I have learned. Life and death—and all others—are partners with whom we dance from beginning to end and back to beginning.

It suddenly seems clear to me—and I'm embarrassed it took a bumblebee, or anyone, really, to point this out to me—that if you don't fear life, and instead are present to life, as it's clear that bumble-bees, spiders, sweet clovers, ponderosa pine don't fear life and are present to life; if you don't perceive yourself as living in a cage, be-cause you're not living in a cage, you'll feel more intensely, you'll *be* more intensely, you'll be more alive. There's a reason we call them wild, and there's a reason the ground squirrel chewed her way out of the cage when I was young. Most of us, I think, would have sat down and tried to minimize our discomfort—through drugs, alco-hol, relationships, television, sex, jobs, buying, religion, power, and most of all rationalization—and soon would have told ourselves and anyone who would listen that our cage is no cage, that in fact there is no cage at all. And we would attempt to kill all those who try to show us otherwise. Thus the murder of the wild.

It suddenly seems equally clear to me that if you don't fear death in the same way we fear death—that is, call death an enemy to be defeated or transcended, rather than someone who walks beside us to the very end and with whom we converse one way or another (and who has much to teach us) for our entire lives—then you will both live and die radically differently. I don't mean you will never feel terror, never run away, never lose your nerve. But if death is sim-ply (and complexly) death, and if all of your life is an ecstatic (and mundane) adventure, and if all of your life has the significance and vividness of a long and splendid (and sometimes mundane) dream, then you will not spend your precious days and nights in a state of anxiety, but will perceive your own approaching death as a continuation of that lifelong conversation. That doesn't mean, of course, that you won't fight or run from those who would kill you, but the fight or flight is transformed from the grim desperation of refugees fleeing some implacable oppressor to a free and wild and willing being encountering a new (and old) challenge, whether that challenge is to fight off and kill (or avoid, or placate) a grizzly bear with your hands, feet, and wits; or to die with the grace and dignity with which you have lived. To encounter a grizzly—or the infirmity of old age—under these circumstances would be not merely terrifying, but now also an exhilarating adventure.

The question becomes: Can I do it?

I get up, put on my clothes. I start to leave. I hear a voice. "All that," it says, "is the barest start."

I tell all this to Allison. She smiles big.

I say, "I kept thinking about that Lakota phrase, 'It's a good day to die.' Until today I always pictured that said with a sort of desperate resolve, but now I can see how that could be said almost with a jubilance. Yesterday was a good day to live. This morning was a good morning to make love. This afternoon is a good day to die. A fabulous day to die. Whether it's said—and felt—with desperation or jubilation makes all the difference in the world."

She's still smiling.

I say, "I have no idea how the Lakota mean that phrase, but I do know that's how the bumblebees live it. They taught me that today."

We both sit.

I say, "But there's something I don't understand. What's the difference between death, and death?"

She doesn't say anything.

"Between a bear, or me, killing a fish to eat, and the Starkist or Unilever corporations killing fish to amass a fortune? The fish are just as dead."

"One individual fish, maybe, but not the ocean. One difference is that in the former case it serves the community."

It's true. I've written about that. A few years ago a radio interviewer said to me that Indians exploited salmon, too. I said, "No, they didn't. They ate them."

"What's the difference?" he asked.

I said they give them respect for the spirit in exchange for the flesh, but I knew that wasn't the whole answer. That afternoon I went to the forest near my home and asked a tree, what is the fundamental predator-prey agreement? The tree gave me the answer immediately: when you consume the flesh of another, you now take responsibility for the continuation and dignity of the other's community.

"But there's another difference," Allison says, "between a wolf killing a moose or a moose killing a plant, and the U.S. bombing some group of people or a man raping a woman."

I don't say anything.

"In the former cases the death serves life. In the latter cases it's not about death or life at all. It's about control."

I nod.

"What's the difference," she asks, "between making love and rape?"

"There are lots of differences."

"Right now I'm thinking of one. Making love serves life. It makes love. It's about life. Rape is about power. They share the same form, but the meaning and the process—I don't mean a man moving in and out, but the emotional and spiritual processes, and the memories made—are radically different."

I nod again. She can tell that I still don't quite understand.

She gets up, walks to the bookshelf, pulls down a book, goes to another bookshelf, pulls down a magazine, pulls down another, brings them back, sits down. She says, "This is from a United States pilot who was dropping napalm on Vietnamese in 1966: 'We sure are pleased with those backroom boys at Dow. The original product wasn't so hot—if the gooks were quick they could scrape it off. So the boys started adding polystyrene—now it stuck like shit to a blanket. But then if the gooks jumped under water it stopped burning, so they started adding Willie Peter,'" she pauses, looks at me, says, "Willie Peter means white phosphorous," and then she continues reading, "so's to make it burn better. It'll even burn under water now. And just one drop is enough, it'll keep burning right down to the bone so they die anyway from phosphorous poisoning.'"

She puts down that magazine, picks up another, thumbs through it, says, "This is what Canadian Minister of Natural Resources John Efford says to those who wish to stop the slaughter of seals by Canadian sealers, 'I would like to see the six million seals, or whatever number is out there, killed and sold, or destroyed or burned. I do not care what happens to them. The more they kill, the better I will love it.' Or in the US invasion of the Philippines, soldiers were sent into the field 'for the purpose of thoroughly searching each ravine, valley, and mountain peak for insurgents and for food, expecting to destroy everything I [found] outside of towns . . . all able-bodied men [were to] be killed or captured.'" Allison pauses, says, "Now here is the point, and remember what the man said about seals. General Jacob H. Smith gave orders that, 'I want no prisoners. I wish you to kill and burn; the more you kill and burn the better you will please me.' When a subordinate requested clarification, Smith said he wanted all persons killed who were either hostile toward the United States or who were capable of bearing arms. This latter category explicitly included children down to the age of ten.'"

Neither of us says anything.

She says again: "'The more they kill, the better I will love it.' And, 'The more you kill and burn the better you will please me.'"

"My God," I say.

"Of course," she responds. "Who else?"

"That's everything," I say, "isn't it?"

"That's the culture in a nutshell, yes."

"The *wétiko* disease."

"Yes."

"We're reaching the end, aren't we?"

"It can't go on much longer."

"No."

"It can't."

I understand, but I don't. I want to understand better the difference between death and death. And I want to know more what it's like to be a forest, not just anytime, but now, faced with this culture.

Allison says, "You can ask me, and I'm glad to make up an answer, but if you want to know, why don't you ask the forest?"

Allison comes with me. We're in the forest. She's lying on the ground and I'm on top of her, pushing into her as she pushes against the soil and the soil pushes against her. She wraps around me as the roots of trees reach from beneath the ground to wrap around us both. She comes, and so do I. The earth beneath us comes, as do the stones and trees.

nine
teen

to be a forest

I sit, back against a tree. I ask, "What is it like to be you, facing this culture? And what is the difference between death and death?"

The answer comes immediately, and so clearly I have to look at Allison to see if she heard it too.

Her face is blank.

I say, "I'm supposed to go to the river."

"Do you know why?"

"I'll find out when I get there."

There are a bunch of reasons I don't talk much with Allison about my previous romantic relationships, not the least of which is that I've found that to talk very much about exes almost never helps the current relationship, or more specifically, the current partner. I can still hear my mother say to me when I was very young, "Help each person—whether grocery clerk or best friend—feel good about themselves, help them to feel like the only person in the world." I remember her encouraging—even enforcing—this behavior when I was six, seven, eight. This must have been something my entire family learned, because I remember years later asking my sister if she thought I should discuss with my current girlfriend some problems I'd had with an ex, and I remember her saying, "Why would you want to do that? If you need to work through those issues, do it with someone not involved, with *anyone* other than your new girlfriend. Trust me on this. The questions to ask yourself before you bring up things like this are: How will talking about this make her feel about herself? Will it make her feel special? How will talking about this make her feel about you? How will talking about this make her feel about your current relationship? How will talking about this help the relationship itself? Are there other ways you can get across the same points without planting unnecessary memories?"

Memories are alive, and once planted they grow. Allison remembers every detail, no matter how trivial, I've ever told her about anyone I've ever dated. The same is true for me, and the same is true for more or less everyone I've ever known. Mention that you once had sex on a train—and just for the record, I'm speaking theoretically—and I can guarantee what your partner will think about when she next hears that lonesome whistle blow. Talk about your hot weekend in Vegas where you were lucky both in cards and in love—once again, I'm making this up—and I'm guessing your partner's enthusiasm for hearing you talk about poker might dim just a little.

Several years ago I knew a woman whose boyfriend talked incessantly about previous girlfriends. All roads, she said, led to exes. There was no place they could go without him saying, "Oh, I brought Samantha here on our first date," or "I used to come here all the time with Hope," or "I used to date a Vietnamese woman whose favorite soup was pho, and she taught me how to pronounce it. She's the only Asian woman I've ever had sex with."

She told me she'd gotten tired of never being alone with him, because he always brought along these ghosts. "It got so I was afraid to talk about anything," my friend said, "because I was always waiting for him to conjure another woman into every conversation. I should have known something was wrong when right after the first time we were together, even still in bed, he started talking about old lovers."

I asked her what happened.

"I got him to stop."

"How?"

"We were housesitting for some friends who had a hot tub, and he and I were going to get in. Just before we did, I told him this reminded me of the time I'd had sex with some guy in a hot tub. I told him how wonderful it was, and I told him all the details, every last one, blow by blow, thrust by thrust."

"Was that true?"

"Are you kidding me? I'd never even been in a hot tub, much less had sex in one. But my details were evidently convincing because he got very quiet and remembered there was a movie he wanted to watch instead. After a while I went inside and asked him if he liked how that felt.

"And it worked?"

"Absolutely. But a few months later we broke up anyway."

It is in the nature of memories, if they live, to grow and spread like plants. They can be fed and watered by, among many other things, tangible reminders. This is true of pleasant and unpleasant memories, memories we'd rather see flourish and memories we wish would die. It is true of personal memories, and it is true of memories who live among us collectively. Like plants, like humans, memories wish to stay alive, unless they don't. And like so many others, they are hitchhikers: they live in humans, in rocks, in trees, in air, in the spaces between all these.

I have not always understood this. I remember when I was an early teen, the husband of one family friend was caught cheating with the wife of another family friend in the former's bed. Both marriages ended, and the aggrieved woman threw away her bed. That made no sense to my thirteen-year-old junior scientist mind. The bed hadn't done anything. And it was just a bed. But I did not understand the nature of memories, how each time she saw that bed would feed and water that memory, how the memory would live not only in her but in her bed, too.

Memories can spread from place to place, spawn connection after connection. I knew a man whose girlfriend cheated on him in the ski resort of Vail, Colorado with a man named Mike. For the rest of the time they were together, the town of Vail carried that memory, as did skiing, and as, oddly enough, did the Chicago Cubs when he discovered the name of one of their outfielders: Mike Vail.

It's easy enough to laugh at the absurdity of someone skipping the sports pages so he won't be reminded of something he's trying to forget, but we all do that all the time. For a while I taught writing at a prison, and I was always careful not to talk to my students—unless they asked—about sex, walks in the forest, or anything else they would never again get to do. Many of the guards would intentionally stand near prisoners and talk loudly among themselves about what they were going to do with their families over holidays, thus feeding, always feeding, the memory of where the prisoners were and what they could not do. On the other hand, I once saw a prison librarian apologize profusely for accidentally mentioning to a prisoner that she was going to spend Christmas with her family.

Now, I know that what's past is past, and I know it's not supposed to bother Allison that I told her about making love next to a cemetery—I still don't understand that, by the way, because I'd still swear that was her, although of course there is precisely zero chance of me raising the issue again to clarify—and I know I'm not supposed to attach mental tags to anything Allison says about an ex either. But I know what I experience, and I know what Allison tells me about her experience, and I know what at least some of my friends tell me.

I had one friend who was normally as tight-lipped as either Allison or me, who in two consecutive relationships was talked into giving details he soon regretted. In one, his girlfriend asked him if the first time he made love was planned or spontaneous. He said he wasn't going to tell her. She begged. He said it didn't matter: it was a long time ago. She pleaded. No. She pouted. No. She swore it wouldn't make her feel bad. He told her that it had been planned for a couple of months, that they'd made an event of it. She burst into tears. He asked why. She said she felt bad because the first time *they'd* been together hadn't been planned, so it obviously had not been as special. Then the next woman he dated, a couple of years later, insisted that in order to get to know him better she wanted to know his past. "I won't be threatened at all. I just want to know you, and that means knowing all about you. Why don't you bring out your pictures and we'll talk about your history?" The idea seemed bad, but she was persistent. He brought out the pictures—"No, *all* the pictures, not just the ones of you by yourself"—and they had what he said was a very frank and intimate discussion. *That wasn't so bad*, he thought. That's what he continued to think until the next time he told her he didn't want to do something with her—she wanted him to go swimming, if I recollect—when she said, "You used to do that with Stephanie, and now you won't do it with me? You must have liked her better than you like me."

I don't want to make it seem like not talking about exes is some sort of religious stricture that Allison and I have to follow for fear of eternal damnation. Of course we talk about exes when necessary. But the key—and this applies not only to talking about exes, but to everything—is always asking the questions asked by my big sister: How will my making this comment or asking this question or performing this action affect the other person? How will it affect the relationship?

Of course asking these last two questions applies not only to one's lover, but to all relationships, including one's relationship with the land.

It's all pretty simple, but not many people do it. Almost no one within this culture asks these questions about their relationship to the land.

The point is not to avoid all unpleasant memories. The point is to ask yourself whether the planting or feeding of a memory is what you want to do.

There are those whose avoidance of unpleasant memories causes great harm. One reason my father abused us was that by simply being happy and free children, we reminded him of who and how he was before his parents destroyed him by abusing him. Because he did not wish for that memory—of who he was and what they did to him—to grow (although of course in this case it had already grown to overshadow his whole life, and ours, too) he had to destroy that which reminded him of it, that which fed the memory. Us. That's one reason God similarly must destroy all life: it reminds Him that

He has no body, and that bodies bring great joy, two things He tries desperately to forget. And why do you think so many *wétikos* spend so much time and so much energy destroying non-*wétikos*? So they, too, won't remember. And why was I so afraid of lying naked on the ground? What memories was I trying to not allow to come up? What was I afraid I would learn if I asked the forest what it was like to be a forest, and what was I afraid I would learn if I asked the forest what it is like to face down the wétikos?

Perhaps I would learn some of those answers at the river.

We go to the park where I saw the man die. I drive. Allison rides. I know I'm not going to fall through time on the way there. We stop, get out, walk the overgrown road toward the river, come to a small overlook with a ten-foot drop-off. This seems as good a place as any. We sit, feet dangling over the edge. The river makes soft sounds: gloops and laps and hisses. I don't know how to read them. I don't know what I'm supposed to read. I don't know what I'm supposed to learn. Is it the old Heraclitus line about how you can't step into the same river twice, because it's not the same river, and you're not the same person? Maybe the forest is trying to say that a forest is a process, like a river, like any other being.

I see gnats hovering. I see a fish jump. I see swallows flying low over the water. I see one open its mouth, maybe take a drink. I wonder if I'm supposed to learn that a river is not just water but insects, fish, birds, and that a forest, too, is not just trees.

I was expecting something more dramatic.

I turn to Allison. She raises her eyebrows.

"Nothing," I say.

I look at the river, lean back a little, rest my weight on my hands, slightly behind me and to the side, arms straight, elbows locked. I close my eyes.

When I open them it's dark. I see very little. There's no moon, and the only light is from the city. I can't imagine I fell asleep so suddenly. I've never done that before. I say, "Allison."

No response.

I say it again.

Still no response.

I don't think she left me while I was sleeping. I don't know why she would. But she's not there.

I hear a vehicle behind me and I scramble off to the side. Bushes scratch my arms. I see headlights. After the dark they blind me. The vehicle stops. The lights go out. The door opens. There is no dome light. Someone—I think a man—gets out, turns on a flashlight, walks to the overlook, shines the flashlight down. Apparently satisfied, he moves to the rear of the vehicle. It's a truck. He opens the tailgate, pulls out something heavy, carries it to the edge, sets it down, rolls it over. I hear a splash. I creep out to look. He again shines his flashlight on the river. I see a woman in the water, her long hair spread like a fan. The man returns to his truck, gets in, starts it, drives away.

I close my eyes.

When I open them it's bright. I blink, can't see anything. Finally I see I'm standing near where I was sitting before. Allison still sits. She looks at me, concerned. I tell her what I saw.

"Was it Nika?" she asks.

"No, her hair was different."

"Was it the same man?"

"I think so."

"How do we stop him?"

"I don't know." I stay standing, stare at the river. There's too much death. I don't know what to do.

After a time, I begin to wonder what this has to do with what it's like to be a forest. I still don't understand.

I close my eyes.

When I open them it's dark. I hear the river. A truck is parked close by, and even closer is the man with the flashlight. His breath is heavy from exertion. He plays the light over the water, and I look for bodies. I see none. He turns off the light. He's still breathing heavily. I don't want to move, for fear of him noticing me. I somehow know that if he notices me, even the slightest, I'm dead. I shift. My foot feels something slightly soft. I think I know what it is.

Finally the man's breathing slows. I don't know what he's going to do. I sense him look up, and I look up, too. I see a few stars, beyond the trees, beyond the refracted lights of the city. He looks back down. Something's going to happen.

He turns on the flashlight, points it toward the ground.

There is not one body there. There are two. They are on their backs. I see their faces. Suddenly I know what it is like to be a forest, what it is like to be a forest faced with this culture. One of the bodies is Allison's. The other one is mine.

twenty

h e l l

We're at home. We're sitting on the couch. I haven't told Allison what I saw. The only words I've said to her are, "We need to go." I said this the moment I got back to the daylight, with me blinking in the brightness, barely seeing the figure of Allison sitting on the overlook. She stood, took my arm, turned me toward the vehicle, led me up the path. She asked a couple of times what I saw that made me so pale, that made my whole body a mask, that made me unsteady on my feet.

I shook my head. I couldn't speak. I couldn't even think.

Allison drove. I sat. She was silent. I tried to think, tried to clear my mind.

First I tried to convince myself I had not seen what I had seen. But I had. I knew that. I have seen Allison's and my own faces enough to know them, even cut and bruised as they were. Or rather, cut and bruised as they will be, when this comes to pass. Cut and bruised as we will be.

We're sitting on the couch. Allison is crying. She is holding my hand. She squeezes. I haven't told her anything. I can't. I won't. I don't want to plant those memories inside of her. I don't want them to grow as they're already growing and twisting and climbing and reaching out inside of me. I don't want for her to be able to picture the mutilations, the disfigurements, the pulpy, bloody masses where before were flesh and organs.

She squeezes again, says, "What did you see?"

Silence.

We're sitting on the couch. I wish I'd never gone to the river. I wish I'd never asked what it's like to be a forest in the face of this culture. A river. A mountain. An ocean. A nonhuman. A human being. I no longer want to know. I want to go back to the way I was before: ignorant, dead to the world. I wish I had never fallen through time. I wish I could pretend none of this was happening. I wish I could pretend I was not going to be tortured and murdered.

There is a difference between death and death. I feel like a fool for even asking that question. The question is theoretical, abstract, absurd, the sort that could be asked only by someone who does not live in the real, physical, world, who is not paying attention to the meaninglessness—the absolute meaninglessness—of the suffering and death—the utterly needless suffering and death—caused by this *wétiko* culture and by individual *wétikos*. It could only be asked by someone who has no experience of the real world. It could only be asked by someone who is hiding from the real world. I wish I were still hiding. I wish I had no experience. I wish I could still ask that question.

We're sitting on the couch. Allison asks again, "What did you see?"

Silence. "We need to leave."

"Why?"

I won't tell her more. I won't plant those memories.

She asks, "Leave this house?"

"This area," I say. "Far away."

Silence. She's not squeezing my hand. She's thinking. I see she is starting to understand. She is anything but stupid. Finally she says, "You saw another body…"

I look straight ahead.

"Another woman."

I feel my teeth press against each other.

"It was me, wasn't it? You saw me."

"We need to leave."

It's odd. You'd think that, faced with our own torture and murder, we would immediately flee. But we don't. After the initial shock wears off, we pretty much go about our lives, now wearing a cloak of dread. I've read that many Jews in Nazi Germany did the same thing, going about their business as though if they ignored the threats diligently enough, the dreadful would never overtake them, as though pretending that nothing was wrong would exempt them from the consequences of their inaction. And it wasn't just Jews.

Many German officers knew the war was lost—and long before that, they knew it was wrong—yet they lacked the nerve to join the resistance. Inertia, cowardice, and short-term self-interest so often trump everything, from morality to sanity to realistic self-preservation.

Most of us do the same.

Oh, I shouldn't say that Allison and I don't change our lives. We start locking the doors at night, we buy guns, and I stop lying naked in the forest (although I don't tell Allison why). But we don't immediately flee.

We do make plans. Allison has a show opening in a month at a major gallery in New York City. Normally you wouldn't catch me dead in New York City, but given that the alternative is for me to get caught dead—for real, not cliché—in Spokane, I'm going to accompany her. After that we'll stay a while with her parents in northern California. We aren't sure what we'll do after that.

I don't tell Allison what I saw. She doesn't ask. I do tell my mother, though. She already knows about me falling through time. I tell her what I saw at the river, everything but the mutilations. I tell her where Allison and I are going.

She says, "I'm glad you're leaving."

"What will you do?"

"I'll take care of your animals and your place until you decide where you're going to live. And then I'll move into the area."

"You won't stay here?"

"In a town where you'll be murdered? Of course not. I don't want to think about you dead every time I think about the river. And if I did stay, I'd never see you: do you think I'd want you to visit if I knew you'd be murdered here?"

I go back to my mom's the next day. We sit at her kitchen

table. The house is on a hill southwest of Spokane. You can see the city out the windows. You can see the valley where the Spokane River runs. She is drinking tea. I am drinking water.

"Is it possible," she asks, "that what you saw was wrong?"

A pause. "No, I saw it was us."

"I'm not suggesting you were mistaken. I mean, just because you saw it, does that mean it's bound to happen?"

I think a moment. "It hasn't been wrong yet."

"I'm still not being clear. I don't even mean wrong. I guess I mean inevitable. Maybe you're being shown one possible future. Maybe it's not the only one. Maybe by acting you can change what only seems inevitable."

"That's why I need to leave."

"Yes, I understand."

I am not simply telling the truth when I say that the inevitable end that I most want to change is not my own torture and murder, nor even Allison's, but rather the torture and murder of the planet. Compared to that, our own is very small.

We bid temporary farewell to my mother, our friends, and our animals, and we say good-bye to the forest, hugging and caressing trees we have grown to know and love over the past years. We're glad that at least we were able to get them a temporary stay of execution before we ran away. We say good-bye also to the apple trees, and to Latah Creek. We do not return to the Spokane River.

During all of this I do not fall through time.

On the last afternoon in Spokane, I see a small snake curled on the kitchen floor. I pick her up, carry her outside, put her on bare ground in the partial shade of a clump of wild grasses. I watch her. She stays coiled, and flicks her tail several times. I leave for a few moments, and when I return she is gone.

We all have our own large and small delusions by which we live, delusions we wear like undershirts to keep ourselves from feeling the discomfort—the agony—of the cloaks of dread and terror that accompany and characterize this culture. One of my own delusions is that because I live next to a forest that there are forests everywhere, and even that the forest I live next to is not itself horribly wounded: remember, a forest is more than just trees (and young trees at that). But whenever I leave my home I'm reminded that even small areas of wild have become an exception. What was once everywhere now persists in patches. This reminder slaps me even harder each time I fly.

We fly to New York City.

In the West we fly over clearcuts, patchwork quilts of relatively bare ground alternating with sanctuaries of green that are smaller each time I see them. I've walked those clearcuts, and they look as bad from the ground as from the air. Worse, even. Sometimes moonscapes, sometimes patches of invasive weeds, sometimes intensive replantings of monocropped seedlings. Never a forest. There is no rest.

In the Great Plains it's field after field after field, circular patches of irrigated green in a landscape that should be tall- and short-grass prairie, that should be brown with bison. I've walked those fields, too, those killing fields where giant sprinklers suck the life out of rivers, streams, aquifers, where any nonhuman who threatens the production of saleable goods—anyone who threatens the production of money—is "treated" with herbicides, insecticides, rodenticides, is killed. Humans who threaten production are arrested, labeled as terrorists.

When we cross the Missouri the fields start to give way to towns and cities, until no matter where we are we can see the artifacts of this machine culture, shiny towers and ribbons of black asphalt, great masses of land devoid of any living being not surrounded by concrete, by stasis.

We're in New York City. I have seen the future, and the future is hell. It is a hell of concrete, steel, glass, asphalt, and people. It is an echo-chamber hell where the distorted voices of distorted human beings—and most especially the voices of the machines to which these humans have enslaved themselves—echo and re-echo and re-echo until they literally overwhelm with their deafening and deadening sameness, until there is no escape from this sameness, this constant repetition of the one overriding and underlying message of the supremacy of the manufactured, of the produced, of the artificial, of the machine-made over the living and the wild. It is the hell of a hall of mirrors reflecting back who and most especially what we have become.

It becomes easy to see why so many people are insane. Sensory deprivation can cause hallucinations, and in the city every sensation we receive—save that coming from pigeons, rats, roaches, and trees encased in concrete—is created or mediated by humans. It's no wonder, given the hellish church in which they worship, the hellish house in which they live, that so many people in cities lose the ability to perceive reality, lose the ability to perceive that anyone exists other than themselves and those just like them, and that they wear this narcissism like a suit of armor, never acknowledging that this armor weighs them down, that it constricts and ultimately kills them at the same time that it protects them from ever perceiving physical reality.

So many humans in cities are infected by the insane spirit of an insane God, and come to see themselves in the life-negating image of this life-negating God, and come to believe that there is no god but God, that there is no god but Man.

So many humans in cities are *wétikos*. It would be hard or almost impossible to survive in a city without becoming infected yourself, surrounded as you are by *wétikos* and their creations, their totems, their fetishes—from tall buildings to banks to razor-wire-topped fences to flattened sidewalks to dogs and humans whose paws have never touched the ground—with no wild available to heal you, replenish you, to help you remember what it is to be alive and to be human, to be wild, to remind you that this city is not all there is, that these wétikos are not all there are, that a real, physical world still lives beyond the reach of those who would control or destroy everything.

I'm walking down the street. I have no skin left. It's been worn off by sharp corners of buildings and too many people. This is how I feel every time in a city. The pain is physical.

I see a billboard of a man reclining in a chair, holding a beer bottle, base at his groin. The bottle stands like an erect penis. A semi-nude woman sprawls between his legs. I'm surprised they don't show her sucking on his bottle. Another billboard shows a woman, an erect whiskey bottle, and an invitation to slip into something smooth.

I hear a horn blare, and another, and another. A siren. I'm at the edge of a park. I hear the rhythmic thumping of a woodpecker and I marvel at the ability of any creature to survive this environment.

"That's not a woodpecker," Allison says. "That's a helicopter."

She's right. I soon hear it more clearly, and finally I see it.

We walk. I remember an analysis I read of cities saying that if you pack any other mammal this tight the gutters would constantly run with blood. Rats packed this close begin to cannibalize each other. And the humans I see *are* eating each other, just not always physically.

Allison asks, "Have you noticed how skinny so many of the women are?"

I nod.

She continues, "And how disproportionately large their breasts are?"

It looks freakish. I respond, "I wonder how much of this is real."

"This?" She points at the buildings, the cars, the people. "Almost none of it."

We're in a hotel. Allison sits on the bed. I sit in the room's lone chair. "I've been wondering," I say to Allison, "if maybe I haven't been falling through time at all."

She looks at me out of the corners of her eyes.

"Maybe I'm not falling or going *anywhere*."

She waits.

"Maybe I'm staying right where I am, and the land is showing her memories to me. Maybe the land is moving inside of me."

She thinks about it.

I say, "I've read lots of accounts of plants hitchhiking into people. That's a standard part of some indigenous peoples' experience. A plant might jump inside of you and ride along with you for a while, then go back to its own body."

"Kind of like your or my muse," she says, excited.

I nod. "I once asked an Indian friend where dreams come from, and she said, 'Oh, everyone knows the animals give them to us.' I think it's plants, too."

"And dreamgivers, and muses, and others."

"And others." I pause, then say, "In areas with a lot of plants, this joyriding—which I've read is often beneficial or at least entirely benign but sometimes harmful—can get to be incredibly distracting, almost like being with someone you love to make love with, but at some point you've got to carry in the firewood for the winter. . . ."

"I know that one," she says.

"Me too." I think a moment, smile, then continue, "I've heard that in some places that constant joyriding has led people to incorporate into their cosmologies certain spiritual practices necessary to keep the plant and animal joyriding manageable."

She laughs. I love her laugh. Then she says, "Why does the land share memories specifically with you?"

"I think this might happen to everyone, but most people

don't notice, at least consciously. Most people don't even pay attention to other *humans* around them, much less plants."

"That's one reason," she says, "that I always touch and say hello to trees in the city. I want to acknowledge their existence, let them know that *someone* thinks they're beautiful, that someone's sorry they're in prison.

"Yes," I say. "Me, too."

"But why don't *I* perceive the land's memories?"

"You probably do. Just not the same way I do. And remember, I didn't start perceiving them this clearly until a couple of months ago. Why did I start then? I wish I knew."

Suddenly I hear a voice, clear as Allison's, yet different: solid, sharp, short, certain, slightly hissing, male. It says, "You will."

I say, "Did you hear that?"

"What?"

I tell her what I heard. She didn't hear it.

Silence. Finally Allison says, "What about seeing the future? If you're seeing memories, how do you see the future?"

I bring my hands directly in front of me. She catches on before I can do anything, and brings up her hands to make the circular motion the Indian elder made to show me how time winds around itself. I think of the snake who was curled around herself in our kitchen.

Allison says, "I don't mean to be contrary, but I've got another question. What about the man who grabbed you at the river, the man who died? If it was a memory, how did he grab you? You wouldn't have been there at the time."

I make that motion with my hands. I say, "That's part of the answer. But also, if a memory is alive, why can't it affect us physically, just like any other hitchhiker? A virus can affect us physically."

"You're right," she says. "Memories do affect us physically."

I'm thinking of what I saw at the river: Allison's body, mine. I feel the memory tightening its hold on my back, the sides of my neck, my stomach. I say, "They can grab us tight, even tighter than the man grabbed me."

"Or," she says, "they can make us smile. Sometimes memories of you and me make me smile. They touch me."

We take a walk. It begins like any other stroll through hell. Heat. Pavement. Concrete. People on cell phones. People driving cars. People in line for restaurants. Billboards. Advertisements. Automobile exhaust.

In the middle of our third block I stop, take Allison's arm, say, "It's happening."

"Do you want to sit?"

"No." I step to the side, out of the stream of people, against a building. The building becomes a deciduous tree that stretches up through thick leaves farther than I can see. I'm instantly cooler. I touch the smooth bark, look down at the duff and forest litter. I am transfixed by the beauty and by the embodied knowledge that this place was not always hell. Not even so long ago it was someplace completely different. I see oaks, tulip trees. In front of me I see a meadow, and a reach of open sky. I close my eyes and breathe deeper than I have since we arrived in this city. The air smells so good, so rich, so moist, so clean. I hear the delicious sound of a slight breeze in the trees, and I open my eyes. I take two small steps so I can hear the leaves beneath my feet.

And then I hear something else. Distant thunder, perhaps, but it doesn't stop. A train, but I know the land is sharing with me a memory of a time before trains. The sound grows louder, and louder still. I can't imagine what's making it.

And then I see a dark river in the sky, moving like clouds, but ever so much darker, and moving ever so much faster. This mass pulsates, splits, rejoins, covers the sky from horizon to horizon. The thunder, the train, the roaring, the tornado, grows louder and louder still.

And then I see what they are. They are birds. They are passenger pigeons. Millions, tens of millions, hundreds of millions of birds. And they are flying closer and closer. The mass is tumbling, shimmering, covering the entire sky.

I have spoken before of seeing god in Allison, and hinted at seeing god in salmon. Now, as much as ever before, I know that once again I am in the presence of the divine.

I begin to sob.

And then. . . .

I am back in hell. I am still sobbing. I cannot catch my breath.

I cannot live like this. I cannot live in hell.

Allison asks, "What did you see?"

"The beauty. The beauty." And I know that this place was not always hell. And I know also that seeing this land's memory, just like seeing other lands' memories, has made this hell even less tolerable for me than it ever was before, has made me understand more than ever before that this hell cannot, will not, must not last.

twenty one

dr. kline

That night I dream of Dr. Kline, whose name I've never heard before. I dream I'm supposed to go to his office, and I'm supposed to go alone. I dream I know where it is. I dream that when I get there I am surrounded by many sad women. They do not want to be sad.

When I wake up, I know what I need to do.

I do it.

That evening, I say to Allison, "Dr. Kline was the professor who raped you." It's not a question.

She blinks, starts to ask, "How . . ."

"I went there today."

Silence.

"When I was there, I saw others."

She takes a deep breath. "Why are you doing this?"

"I'm just telling you that you weren't the only one. This has to do with more than you."

"How many?"

"Lots."

"Why did you go without asking me?"

"A dream."

She thinks a moment, then says, "I want this to stay buried."

"Okay," I respond. "I'll help you re-bury it, or I'll butt back out, whatever you want."

"No. . . ." she says.

"Okay."

"I don't know what to do with this information."

I don't say anything.

Finally she asks, "Are any of them recent?"

"Yes. I could tell when different memories took place from his calendar on the wall."

"I remember that calendar," she says. Silence, then, "What else did you see?"

"More than I wanted."

"Did you see. . . ."

"No."

A pause before she asks, "How are you doing?"

"I'm not the same man I was this morning."

"And there were a lot of them?"

"Yes."

"And recent?"

"Yes."

She doesn't speak for a while. Then she asks simply, "Did you write down his office hours?"

Allison and I are outside Dr. Kline's office. It's late in the evening. Apart from Kline, we're probably the only people in the building. Allison and I are acutely aware of the irony of this. We're also acutely aware of the reason Kline schedules his office hours so late.

The door is slightly open. I can see Kline's back. He wasn't here when I entered his office before, but I know what he looks like from the memories.

Allison looks at me, takes a deep breath, and silently pushes the door a bit more open. She quietly steps inside, leaves the door cracked, and moves to the left. I stay outside. I can see him clearly. She is not in my view.

She says, "Dr. Kline."

He jumps, turns in his chair. "Good God. You startled me." His face softens, moves from her face to her breasts to her hips, back to her face. She's wearing a loose-fitting long-sleeved shirt and baggy pants.

She asks, "Do you remember me?

He looks at her more intently, then slightly shakes his head. "Remind me," he says.

"You said I was beautiful."

He laughs. "And?"

"Do you remember what you were doing when you said that?"

"I'd hate to venture a guess."

"I'll tell you."

He raises his eyebrows.

"You were holding me against. . ."

She continues, "That wall. You were raping me."

His face slightly hardens. That's his only external response. Then he says, "I have no idea who you are."

"I was your student."

He responds, "I've had many."

I wonder if I should step in. Allison and I didn't script any of this. She'd just said she wanted to go in first, and that I should be there to help if necessary.

"You raped me," Allison says, "and you don't even remember who I am?"

He answers, "I never raped you. I don't even know who you are." Then, softly, "You need help. Maybe you *were* my student. Maybe you had a fantasy. I don't know. But it isn't real. And I don't want to be involved in your fantasy. I'm going to stand up now, and I'm going to take your elbow, and I'm going to guide you to the door. I'm letting you know so that when I touch you now you won't think that I'm sexually assaulting you. Are you ready?"

"Don't touch me."

"Then leave on your own."

He stands. But when he stands he's not the man I just saw sitting, a man in his mid-forties. Instead he is as he was fifteen years ago. I hear a voice—Allison's—say, "No." I step in and I see him pressing her against the wall. She isn't wearing baggy pants, but a long skirt. She's much younger. Again she says, "No," and then it is not her saying *no*, but someone else, and Kline is in his late thirties, and the woman has been turned to face the wall, and he is holding the back of her neck with one hand and hiking her skirt with his other. And then she is another woman and she has been pushed back onto the desk. And then she is another and she is on her knees and her eyes are closed and she is eager, but there is still something wrong, and when the memory shifts I know what it is, and I see him leaving the office and I see her alone in the room standing up and then blinking hard several times, then wiping her hand across her eyes to keep away the tears. The memory shifts again and I see another woman, it's Allison against the wall, and again she says, "No."

And then I'm standing next to Allison.

Kline looks at me, says, "Who are you? Get out now. Both of you."

I shut the door.

He reaches for the phone.

I say, "Not a good idea."

He picks up the handset.

I say, "Does the name Theresa Ray mean anything to you? She was last fall. Or how about Dee Miller? She was this spring."

He holds the handset.

I say, "Dee Miller was against the wall there. Theresa Ray, on the floor here."

"You don't know what you're talking about."

"Then call security. Call the cops while you're at it. We'll wait." I pause. I hear the dial tone. When he doesn't move I say, "Do you want more? Jennifer Hancock, six years ago. Before that there's Melanie Marshall. She slapped your face."

"I don't know who you are or what you're talking about."

"Then make the call."

He says to me, "She says I raped her and you buy her story. Or are you going to say you're a former student and I raped you, too?"

"You should know," I say, "that we put up flyers all over the city saying that you're a rapist."

"What?"

"We didn't use the women's names, but we used yours, and your face."

"This is too much." He slams down the phone, steps toward Allison.

She says, "Don't touch me."

He grabs at her left arm with his right hand. She bats away his hand. "For the last time. . . ." I see her demeanor shift the way I've seen it shift when she trains for self-defense. He reaches for her again. She blocks his hand easily and hits him in the face, then gut, then face. Her last punch throws him against the same wall where he once held her, and she stops, pulls him up by his shoulders, and knees him in the groin.

She lets him drop to the floor. She says, "You're lucky I don't kill you."

I say, "The reason you're not going to call the cops is the reason you didn't call them already. The names I've given you are just a start."

He looks up, gasps. "Why?"

"Payback," says Allison.

I ask Allison, "Do you still have that knife in your backpack?"

"Yes."

"Could you hand it to me please?"

She opens her pack, hands me the knife. I open it.

He says, "You're all wrong."

I say to Allison, "You could beat him to death, and you'd *never* get the truth. That's just not possible. Or if you did get an apology it'd be phony and manipulative."

I turn back to Dr. Kline, say, "I don't care whether you believe you've done nothing wrong. And I know you don't care about the pain you've caused, so here's the deal. If you ever again have any inappropriate interaction with any woman—our definitions of inappropriate, not yours—we'll come back and we will make certain you never do it again. Is this clear?"

"You're fucking crazy."

I look at Allison.

She says, "I think we're done here."

"For now," I respond. I turn to Kline, say, "See you later."
We leave.

On the way to the hotel, I ask Allison how she feels.
She says. "It feels so good to fight back."

Of course we were bluffing. I wasn't going to kill him. If I
killed him there would be a body, and if I didn't kill him he wouldn't
go to the cops: he had more to lose than we did from the police. But
if he had called the police, we would have run away: I knew what
happened to the other women, but I didn't know *them*, and even had
Allison and I known the women there's no way we would have asked
them to submit themselves to re-rape by the court system.

It wasn't a bluff, though, about coming back to check on
him. The next time we were in hell, we would be sure to visit.

twenty two

demons

Allison has finished installing her work at the gallery, and the opening party is (thankfully) over. She's going to spend the next few days introducing herself to a bevy of other gallery owners, and then she has one final commitment: a couple of free art and feminism classes for kids at an alternative high school. After that ends our tenure in hell.

We take another walk. We see the same sights: cars, billboards, people, more people, and still more people. Stores, more stores, and still more stores. The place is one giant shopping mall. The point of city life, it seems, is to shop.

We start back to our hotel.

I smell something burning. I mention this to Allison, who says she doesn't smell anything but car exhaust, pavement, and fried food. She normally has a stronger sense of smell than I. But I'm not wrong. I smell it.

We walk another block. The smell gets stronger. I ask Allison. Still nothing.

I'm scanning for smoke when a woman catches my attention. She is a block ahead of us on this slightly crowded street, but still I see her clearly. She is staring directly at me. I immediately know who she is. I take Allison's hand, say, "Let's go."

We walk toward the woman.

Allison asks, "What do you see?"

"My muse."

When we're half a block away the woman turns and walks down the cross street. We get to the corner and I look right. I see her, standing in the middle of the block, again looking at me. Allison doesn't see her. We walk more quickly now. When we get within about ten yards she points to the far side of the street. At first I only see a man and a woman on a bench. Then I see a small line of smoke creeping along the ground in front of them. The man and woman don't seem to notice, although it's directly in his vision. She continues on her cell phone, he continues to stare absently. I look back to the muse. She points and points and points. Each time I see another line of smoke.

I look away, see a tired horse pulling a carriage, and I see a tired woman walking a poodle. I see lots of dogs. Lots of people. And then more smoke.

I say to Allison, "I don't. . . ."

She doesn't say anything, and I turn to look at her. She's gone. So is the muse. So are the people on the bench. So is the woman with the poodle. So is the carriage. But there's another carriage, another tired horse. Another couple on the bench. Different people. Different dogs. Different cars. I see more lines of smoke crawling along the ground. I hear a hissing I recognize from somewhere I cannot place. I hear a voice I similarly recognize but also cannot place. It says one word: "Feed."

A man in his twenties walks by me. The back of his shirt reads *The Best FCUK Ever*. A line of smoke emerges from the ground through the solid sidewalk, stays low as it moves in his direction, then begins to rise up just behind him. Out of the corners of my eyes I see lines of smoke everywhere, hugging the ground, then rising in swirling, curling columns. They begin to coalesce.

No one else seems to pay attention. People talk. They eat. They smoke cigarettes. They walk their dogs.

The smoke continues to take form. The carriage horse stops, looks. The driver hits it with the reins. A few dogs pause, sniff, raise their snouts into the air, raise their ruffs and tails the way country dogs do when they smell bears, behavior I've never quite seen in city dogs. I nod. The dogs smell it too. So does the horse.

Oddly, I'm not scared. Apprehensive, yes. But not scared. I know the muse would not lead me into danger. And suddenly I know what is coming, and I wonder what could ever have taken me so long to understand, and wonder even more that no one else seems to notice.

The man in the obscene shirt stops. His hair is short and

black. He wears it greased, as seems to be the fashion here. The smoke rises, swirls, forms a solid mass.

I hear that same hissing, but now I know where I've heard it before. It grows and grows until it fills the entire street. It comes not just from this column of smoke, but from all of them. The columns are everywhere. No one else notices.

When it seems it can grow no louder, it stops. A dog barks. Another whimpers and drops into a submissive pose. Owners jerk on leashes. The driver hits the horse. The man with the shirt talks to a woman.

I hear a loud pop, and the column of smoke takes solid form. It is a demon from that dream—that visitation—of so long ago. With a quick flick it draws one clawed finger across the man's throat. Blood spurts. The woman screams. The demon yanks the man's head to an impossible angle, rips the skin on his neck with one hand, attaches its mouth, and begins to suck.

I can't breathe. I force vomit back down my throat. I want to run, but I hear another pop, and another demon stands in front of the couple on the bench. One swing takes off the woman's head. Another opens the man from throat to navel. Yet another demon grabs a man in a business suit, plants its mouth over the man's mouth and nose, and sucks. The man collapses. The demon keeps sucking.

I stagger, then freeze. I think over and over, *The muse would not lead me into danger. The muse would not lead me into danger.* But I am sheer animal panic. If there was someplace I could go I would run. If I could make my legs work I would run.

People scream, run, trip, cower. Demons leap person to person, killing, eating only the choice bits—like bears in a run of salmon—and dropping the rest for later or to be eaten by someone else.

People try to escape in cars, but demons break windows to get at them, to pull them out, to kill them, to feed. Drivers run over other humans too slow to get out of their way. But these drivers too do not escape, as there is no room for them to make a break, and somehow I know that no matter where they go, there will be nowhere to hide.

I want to close my eyes, but I cannot. I want to look away, but each time I do I see some new horror.

Bodies fall from buildings. I do not know if they jumped or were thrown, but this tells me that there are demons inside the buildings.

A few people pull out guns, but every demon hit merely turns back into smoke, then disappears—seeming to go back where it came from—to be replaced by more and still more demons.

The driver furiously beats the horse, who refuses to take a step. A demon leaps onto the carriage, picks up the man, breaks his back, then throws the man to the ground. The man moves his arms weakly. The demon jumps off, looks in all directions, looks at the horse. With quick motions the demon uses a claw to cut the traces, cut the bridle. The horse spits out the bit, shakes her head. The leather falls to the ground. The horse turns toward the demon. They lock eyes. The demon walks away. The horse steps toward the driver, looks into the man's face. The horse raises a hoof, places it on the man's head.

I see a woman holding a Scottish terrier. A demon moves toward her. She throws the dog at the demon, who bats the dog away, then advances on the woman.

Some dogs defend their owners. These are killed, dropped. Some dogs cower. Others, like the horse, turn on the humans. All these dogs are ignored.

I see a very old dog, a yellow lab/spaniel mix, walking through this abattoir—this city that has been an abattoir as long as it has been a city, though we never seemed to notice since we were the butchers, not the victims—walking slowly with an arthritic gait, bobbing her head with every step. She pays no mind to the slaughter, but walks. A woman in heels trips over her, knocks the dog down. The dog struggles to her feet, continues plodding. A demon stops in front of her, stoops, reaches with one clawed finger toward the dog's nose. The dog stops, looks through clouded eyes at the demon, sniffs, touches the finger. The demon stands, leaps over a grated wall into a restaurant, overturns a table, and reaches down to kill a child left behind when his parents fled. The dog continues to walk.

I wish I could walk. I wish I could run. I wish I could move. I do not want to be noticed. I'm hoping they cannot touch me. But an older man with a briefcase runs into me, almost knocks me down. A demon follows, brushes me on its way past, pulls off the man's head with one twist, and turns toward me. *I can't die here*, I think. *I'm supposed to die in Spokane.*

The demon speaks, in a hissing voice I hear inside my head: "It doesn't work like that."

I can't breathe. I don't know what that means.

It takes a step, looks me in the eye, and shakes its head. It reaches out one finger, then it turns and runs after someone else. It does not lessen my terror, but I know I am safe for this moment. Someday they may come for me, or they may not. I understand that now is not my time to die. Now is my time to watch.

It's done. The demons are gone, moving back through the same passageways they'd used to get here. I can now breathe. I no longer want to vomit. There are dead humans everywhere, on the street, in cars, hanging out of buildings. None of this scares me. It is the killing that troubles me, not the dead. Dogs run, pigeons fly, leaves of imprisoned trees talk in the breeze. I hear a few moans, some screams. After the longest time I see a very few people—a very few crazed, stunned people—wander from buildings and stand amidst the dead. I see one of them shake his head, as though to clear it, and then I see him walk into a store and pop open the cash register. I see him reach into the pockets of the dead for their wallets.

I somehow know—as though I was told—that this outbreak was not merely local, that these demons came in everywhere, that they covered the planet, they fed, and they returned to wherever they came from. I know they will return.

I don't know how many humans are left alive. I don't know *who* is left alive. Because this is in the future, I don't even know if

I am left alive—presuming the psychopath in Spokane hasn't killed me first—and I don't know if those I love are left alive. I do know that most people are dead. I know, too, once again as though I've been told, that neither technology nor religion nor morality nor immorality nor wealth nor poverty protected people from the demons. The demons were in that sense indiscriminate—or discriminating in ways beyond my understanding—like a tidal wave, like an epidemic, like an explosion, like a fire.

I look at the buildings around me, and time again begins to shift. It moves quickly, as months and years pass, and I see plants reach up, see them climb the sides of buildings, see them pull down these buildings as surely as the demons pulled down the people. The buildings fall, trees rise. And in the south I hear a roaring.

And then. . . .

I'm standing next to Allison. Drops of sweat hang from my hair. My shirt sticks to my back, to my sides. My fingers are sore from clenching, and my palms are white, then red, when I release them.

Allison doesn't ask what I saw. She takes me by the arm, and leads me to the hotel, to our room.

For several days I cannot tell Allison what I saw. I cannot think about it, and I cannot keep from thinking about it. I am too scared to stay in our room, and I am too scared to go outside. I am scared of smoke, and I am scared of hissing, and I am scared of pops. I am scared of carriages and I am scared of obscene shirts. I ask for a dream, and I get one that consists of the sentence, "I am trying to tell you something." That's all. Somehow that makes me less afraid.

I tell Allison what I witnessed.
She doesn't say a word.
I ask what she is thinking.
She says, "Keep going."

I say, "I know what I am supposed to feel about this, and I know what I do feel."

"What are you supposed to feel?"

"Well, it terrifies me. That's just the truth."

"It should."

"I didn't want to witness what I witnessed."

"No sane person would."

"But there was something I didn't feel."

She doesn't say anything.

"I felt the same horror I feel at any massacre site: any clearcut, any factory slaughterhouse, any fishing factory, any city."

She still doesn't say anything.

"And I was scared for my life and I wish I didn't have the images inside of me, just as I wish I didn't have images of clearcuts or industrial fishing nets inside of me."

She nods.

"But I couldn't muster outrage toward the universe for this—what do I call it?—this blasphemy. People think they're at the top of some hierarchy . . . people think that there exists some hierarchy to be on top of . . . and violence is supposed to flow down. But I didn't . . ."

Silence.

I continue, "The whole time I kept hearing a voice say again and again, '*This* is what it feels like to be a forest faced with this culture.' And then the voice would say, 'This is what it feels like to be a river. A mountain. A wild animal. A factory farmed animal. This is what it feels like to be indigenous.' The only difference is that this slaughter lasted minutes, and the other slaughters have gone on and on and on for thousands of years, since the beginning of this culture. Six thousand years of relentless slaughter. Six thousand years of unremitting terror."

She takes a breath, lets it out.

I go on, "No. There's another difference. The demons at least ate the people. They didn't kill them to make money. And there's another difference, too. A forest does nothing to deserve this. The salmon do nothing to deserve this. Tormented chickens in factory farms do nothing to deserve this. Vivisected monkeys do nothing to deserve this. But none of the civilized—none of the *wétikos*—are innocent. Children, I suppose, and the extremely poor. Subsistence farmers. The remaining traditional indigenous."

Silence.

"I don't know."

More silence.

"I need to know what you're thinking."

Finally she asks, "How do you stop a rabid dog?"

I don't know what she's talking about.

She says, "I just read that the US military has scattered 2,200 tons of depleted uranium all over Iraq. Background radiation levels are now so high that simply to exist is to receive the equivalent of three chest X-rays per day. Depleted uranium has a half-life of 4.5 billion years. How do you stop them?"

I blink.

She continues, "What if the cannibal culture stuff—the *wétiko* stuff—really isn't a metaphor? What if the reason members of this culture are so destructive is that they really do have a highly contagious spiritual illness that causes those infected to consume the souls of others, causes them to destroy? How do you stop them? How do you stop a rabid dog? Do you see those in power stopping the use of depleted uranium because we ask nicely?"

My mouth forms, "No," but no air comes out.

"I also just got an email from my friends Tom and Rene in Georgia, the ones doing that documentary about the collapse of civilization. They interviewed some climate change experts, and said they were. . . ." She steps to her computer, which is on the hotel room table. She opens a program, reads, "'both big-brained scientists, and both seemingly unable, or unwilling, to really look at the world situation as a whole. No surprise there, I guess. They'd acknowledge some really horrible bit of info about the changing climate, and then they'd say there's nothing to worry about "unless you really love polar bears." They just can't seem to put it all together. For all of the usual reasons.'"

She turns back to me, says, "What if 'all of the usual reasons' includes brain damage from this spiritual illness? It doesn't take much intelligence to see that this culture is killing the planet. It doesn't take much intelligence to see that an economic system—any economic system—is less important than a landbase. It doesn't take much intelligence to see that changing the climate is a really bad idea. And yet is anybody doing *anything* significant to stop global warming? We all know what needs to be done: we need to shut down the oil economy. We need to shut it down completely. We need to dismantle everything we see around us. Now. This isn't a fucking computer game where you get to save and go back and try again. This is life on the planet we're talking about. Why aren't people shutting down the oil economy? Because we're fucking insane. We're rabid dogs.

"What if God is real? What if God hates life? What if God infects people, causes them to hate life as much as God does, causes them to want to infect other people with this hatred, causes them to propagate this sickness? Can you explain the insanity any other way, Derrick? They're killing the planet, and oh, by the way, the Yankees won today, so life must be good.

"How do you stop a rabid dog?

"Leatherback turtles are going extinct. We can say the same for so many others. Who cares? The stock market went up today. Life *is* good. How, Derrick, how? How can anyone be so cruel? And how do we stop them? What did you say to Dr. Kline? How did you put it? How do you stop a rapist? Only now it's not just this or that woman. It's the planet. It's everything. How do we stop them?

"How do you stop a rabid dog?

"Just today the National Oceanic and Atmospheric Administration reduced protection for salmon in the Northwest by about 90 percent. Why? Because the National Association of Homebuilders asked them to, acting in proxy for big timber. This is how it goes, Derrick. Every time. Every fucking time. You know this. I know this. We all know this. They're fucking rabid dogs, Derrick, and they need to be stopped.

"As we speak the fish are all dying in the Black River, here in New York. Do you know why? Because three million gallons of cow shit spilled from a factory dairy. The cows are tormented, the land is destroyed, and now the river. And did you know that workers in factory slaughterhouses have to wear earplugs or they would go deaf from the screams of pigs being hacked to bits while they're still alive? What will it take to make all of this stop?"

She's crying now. "I don't think salmon will be outraged by the arrival of the demons. I don't think the few remaining leatherbacks will either. Nor redwoods. Nor white pines. Nor cows in factory farms. Nor pigs. Nor any others. Nor will I. I'd imagine most nonhumans are praying day and night for the demons' arrival, and the question most nonhumans—and most indigenous, and those others who love life on this planet—are asking is: Why are you taking so long?"

twenty three

on the run

We're on the last leg of our journey back west, flying from San Francisco to Crescent City, California, on a plane that holds about twenty people. I'm looking out the window. The propeller spins, shredding the flesh of thick clouds. I wonder how much it hurts.

I turn to Allison, say, "You're right."

"Of course I'm right. I'm a woman, remember?" She smiles. "About what?"

"I think the *wétiko* disease causes brain damage. You know that question I always ask about whether politicians and CEOs and corporate journalists—and in fact most members of this culture—are stupid, or are they evil?"

"Or both."

"Maybe the disease causes people to become really stupid."

"Public discourse would suggest this is the case."

"Maybe it causes them to act against their self-interest, like the ants who climb to the tops of blades of grass and clamp on tight. Certainly people are clinging just as tight to systems that are killing them. And maybe it turns them into idiot savants, into people who can't think clearly but who can send a rocket to the moon. . . ."

"And who can build really big bombs."

"And who have a gift for making money."

"And maybe it causes them to hallucinate, to *actually* perceive money as worth more than life, to *actually* perceive heaven as worth more than earth. It's not that they're poor deluded souls who just don't quite understand. They are *incapable* of getting it, just as people with Alzheimer's or Mad Cow are incapable of remembering or thinking clearly, just as humans are incapable of seeing ultraviolet and bees are incapable of seeing red."

"One characteristic of sociopaths" she says, "is that they're incapable of feeling certain emotions, including joy, sorrow, regret, and especially empathy or compassion. Incapable. If, at a very young age, your caregivers don't nurture you—if they don't bond with you and you don't bond with them—you may very well not develop the capacity to care, to *feel*. If that's the case, it doesn't matter what therapy you get later, the neural pathways simply aren't there."

I respond, "I once had a friend who contracted measles as a fetus. The disease scarred her eyes. She has something like three percent vision. You and I could talk to her all we want, we could sign petitions, we could file lawsuits, we could beg, plead, bribe, but it wouldn't matter. It *couldn't* matter. She is incapable of seeing. Of course in her case she can empathize, very well, actually. But the point is that when certain diseases cause certain damage, there is nothing you can do about it."

We deplane on land that used to belong to the Tolowa and Yurok, to the salmon, the steelhead, the redwoods, the grizzlies. Now it belongs to the *wétikos*. Or at least they claim it.

Allison's parents—George and May—pick us up, drive us home. May has—as she always seems to—cooked a delicious meal, this time carrot soup, homemade bread, mashed potatoes, and chicken with homemade noodles. Over dinner George tells us stories. I've heard most of these before, but he tells them well, and so long as it's only the fourth or fifth time, I don't mind.

I remember one of the first times I met him he told a long, elaborate story about a premonition of death he'd had when he was a teenager, and how a dog and a cat had saved his life. I'd been utterly fascinated and unable to understand why everyone else fled as soon as he began: Allison to clear the table, May to wash dishes, and Allison's sister Vi to feed the cats. Eleven or twelve retellings later I understood, and began helping May to dry dishes and put them away.

Tonight he tells a story I've never heard. May helps. It's from Allison's childhood.

"We always encouraged Allison and Vi to take as much freedom as they could handle," George says, then turns to May. "Do you remember the time Allison decided to sleep in a cardboard box in the basement?"

"Oh, yes," she says. "You got her a box from the appliance store and I made up a little bed for her, and she took her stuffed animals."

George continues, "She slept down there for probably two months, then one day she said she wanted to come home."

"How old was she?" I ask.

"Twenty-three," says Vi.

"Oh, she was not," responds May. "I think she was six or seven. She said she wanted to go on a trip, and every day she would tell us where she and her box had gone the night before."

"And then do you remember," George says, pointing his fork at no one, "the time we gave all her toys to the McNallys?

"Why?" I ask.

"Oh," May says softly, "the McNallys were so very poor. The father used to be a roofer. He was working at some business and fell through the roof, landed flat on his back. He fractured his skull, broke his back, and then got a terrible attorney who talked him into settling for about $5000. This was a long time ago, but that was still not nearly enough for them to live on."

"And then do you know what the attorney did?" George asks. "He got a job with the insurance company about three weeks later."

May continues, "So George used to go down to the grocery store—this was before they were all big and automated—and he sometimes told the owners to just charge us the next time the McNallys came in."

"So Allison donated her toys? How nice!" I say.

Everyone laughs. Allison rolls her eyes.

George says, "Not hardly. We took them from her."

"Why?"

"She was a messy child," says May.

George says, "You should have seen her room. Games and books and clothes all over the floor."

"That was normally okay," May adds. "We usually just closed

the door."

"But it got to be too much," George continues. "We couldn't even get the door shut. And she started leaving her stuff everywhere. In the living room, the kitchen, our room, Vi's room, grandma's room—this was before she died, obviously. So we told her to clean up her mess."

"What did she do?"

May answers, "She ignored us."

"How old was she?" I ask.

Predictably, Vi answers, "Twenty-three."

"Oh," May responds just as comfortably, "she was not. I think she was nine."

"I think she was ten," George says.

"No, it was the summer Vi got chicken pox, so she must have been. . . ."

Silence.

I say, "What happened?"

"Oh, Vi was really sick. I remember giving her oatmeal baths to help her feel better."

Allison sighs, then says, "I think he means with the toys."

George says, "We gave them away. We kept saying, 'You need to clean up your mess,' and she kept ignoring us. Finally we said, 'If you don't clean it up we will. And everything we have to clean up you're going to lose. You'll never see any of it again.' She didn't believe we would do it."

"We realized," May says, thoughtfully, "that it was time to teach her about consequences, and about responsibility."

George again: "So we cleaned it all up, and everything on the floor we gave to the McNallys."

May adds, "Oh, how Allison cried. She cried for a couple of days, and afterwards pouted until she realized that wasn't doing any good. The toys were gone and she wasn't getting them back. At that point she got on with her life."

The next day I tell George about the demons. He already knows about me falling through time, but we haven't yet told him why we left Spokane. I'll leave that to Allison, if she so chooses: they're her parents.

George listens carefully, then says, "Let's go outside."

We do. It's a sunny day, hot for the cool coast of far Northern California, maybe seventy degrees. George and May moved here five years ago when he retired. Vi moved to live near them. George and May live in a meadow on about forty acres of second growth redwoods which they bought to keep them from being cut. The land has become something of a sanctuary for wild plants and animals increasingly surrounded by lawns—which are nothing more than heavily poisoned clearcuts—and houses. They routinely see bears, foxes, and other wild creatures who have been pushed out of their homes.

He takes me to a huge brier at one edge of the meadow, says, "You know what these are."

I nod. "Himalayan blackberries."

"Invasives," he says. "They take over everything, and if you try to cut them out the thorns get into your hands. And have you ever stepped on a blackberry with bare feet?"

I acknowledge I have not.

"You don't want to do that. I know someone who got infected that way and the red lines started moving up his leg. He had to go the hospital and have surgery."

Even without the infection I can't see wanting to step on a blackberry thorn. They're huge.

He says, "Living on the East Side"—that's what a lot of people on the coast call the areas east of the Cascades or Siskiyous—"you probably haven't encountered these plants very much, but they're everywhere out here, and they crowd out a lot of native species. It's a big problem. And even if you do pull them they just come right back. The roots are very persistent."

I'm wondering what this has to do with demons killing people.

He asks, "How healthy do these plants seem to you?"

I look more closely. "They look terrible." I've seen enough blackberries to know that normally the leaves are deep green, solid, vigorous. These are limp, fading, growing transparent, with holes and red and black splotches.

He turns over a leaf. The underside is covered with yellow and black pustules. He says, "Himalayan blackberry rust. It's a very targeted disease, only affects this species. It arrived a few months ago, and you can see it's already killing the plants."

I don't say anything. I still don't see the connection.

He makes it for me. "This is what happens to noxious invasives. They take over for a while, but at some point the land finds a way to get back in balance. When you overrun an area, eventually some disease kicks in, brings you down. That's just the way life is. And we're not exempt, no matter how much we like to pretend."

I understand.

He continues, "What you say doesn't surprise me at all. And in some ways it doesn't matter whether we're talking about real physical demons sucking out people's insides or whether these demons are symbolic representations of what some disease is going to do to us. Either way it's going to happen."

I nod.

"The big surprise to me," he says, looking at the wilted blackberries, "is that it hasn't happened already."

Allison is so very much her father's daughter.

Allison and I drive north of town. We park at a trailhead. She walks to a beach to sit and read. I walk parallel to the ocean, always a half-mile or so from the shore. I can hear the waves, and when the dunes turn to sandy forest I can hear the slight breeze in the trees. It's hot. I walk. The path climbs, then levels off. Below me to my right, on the inland side, I see some large ponds. I sit. I look at the water. I feel as though I'm going to fall through time, but I don't. Still, I feel something I can't quite identify. I walk back to the trailhead, then down to the ocean. I see Allison sitting. She doesn't see me. I look at her for a few moments, enjoy her profile, the texture and color of her hair blowing in the wind coming off the ocean. I walk up to join her.

The next few nights the place makes itself the setting for my dreams. In one, I'm running along the trails by the ponds. In another, I'm beneath a pond's surface, using a reed to breathe. In yet another, I'm in the middle of a great ocean, and the land there rises to make an outcrop, an island, a continent. Grasses, then trees, grow in the soil. Birds fly in to land on the branches.

I don't know why I'm having these dreams. I don't know what they mean.

Still more dreams. I see great auks. I see Carolina parakeets. I see passenger pigeons. I see Eskimo curlews. I see Quagga. I see Steller's sea cows. I see silver trout. I see Ridley's staghorn ferns. I see marbled toadlets. I see Rodrigues little owls. I see Sampson's pearly mussels. I see Crimson Indian paintbrushes. They have all gone away, because they don't like how they are being treated. They've gone to the other side, to the other sides, to where the muse lives, where the dreamgiver lives.

They are waiting, waiting until it is safe to come back to this side. Sometimes one or two come to check whether things are better here, but then they go back and let the others know that things are not better, that things are worse, and worse.

This is what I dream after I walk at that place.

I wake up. It's dark. Allison is next to me. I say, very softly, "Are you asleep?"

Her voice, clear, "No."

"I know why the demons haven't come."

Silence.

"They're waiting to see if humans are redeemable. . . ."

More silence.

". . . or if we've all either been killed or lost to the *wétiko* sickness."

Still more silence.

"We're being given one last chance to clean up the mess humans have made. If we don't clean it up, the demons will. And if they do, they won't discriminate. They'll kill as many of us as necessary, and if that isn't enough, they'll come back and kill more, and they'll keep coming back to kill us until the *wétikos* are gone."

I hear her take a deep breath, then, "What does that mean?"

"It means we have to stop the *wétikos*. It means we have a lot of work to do."

Another deep breath, before I hear her say, "You're right. We do."

The day is gray and windy, and cold enough for us to wear jackets. We drive back to that trailhead, and this time walk together toward the ponds. I feel the same things I did before, but still I do not fall through time. We turn east, drop down, walk a maze of paths. The day is still windy, still cold. We walk, sometimes hand in hand, sometimes not.

It's been a while since we've made love. Her parents' home has an open design, and privacy has been at a premium. We've snuck into the forest a couple of times, but our daily average is plummeting. My prostate is by now much better, and I'm fortunately no longer bound by Dr. Lu's prescription. Not that it's mattered the last few days.

We both notice something as we walk. Have you ever been to a place where the land demanded you make love? Even if Allison and I had already made love several times today, even if we were both sexually exhausted, we both would have been compelled—*compelled* is not too strong a word—to intertwine our naked bodies. We would have been compelled not solely by our selves, not solely by our respective muses, but by the land.

We don't talk about it. We don't have to. The only thing Allison says to initiate is, "How about there?"

We walk to the spot, a bed of moss and tall grass at the edge of some trees. We face each other, hold both our hands. We kiss, and my hands slip out of hers, reach behind to pull her close. After an embrace we step apart, remove our jackets, our clothes. I start to lay down my coat for us to lie on but she says she wants to feel the moss on her back.

"That's cold," I say.

"I don't care," she says. She sits, shivers, lies back, says, "Will you cover me, please?"

I do. She wraps around me and I fold into her. We stay like that, not moving. I close my eyes, feel her, then open them to see she's looking over my shoulder. "What do you see?"

"The sky," she says. "The trees. They're all so beautiful."

I move slightly, keep staring at her eyes. I say, "You have the face of an angel."

She smiles. "Would you like to see god?"

"I already do."

"I want you to see the sky, the trees. Like this. Together."

We roll over, still on the bed of moss. I look at the sky, the trees, a distant hawk. She's right. I've never seen anything so beautiful. She moves her hips, rises up then down, softly, slowly. I look at her face. Her eyes are closed, her expression soft, her lips slightly parted. My eyes move down, to her neck, shoulders, breasts, ribs, belly. I see goosebumps. Further down I see where we come together, see her moving slowly, softly, up, then down, up, then down.

Her pace quickens. So does mine. She opens her eyes, looks straight ahead at the trees, the tall grasses. She says, "Oh."

Faster, and faster. I look at the sky, the trees. I close my eyes and still I see them, still I see her, still I see us.

The trees close in, the grasses join us, the mosses, too, and the soil beneath them, all of them join as we move together, slow, then fast, then slow, then fast.

"Oh," she whispers. "Oh."

And I hear the trees whisper in return, and the grasses. "Yes," they respond. "Yes."

Afterwards we don't spend much time basking together. It's too damn chilly. We whip on our clothes and continue walking the path.

It heads sharply uphill. At the top we see a small fence surrounding a forty-by-forty-foot area.

"Oh," she says.

"Oh," I say.

She says, "You were right."

"What?"

"It was me."

"What was you?"

"At the cemetery. Making love. We just hadn't been here yet."

I look inside the fence. There are small markers. "You're right."

She says, "I'm sorry I got upset."

"That's okay. I probably would have done the same."

She stops, then says, "But in your dream we lay atop the coats."

I think, say, "Yes."

"What do you think that difference means?"

We stand silent a moment, then she says, "You said *Oh* too. For the same reason?"

"No. I said it because I've read about this place. It's called Yontocket. For the Tolowa people, this is the center of the universe, where land first came up from the water."

"Your dream a few days ago."

"Yes. And each year they'd have their world renewal ceremonies here. They'd dance and sing and perform rituals to help the world renew itself. But one year the whites. . . ."

"What?"

"I need to sit. It's happening."

She helps me sit on the short grass.

It begins. I see people dancing, and I see a fire. The fire is alive, and it is speaking, to the Tolowa, to itself, to the wood it consumes, to the land. It is speaking in the language of fires, a language I do not understand. But it is speaking. The Indians are dancing.

And then they aren't. They are screaming. They are falling. They are dying. They are running. I see men—white men—shooting them, stabbing them, throwing Tolowa regalia into the fire, throwing Tolowa infants into the fire. I hear the same laughter I heard in Spokane at the murder of the horses. And I hear the voice of the fire, different now, saying something different, something I still don't understand.

I see the whites bashing out the brains of the old, young. I see them holding children by their feet and swinging them against trees. I see them chasing adults who run down paths toward the ponds, and I know the Indians will dive in, hide, breathe through reeds.

And now I see Allison, wearing her jacket the color of camel skin, and I see the pale gray sky, and I see the short grass, and I tell Allison what I saw.

She doesn't say anything.

Suddenly again I don't see her, and instead I see Indians dancing. I see fires. I see days and nights and years of celebrations and mournings. I see people making love. I see the same for all kinds of animals, all kinds of plants. I see them living, dying, loving, hating. I see generation after generation of human, generation after generation of cedar, generation after generation of porcupine, generation after generation of ant, generation after generation of grasses, mosses, generation after generation of fire.

And suddenly I see even more. I see generation after generation of muse, dreamgiver, demon, walking back and forth between worlds. I see geese and martens and wrentits moving between worlds. I see fires moving between worlds. I see humans moving between worlds. I see the living and the dead.

I see all these worlds being renewed by this intercourse, this movement across borders porous and impenetrable and permeable and impermeable and breathing and alive as skin. I see these worlds winding and unwinding, tangling and untangling like the lovers they are, and I see moments in time, too, winding and unwinding, tangling and untangling like the lovers that they are, too. These worlds, these moments, they are not one, they are not two. They are lovers, like any others.

I see Allison. "Hold me," I say.

She does.

I say, "There was a horrible massacre here. . . ."

"Yes."

"But this land is not the site of a massacre."

She holds her breath.

"That was one night among thousands and tens of thousands of years of nights. Yes, it was horrible. Yes, the massacres of the wild continue everywhere. But that's not how the land identifies. That's not who the land is. . . ."

"No more than Dr. Kline raping me is who I am."

"Yes. There are thousands of years of humans making love here. Hundreds of thousands of years of nonhumans making love here. Fires making love. Everything."

"That's why the land wanted us to make love."

"The land misses us as much as it misses the salmon, the grizzly bears. It misses our touch, our participation as much as we miss the touch of the land."

"Or as much as we would miss it if we were in our bodies."

We stand, begin to walk a trail across a meadow, away from the cemetery.

Allison asks, "Do you think the demons are real? Do you think plants and animals really don't go extinct, but instead they go away, and they will come back when we are either gone or have learned how to behave? Or do you think we're just making all this up?"

"I don't know." I pause, think, say, "But I don't think it matters whether we're stopping *wétikos* so the passenger pigeons can come back or stopping *wétikos* so the salmon aren't driven extinct or stopping *wétikos* so the demons don't kill us all. Our actions are the same. We're still stopping *wétikos*."

"Of course." She pauses, then says, "What if God is stronger than life?"

"I don't know that either."

We walk.

I say, "Let's ask."

"Who?"

I point with my chin at a hawk sitting atop a dead tree at the edge of the meadow. "That hawk was above us when we made love."

I look up, see no other birds, then say, very quietly, to the hawk, "If plants and animals are waiting for the demons to do their work so they can come back, will you please fly up and circle us?"

The words are barely out before the hawk opens her wings and with two powerful beats takes off. She flies behind us in a semi-circle, then lands in a live tree on our other side.

I say, "Maybe that means we're half right."

Allison gasps, grabs my arm, points with her other hand to the sky in front of us. I look, see a single vulture coasting to finish the circle.

She says, "The demons—the predators—aren't the only ones they're waiting on. That's only half of what's necessary. When the demons are done someone still has to clean up the mess. That's who the vulture represents. After that the plants and animals and fungi and rivers and everyone else will come back."

"I hope you're right."

"None of which alters the fact that we need to stop the *wétikos* now.

Allison says, "I need to go back to Spokane."

"To get some of our stuff?"

"No. To live."

"I don't understand."

"We can't live on the run. I can't live on the run. I won't live on the run."

"If we're going to fight the *wétikos*—if we're going to fight the culture—we've got to start somewhere."

"I agree, but. . . ."

"And just because we're running away, just because we look away, just because we pretend it isn't happening, doesn't mean he isn't still killing women."

"Yes, but. . . ."

"And if you and I—you and I, Derrick, with what we know and believe—can't stand up to one person, take out this one person who is doing so much harm, how can we expect anyone else to stand up to the whole culture, to take out this whole culture that is doing so much harm?"

"Yes, but. . . ."

"But what?"

"But we don't win."

"Don't you see? Somebody's got to take a stand."

"I'd agree with you if I'd seen *us* dumping *his* body, but I didn't."

"This isn't negotiable, Derrick. There is too much at stake. You said the demons were waiting to see if humans are redeemable, if humans can clean up this mess. Well, here's one human who is still human, who is redeemable. I'm going to fight back. I may die, but I'm going to go down fighting. I will not live my life on the run. This is who I am. This is what I am."

I suddenly understand that she is right. This is who and what she is. This is what it is to be a human being. I'm suddenly very glad I never told her about seeing my body at the river. I know she would do what is right at the cost of her own life, but I'm not certain she would do this at the cost of mine as well. I say, "I'm going with you."

twenty
four

Allison tells her parents why we left Spokane, and why we are returning. She wants to do this alone, so I take a walk.

When I get back, their eyes are red. Her father, who normally shakes my hand, hugs me. Her mother hugs me, too. She says, "We tried to raise our daughter right . . . sometimes it's not easy."

There's really nothing I can say.

◉

Picture this. Your name is Axel Freiherr von dem Bussche. You are a Captain in the Wehrmacht. It is 1942. You are a very good soldier. Later you will win the Iron Cross 1st and 2nd Class, the German Cross in Gold, the Knight's Cross, and the Golden War-wounded Badge. But now, in October of 1942, you see something that disturbs you deeply. Entirely by accident, you are at an airfield, Dubno, in the Ukraine, and you see several thousand human beings—men, women, and children—being herded by SS men carrying pistols and submachine guns. The SS men force some of these human beings—Jews—to strip and lie face downward on the ground. The men then shoot them in the nape of the neck. After this another row of human beings—Jews—are forced to strip and lie face down on top of the still-writhing bodies beneath them. These people then are also shot. This continues, and the pile grows.

You have heard rumors of this before, and you know enough about how the government works to know that these men are acting under orders, and that there are many other groups carrying out similar actions all over Russia.

What do you do? Do you invoke paragraph 227 of the code of common law, which states explicitly one's right in an emergency "to defend oneself or another against unlawful attack," and in doing so hope to halt the operation? Of course this would have been impossible. Even if you were able to get the SS men to take notice of you—improbable at best, considering that you're a mere captain—you know that the "special treatment" would just have resumed as soon as you left, and in any case would have stopped nowhere else. In other words, you recognize almost immediately that you are witnessing one manifestation of a much larger problem.

What do you do?

Now, picture this. It is the present. You are who you are. You see a clearcut, with several thousand trees cut and stacked. Or you see a factory trawler, with several thousand tons of fish killed and containerized. Or you see an entire economic and social system that is changing the climate of the planet, that is deforesting the planet, that is killing the oceans, that is toxifying everything it touches, that is killing humans and nonhumans alike.

You know enough about the system to know that the people who are deforesting, who are murdering the oceans, who are changing the climate, who are rendering the planet toxic, are acting consonant with an entire social system that values money and power over life itself, and that there are many other groups of people carrying out similar actions all over the world. In other words, you recognize almost immediately that you are witnessing one manifestation of a much larger problem.

If you are in this situation—which of course you are—what do you do?

Axel Freiherr von dem Bussche determined to kill Hitler. As with Colonel Freiherr von Gersdorff, he and other plotters decided they would blow him up during an inspection. Bussche would bring a hand grenade, and would use his movements as he modeled a uniform to disguise igniting the fuse. Then he would cough to mask the fuse's distinctive hissing, and at the last moment throw his arms around Hitler and blow the both of them up.

The plotters obtained a hand grenade—once again, no easy task for someone not at the front—but while they waited for Hitler to commit to a day and time for the demonstration, an Allied air raid destroyed the railroad car holding the uniforms. Bussche was sent back to the front, where he lost a leg and was thus unable to participate in any attack on Hitler.

After Bussche lost his leg, someone else came forward to try to kill Hitler. His name was Ewald Heinrich von Kleist. He was a lieutenant. Kleist asked his father for permission to give his life for this cause. His father said that under no circumstances must he let this opportunity slip to perform such a crucial duty. Kleist, like Gersdorff and Bussche, was to carry an explosive into a demonstration, killing both himself and Hitler. For reasons unclear to this day the demonstration was never held.

Yet another person came forward to kill Hitler. His name was Eberhard von Breitenbuch. As an aide to Field Marshall Busch, Breitenbuch had routine access to Hitler during briefings. On the day Hitler was supposed to die, Breitenbuch sent his wristwatch and rings to his wife. She knew what this meant. He arrived at the site, left his service revolver in the coat room, and carried a briefcase full of Busch's papers into the anteroom. Unbeknownst to almost everyone there, he also carried a loaded 7.65 mm Browning, this in his pants pocket. It was rumored that Hitler wore a bullet-proof vest—(these rumors came about in part because Hitler walked hunched over, as though carrying a heavy weight; he may or may not have worn armored vests, but the reason he hunched, known only to his physician, was that he had scoliosis)—so he would have to aim for the head.

At last the doors to the conference room opened, and an

SS guard invited the men in for the briefing. Because Breitenbuch was the most junior officer present, he waited last in line. As he reached the door the SS man grabbed him by the arm and said that on this particular day no aides were to be allowed into the room. Both Breitenbuch and Busch protested that his presence was necessary. The SS man had his orders, and would not be swayed.

Breitenbuch sat alone in the anteroom. Occasionally an SS guard would enter the room, then leave. Each time, Breitenbuch was certain he was about to be arrested. He knew what would happen then.

But no arrest ever came, and no explanation was ever made for Breitenbuch's exclusion. Saying, "One can only do that sort of thing once," Breitenbuch never made another attempt.

If people know only one thing about German resistance to the Nazi regime, it is that on July 20, 1944 Lieutenant Colonel Count Claus von Stauffenberg set off a bomb that very nearly killed Hitler.

Stauffenberg had himself nearly been killed fourteen months earlier, when American P-40f fighters attacked a column of the 10th Panzer Division in Tunisia. Stauffenberg's scout car was riddled with machine gun bullets, and Stauffenberg lost his left eye, his right hand, the third and fourth fingers of his left hand, and part of his hearing. After surgeries and stabilization at a military hospital in Carthage he was transferred to a hospital in Munich. His wounds became infected, and he was delirious for weeks. Once through the delirium, and through further surgeries on his head and hand, Stauffenberg began to teach himself how to write with his left hand, and to dress himself with his remaining fingers and his teeth.

Stauffenberg became convinced that his life had been spared so that he could help rescue Germany by assassinating Hitler. Long before, he had complained to one fellow soldier, "Is there no officer over there in the Führer's headquarters capable of taking his revolver to the brute?" And now he said, manifesting perfectly the transition from outrage to accountability and from there to action, "As General Staff officers we must all share the burden of responsibility. . . . I could never look the wives and children of the fallen in the eye if I did not do something to stop this senseless slaughter."

The doctors wanted to keep Stauffenberg at the hospital to fit him with an artificial eye and hand, but Stauffenberg had no time for this: he had work to do, and so chose merely a black eye patch and a pinned-up sleeve.

On the second finger of his left hand he wore a ring with raised lettering: Finis initium (Finish what you begin). This is what he would do.

He began working with General Friedrich Olbricht, who was already part of the conspiracy. Olbricht's work brought Stauffenberg into regular contact with Hitler's inner circle, whom he described to his wife as "rotten and degenerate," and as "patent psychopaths." He also noted how poor was their security: neither he nor his briefcase were ever searched.

Stauffenberg and the rest of the conspirators continued to look for opportunities to kill Hitler, and continued also to make plans for an armistice with the Western powers after their coup. These plans were dealt a blow when the Allies invaded France. Everyone who was not entirely delusional knew then even more than ever before that the current regime could not last. (Of course those who come after will say the same about us and our time.) Stauffenberg sent a message to Tresckow asking whether there was any reason for them to proceed with their plans, now that the end was so obviously near. Tresckow responded immediately, "The assassination must take place, cost what it will. Even if it does not succeed, the Berlin action must go forward. The point now is not whether the coup has any practical purpose, but to prove to the world and before history that German resistance is ready to stake its all. Compared to this, everything else is a side issue."

Would that we now had the same courage.

So Stauffenberg moved forward, recruiting more than a hundred officers into the conspiracy. Twice he carried a bomb in his briefcase into Hitler's presence, but each time he did not detonate it. The first was on July 10, 1944. He did not set the fuse because he saw that Reichsmarshall Hermann Göring and Reichsführer SS Heinrich Himmler were absent, and most of the conspirators agreed that they should try to kill as many of the top Nazis as possible. When it came time for Stauffenberg to give his presentation, he coolly removed the appropriate papers from his briefcase, gave his talk, and withdrew.

Unlike Breitenbuch, this was something Stauffenberg could do more than once. On July 15 Stauffenberg attended another briefing. Again Göring and Himmler were absent. This time Stauffenberg slipped from the room and called his head-quarters in Berlin to ask whether he should proceed anyway. While Stauffenberg stood waiting for an answer, those in Berlin argued back and forth for at least fifteen minutes, finally telling him not to set the bomb. Frustrated at their hesitation, Stauffen-berg decided to move forward anyway, but by the time he re-turned to the conference room, the meeting was nearly over. Be-cause the bomb had a ten-minute fuse, no purpose would have been served by igniting it now.

The next time there would be no such hesitation. On July 20, Stauffenberg flew to Hitler's headquarters in Prussia, arriving a couple of hours before the briefing. He met with sev-eral generals for about an hour and a half, then retrieved from his assistant his briefcase containing two bombs. He asked one of the generals' aides where he might freshen up and change his shirt: he wanted to be immaculate, he said, for his meeting with the Führer. The truth is that he needed some time unobserved so he could use specially-twisted pliers—remember, he had only two fingers on one hand—to start the fuses. A few moments earlier, however, another of the conspirators, General Fellgiebel, had telephoned headquarters to ask to speak to Stauffenberg. A non-commissioned officer had been sent to find him. He did, and asked him to come to the phone. Stauffenberg crossly attempted to send the other man away, but the man remained in the doorway, looking in. Stauffenberg stood with his back to him, busy with something the man could not see. Finally another man approached, and said, "Stauffenberg, come along, please!" Stauffenberg never received the necessary privacy, and only started one fuse. The bomb was only half the strength it could have been.

Stauffenberg briskly made his way to the briefing room. There he asked, "Could you please put me as near as possible to the Führer so that I catch everything I need for my briefing afterwards?" He was placed to Hitler's right. They stood in front of a massive oak table—nineteen feet long, four feet wide, and four inches thick—covered with maps. Stauffenberg noticed that the windows were open. This was unfortunate, since that would allow some of the blast to escape. He placed his briefcase partway under the table, remained a few moments, then murmured that he needed to make a telephone call—something that happened all the time at these conferences—and left the room. He could not remain to make this a suicide attack because he was invaluable to the coup that was to happen in Berlin immediately upon Hitler's death. Soon after Stauffenberg left, a Colonel Brandt moved forward so he could see the maps more clearly. But he felt a briefcase against his foot, and pushed the briefcase farther under the table, against the table's solid oak support. This movement—as well as the telephone call made by a conspirator for Stauffenberg, causing someone to stand in the doorway and watch Stauffenberg's back as he set the fuse—saved Hitler's life. The bomb went off, but protected as Hitler was by so much solid oak, Hitler survived.

The war continued.

Hitler often said that a miracle had saved his life. "I am grateful to Destiny for letting me live," he would say, and he would say that the reason Destiny had let him live was that Providence still had a task for him.

Perhaps this was the same Providence that George Washington invoked in his inaugural address.

Perhaps this is the same Providence that has so far allowed the *wétikos* to overrun the planet.

⊙

When we return to Spokane, my mother is on a deathwatch. She hasn't slept more than a couple of hours in a few days. One of her cats—perhaps her sweetest cat ever—is in the final stages of kidney failure. My mom knows from research she's done that there's nothing she can do. A trip to the vet will only scare the cat and not prolong her life. So she sits with the cat in her last hours and sews a small quilt in which the cat will be buried.

There is something unspeakably beautiful about watching this process. I contrast it with the death of one of my own cats from this same condition, not long before Allison and I left for New York. She too was an extraordinarily sweet cat, and she, too, entered these final stages. Still she purred, still she flicked her tail when I spoke her name. She crawled into a closet, I know now looking for a place to die. I did not yet know there was nothing to be done, so I took her to the vet. She purred and blinked at me as he took her away for tests and hydration. He called later that day to say she was dead. I brought her home and buried her wrapped in some of my shirts. I regret that I did not keep her home to die, and I worried that after her death she might not be able to find her way home. She came to me three nights later, though, and said she was fine, and she was happy, she was glad to be home, that death was okay, and that she had been tired, that's all.

I sit with my mother as she sews, and I think that this is what people have done for tens or hundreds of thousands of years, since the beginning: sit with those they love as they die, and make presents to carry the dying through this transition. Only recently, I think, have we mechanized death, pushed it away, made it the property of strangers and their machines.

The cat purrs, looks at my mother, looks at me. I hold her, pet her, cry. I have been doing this for hours, my mother has been doing it for days. The cat gets no worse, gets no better.

And then my mom leaves to take a shower. I hear the water running. The cat looks at me one more time, closes her eyes, and begins to convulse. She coughs, gags, thrashes, and then she is gone. It is clear to me she had been holding on until my mother left the room. She did not want my mother, her best friend, to see her die.

My mother comes back. She cries. She is done with the quilt. She asks me to bury the cat wrapped in the quilt outside her window. I do. It is raining. As I dig the grave, I find a salamander. I pick him up, look at him, and gently set him down on the soil by a pile of wood. He walks slowly forward, finds a small hole in the ground, and moves back beneath the surface, back to where he lives.

What makes us think that others, too, do not mourn their losses, that rivers do not mourn their beloved salmon, their beloved sturgeon, indeed their own beloved freedom? How narcissistic—how psychopathic, how evil, how infected with the spirit of a life-hating God—must one be to not recognize the sorrow of all those humans and nonhumans who lose their loved ones, their freedom, their homes, their ways of life, to this culture?

Allison and I walk in the forest near our home. We are glad to see it. It seems glad to see us. The day is bright and warm. We meander, make our way to the place I used to lie on the ground. I see two trees I haven't noticed before, two trees growing close together, their branches intertwining. I walk over to one, touch the trunk, and suddenly find myself sitting on the ground.

Allison asks what's wrong.

I can't speak. I'm panting.

She looks worried.

I shake my head, catch my breath, then say, still panting, "You know how I've been asking what it's like to be a forest, and the forest keeps showing me?"

Understandably, she looks even more worried.

I smile, say, "No. This is good. When I touched the tree, I felt this immense orgasm run through my body." I hold out my hand, palm downward. "See. I'm still shaking."

"So. . . ."

"Yes."

"Being a forest . . ."

"Yes, or a river or mountain or desert or ocean . . ."

". . . is like . . ."

"Yes."

Her smile no longer tentative, she says, "That reminds me of something I've read. . . ."

"You've read?"

"Yes. Pathetic, isn't it?"

We both laugh and laugh, me sitting, her standing holding her sides. She starts to lean against a tree, but hesitates to touch it. This makes us laugh harder.

Finally I say, "You read. . . ."

"Oh, yes. The anthropologist Claude Lévi-Strauss described indigenous humans as living in a 'blaze of reality.' Maybe that's part of what he meant."

"I thought you were going to say this makes you understand why so many white settlers ran off to join the Indians."

"That, too."

She sits. We don't say anything for a while. Suddenly I notice a small lizard on a rock a few feet away. I nudge Allison, gesture slightly with my head. She sees him, nods. The lizard sits looking at us for the longest time, then he closes one eye. He opens it, closes it again, opens it, and scampers off the rock.

I look at Allison. She looks at me. We can't help ourselves: we start laughing again, even harder this time than before. As I roll on the ground, I hear Allison say, her voice squeaky through the laughter, "He was winking at us."

twenty five

power, again

No miracles are free. Every miracle carries with it a cost, paid to those who perform this miracle. And who is to say that those millions and tens of millions killed by the Nazis and their wars were not human sacrifices to placate and to nourish those who then provided miracles—fog, a detonator that fails to ignite a bomb, a telephone call causing someone to stand outside a room where someone else is setting a fuse, a briefcase pushed too far underneath a thick oak table—in return? And what of the sacrifices made all along to the God of this culture, this jealous God, this God of stasis? Could not the entire world—and her members large and small—said to be the sacrifice being made now?

Jack Shoemaker reaches one gloved hand into cage A43, picks up the mouse, drops it into a plastic bag. He clamps the opening of the bag to the nozzle of a CO_2 canister, then turns on the gas. The bag inflates, and he turns it off. The mouse from A43 gasps, scrabbles at the smooth plastic, and begins to convulse. Jack writes the mouse's number on the bag, opens the lab's refrigerator, puts the bag inside, shuts the door. He walks to cage B17, reaches in, puts the mouse in a bag, walks to the canister, and so on. Tomorrow one of the graduate students can run the tests on the dead mice.

Through all of this it never occurs to Jack to ask the questions he asks so often of the women he kills: Where do you go when you die? What do you think and feel and see as you die?

Allison and I try to settle back into our lives in Spokane. But this is hard to do when we know what is coming, when we know we need to act. There are moments like in the forest, with the trees and the lizard, but for the most part we go through our days as though we are wearing clothes that are too small, living in rooms too tiny to maneuver. For about a week we don't do anything about Nika's killer.

Then Allison asks what's next.

"I thought you'd have some ideas."

"I only knew it had to be done."

I nod.

She continues, "Committing is the hard part anyway. Everything else is technical."

I say, "I guess the first thing is to go back to where I saw Nika, and see if I learn anything new. We can also go to the river."

"Where you saw him. . . ."

"Yes, there."

We go to where the apple trees are growing over the small stream. The leaves are starting to turn. We sit. Allison reads. I try to will the land to show memories to me. Nothing. I try to will myself to be open to receiving those memories. Still nothing. I lie down, close my eyes, begin to drift. I dream of rabbits and coyotes and I dream of dreaming. I dream that when I dream, the dreams do not come to me but that I go to them. I dream that when coyotes dream, the dreams do not come to them but that they go to the dreams. I dream the same for rabbits, salamanders, trees, rivers, rocks. I dream that dreams are living beings who eat us to stay alive and whom we eat, too. I dream that dreams keep us alive. I dream that without dreams we die, and we die faster even than we die without other foods, without fruits and meats and roots and shoots and leaves. I dream that we are here to dream, and that dreams are here to come into us. All of us. I dream that dreams hitchhike into us, and that we hitchhike into them. I dream that otherwise sleeping makes no sense. Rabbits need to rest, but to sleep is to be vulnerable. I dream that we are here to be vulnerable, that we are here to sleep and to dream.

I dream that we have forgotten how to dream, and that we have forgotten how to live, and that we have forgotten how to die. I dream that if we do not remember how to dream, we will never remember how to live, nor will we remember how to die.

Nika is dead. She is dreaming. She is dreaming that willows grow out of her hair. She is dreaming of rivers full of salmon and she is dreaming her ribs are made of pine trees. She is dreaming of wild roses on her breasts, on her hips. She is dreaming she is making love—something she never before got to do. She is dreaming she is making love with Osip and he is making love with her and he is running his hands through willow leaves and he is holding tight to the trunks of pine trees, and she misses him and her mother and her father and her brother, and she wishes she were home, but it is a long way home, and she will go to visit, but this is where she is now, with willows growing from her hair and pine trees in her ribs.

Nika is dreaming.

We go to the river. Again I do not fall through time. Again the land does not open up to me, or at least it does not in ways I understand.

So we go to Latah Creek, sit on the bank. I lie down. I drift. I dream that I sit up, that I see salmon running thick. I see bears and foxes and birds eating the fish. I see insects eating the fish. I see pine trees eating the fish. I see willows eating the fish.

And then I see a woman. I see Nika. She has willows growing from her hair, she has pine trees in her ribs. She has wild roses on her breasts and on her hips. I dream she is making love and I turn away to not pry, and when I turn back she is gone, and so are the salmon and bears and foxes and birds and insects.

Again I dream. Again I see Nika. I speak to her, ask her how she is. I reach out my hand. "Nika," I say. "Nika."

She reaches out her hand, too, touches finger to finger. I feel a charge run through my body like an electric current. I jump, and when I look again she is gone.

Nika is dreaming that she sees a man who sees her, too. His lips move but she cannot hear his voice. He reaches out his hand, and suddenly she hears him say her name. He says it twice. Or maybe he says it eight or twelve or twenty times. She reaches out her hand, too, and when their fingers touch she feels a flood of memories rush into and out of her, memories of human contact, of hands touching her, of her family, of Osip, and then of others, of all the men, of Jack. It's too much. She pulls back, gathers herself, and when she gains the strength to look again he is gone.

My mother asks me why we came back. She says, "I don't mind making a quilt for your bed, but I don't want to make a quilt to bury you in."

I tell her we came to fight back. I stop, then say, "But I'm scared."

"I am, too."

Silence.

Finally she says, "Just because you saw the future doesn't mean you saw the only one."

"I want to believe that."

"Obviously you do, or you wouldn't have come back."

She's right. Or at least I want her to be right.

She continues, "This isn't like the cat, where there was nothing to be done, and so we just held on to every moment for as long as we could."

Silence.

She says, "This is a terrible thing, to be living in the shadow of a murderer."

"Yes."

"And you *are* going to change the future. You *are*."

"Yes." I wish I were as certain as she sounds.

"So the sooner you do it," she says, "the sooner we can all get back to living."

Allison and I go to East Sprague. The way Nika was dressed makes me think she might have been a prostitute, and we have seen women walking there wearing hot pants and halter tops. We don't know what else to do.

We park. Allison gets out. I stay in the car. Not only is Allison somewhat less introverted than I, we also decided there would be less confusion if a woman approached rather than a man. She's going to pass out pieces of paper with our names and phone number and a request to call if they have information about someone named Nika. She's not going to say anything about Nika being missing, since for all we know she might not yet have been attacked. We also decided that if anyone asks why we want to know we'll just say we're concerned.

I see Allison talking to one woman, then two together, then another alone. After she returns to the car she says the women were friendly and took the slips of paper, but none responded to the name.

She goes back out. I remain in the car. I watch a man pull his car to the side of the road, watch a woman lean into the passenger seat window. After a few moments the woman gets in.

Allison is now a few blocks away. I start the car, follow behind, park again. If it weren't for the memory I saw at the river I probably wouldn't worry if I lost sight of her. I may not even have come down with her. She is perfectly capable of taking care of herself.

This whole process doesn't take long—this stretch of East Sprague is short, the density of prostitutes is low, and neither of us knows where else to go—so when she's finished we head on home.

Kristine doesn't feel good about the slip of paper the woman handed her. She doesn't know what the woman—she said her name was Allison—wants, so she didn't let on she knew Nika. Oh, she'd nodded and smiled and looked at the paper, which she'd folded up neatly and put in the tight front pocket of her pants, and then she'd promised to call if she heard anything, but she wasn't going to act.

Maybe the woman really wanted to do something good for Nika, but then again she'd seen Allison's man—Derrick, the note said his name was—hanging back in a car waiting. Maybe he'd sent Allison to get Nika for a threesome. Fucking coward. He could have just come forward himself. *And why Nika? Why not me? I'm not good enough? Well, fuck you.* Or maybe they were cops, in which case she wanted nothing to do with them. Or maybe Nika made a break for it—Kristine hadn't seen her for months now—and these two fucking sleazeballs were with Viktor. *Yeah, that's it*, she thinks. *They're probably with Viktor*. She's not going to tell those two a goddamn thing.

Kristine wakes up scared. Not scared like when she's woken up with a strange man or men on top of her, or scared like waking up from those dreams where she's running from someone who's going to hurt her and finding safety only to see the faces of her rescuers turn into the faces of those who chase her. Not scared like the time she woke up to see her dealer—to whom she'd owed a shitload of money—sitting staring at her, calmly tossing a small knife from his left hand to his right and back to his left. And not even scared like she wakes up scared every day. This was something new. All night, images of something hitting her in the head kept forcing themselves into her. And images of something pushing into her chest. She'd felt everything about the blows except for the blows themselves. The terror, the impulse to block with no time to make a move, the anticipatory tightening of the muscles. Again and again she'd felt all that, in looped dreams that lasted only seconds but that dragged on all night. And then she'd been awakened by a voice so clear she'd jerked upright and looked around, been surprised to see no one. The voice had said, "Stay."

Fully awake now, she dismisses the voice and especially the message. Staying here is a nice notion, but of course impossible if she wants to avoid another visit from her dealer, who'd promised that next time he wouldn't let her off with a warning.

The thought barely occurs to her—as it sometimes does—to quit the heroin, but she rejects that immediately—as she always does—as absurd, impractical, and undesirable. Almost unthinkable. *The knife*, she thinks *would be less painful than being clean*. And quicker.

She looks around at the weeds dying from the change of season, at the chain link fences, the discarded refrigerators and gutted stoves, the broken glass and crushed cans, and thinks she doesn't want to stay here anyway. She doesn't want to stay anywhere. Nor does she want to go anywhere, mainly because no matter where she would go, she would have to bring herself along. And that's too much weight to carry.

She'd thought, a very long time ago, that by running away from home she'd be able to leave behind everything that happened there and start all over. But she'd learned almost immediately that there was no such thing as a fresh start. The wounds came with her. The memories came with her. The self-destructive impulses came with her. And she had known from the beginning, even consciously, that no matter how clean her rationalizations, too many of her impulses, actions, motivations were self-destructive. The nightmares came with her. The lack of impulse control. The hatred—earned hatred—of men. The hatred of herself.

Even more than scared now, Kristine is tired. She's tired of running away only to find herself still at the same place. She's tired of being tired. She's tired of being.

She cooks up some heroin, thinks very seriously about taking way too much, ending it right now. She holds the knife against the tacky chunk and pictures the knife slicing through, pictures heating it all up, pictures injecting herself again and again, pictures how that would feel to take that one last glorious gasp before going away to feel no more pain, to enter no more nightmares, to see and feel no more flashbacks. How good that would be.

But she can't do it. *Coward*, she thinks. *Fucking coward*. She thinks that has always been her problem, that she was a coward from the beginning. She didn't fight off her brother or her uncle. She's

284 • Derrick Jensen

never fought off any of the men who've taken her. It's as both her brother and her uncle—and so many others—said to her more times than she could ever count, "You won't do anything about it because you're a fucking coward, and a slut besides. You wanted it more than I did. I was doing you a fucking favor by even looking at you."

As always, Kristine puts in only enough heroin to take off the edge. She's disappointed in herself, as she is every time she goes through this, every time she considers ending it but cannot because she's a fucking coward.

She gets up, puts on the same pants as yesterday, rummages through her garbage bag to find her fuchsia blouse, and puts that on. She starts walking toward East Sprague.

"Fuck it," she says. "Fuck it all."

Jack is collecting. He's in his truck. He's thinking about his childhood.

He remembers his parents telling him when he was very young that happiness comes not from being but from striving. You'll never find happiness, they'd said again and again, by gaining some goal or by being in any specific way or place or circumstance, but rather by setting a goal and seeking to attain it. Once it's attained you need to set another. Again and again Jack has found that to be true in so many areas of his life. Certainly in his professional life. His position yields no happiness. Nor do his publications. Happiness is always around the corner, in that *next* promotion, that *next* publication, that *next* bit of knowledge gained through his experiments. And it's just as true in his personal life. Courtship brought him far more happiness than marriage, dreaming of buying a home far more than living in it.

Jack thinks this is what separates humans from animals, or one of the things: this intense restlessness, this need to always conquer always-new and always-larger peaks. If you aren't ever-striving, ever-building, ever-progressing, you're nothing more than an animal.

The hunt is always better than the kill. He remembers that the first time he'd killed someone had been—like the first time he'd had sex—deeply disappointing. His first thoughts in each case had been the identical question: this is what all the fuss is about? The best part is the leadup, and also what this leadup and consummation makes clear about his own power. In the case of sex: this is what you'll let me do to you. In the case of killing: this is what I can do to you, and there's nothing you can do about it.

Kristine is cuffed to the table in Jack's basement. She is naked. She is shaking from fright. He'd picked her up, hit her, drugged her, brought her here.

She doesn't want this. When she'd said she wanted to die, she didn't mean this way. She realizes now she'd meant it metaphorically. She wants parts of herself to die. She wants her awful memories to die. She wants her self-destructive impulses to die. She wants her addictions to die.

But she does not want to die. Not here. Not now. Not like this.

Jack—he'd told her his name—is talking. He has been talking ever since she came to, stopping only to hit her when she screamed. She isn't screaming anymore. She's feeling the pain in her head and not wanting to die. Jack is talking. As he talks he paces alongside the table.

He says, "You're shaking. That's because you're scared, and *that's* because you're a coward. I am not shaking. I am not a coward. You think I'm going to rape you. You think that's why you're naked. You think I want sex. You *want* me to want sex. But I don't want sex. Sex is not the point. Sex is never the point. You think the point is pleasure. The point is never pleasure. The point is power. The point is always power. Not just with me. With everyone."

She's shaking even more.

He continues, "I long ago realized that sex is all about power. This shouldn't be surprising since relationships are all about power.

And *this* shouldn't be surprising since life itself is all about power. Life boils down to one simple consideration: Who does what to whom. And key to all of this is to always—*always*—be the doer."

Kristine begins to sob. She does not want him to hit her. She does not want him to kill her. She says, "Please. . . ."

Jack seems to ignore her. He says, "That's one reason I'm a scientist." He stops, looks through her, asks, "Did you ever wonder why we spend so much time and energy and money trying to make life in a laboratory when there's so much life everywhere?"

"Please," she says.

He slams his open hand on the table. "Did you?"

She doesn't know what to say. "No," she says.

"Of course you didn't. But I did. That's why I'm me and you're you. That's why I'm here and you're there. That's why I do and you are done to. You see that, don't you?"

"Yes," she says, because that is the answer that will not make him hit her.

He takes a deep breath, again begins to pace. He says, "People say we do scientific research to make the world a better place or for progress or for knowledge or for all these other reasons. Some people say we do it for prestige or to make money for our employers. But we know those are just excuses, don't we?"

"Yes," she says.

He says, "No, you don't know. I know. You don't."

"Yes," she says.

"I'm going to tell you why we do it."

"Yes."

"Do you want to know?"

"Yes."

"Power. Science is all about power. Everything is all about power. We do it because we can. Because we are doers. There is us and there is them. We do. They don't. And if you are not a doer your life is nothing. You are there to be used. *You* are there to be used. Everyone is there to be used. That's it. Do you get it?"

"Yes."

"No, you don't. I'll make it simple, for your simple mind. What you create, what comes out of here . . ." He jabs at her pubis. ". . . is nothing. It's just what animals do. It doesn't count. It doesn't come from here." He points at his own head. "It doesn't last. It's not immutable. It's not eternal. It dies. Now do you get it?"

She doesn't know which way she should answer.

He continues, "Because death is a problem. Death is a big problem. It is the biggest problem of all. Because it happens to everyone. Death is the great equalizer, the great doer. Animals die. We should not. Because we are not animals. We *cannot* be animals. Do you see why death is a problem? Even you must see why death is a problem. Do you?"

Kristine is quietly crying. She says, "I want you to tell me."

"Of course you do." He taps lightly on the table, thinks, says, "Death is the only thing we cannot control. *You* cannot control anything. Animals cannot control anything. We can. I can. You are on this table. You are crying because I allow it. If I wanted you to stop crying, you *would* stop crying."

"Yes."

"But I control everything. You live. You die. I choose. You don't control me. I control you."

"I understand."

"Do you?" He stops, then continues, thoughtfully, "Of course there's God. God controls me. I don't control God. But I am *aligned* with God. Do you see? So that is not control because I decide what to do, and it is what God would decide, too. So God decides, and I decide, and it is the same. God doesn't need to control me. I am still a doer, just as God is. I do to you. I do to animals. I do to knowledge. I do. I am a subject. You are an object. Animals are objects. Everything in the world is an object. I am a subject. Understand?"

"Yes."

"And then there is death."

"Yes."

He leans down close, says, "Can I tell you a secret?" Before she can answer he continues, "Of course I can. I decide. You don't.

But I'm going to tell you a secret. Are you ready?"

"Yes."

He stands straight, paces, makes distance before he says, "I have a fear. I can tell you this because you are a coward. I am not a coward. I have a fear. It is that I am afraid of death. My own. Not yours. I can control yours. Of course. I am not afraid of that. But I cannot control my own. I don't know what will happen when I die. God says there is a heaven where we live forever, but God told me that is a lie. God lies to people so they will believe Him, believe *in* Him. Otherwise they wouldn't. But I believe God, I *know* God, I am aligned with God, even though I know there will be no heaven. But I don't know what will happen when I die. And you are going to tell me. You will tell me what you see on the other side."

"Please," she says. She is shaking. "Are you going to kill me?"

"I'm a doer," he says. "You are done to."

Kristine asks, "Why are you doing this?"

"I told you. Because I can."

"Why me?"

"You were there."

Kristine is still alive. Jack is going through her clothing. He finds a scrap of paper in her front pants pocket. He unfolds it, reads. He asks, "Who are these people?"

She doesn't know who he's talking about.

He shows her the paper, asks, "Did you know Nika?"

"We were friends."

"Who are they to Nika?"

It starts to occur to her why she hasn't seen her friend. She asks, "Did you kill her?"

"I cut out her uterus."

Kristine catches a sob, asks, "Why?"

"Because she wasn't a doer."

He asks again, "Who are these people?"
"I don't know."
He hits her. "What did you tell them?"
"Nothing."
He hits her again. "You told them everything."
"There was nothing to tell. How could I?"
"What do they know?"
"I don't know. I don't know."
"I don't believe you."

Kristine is dead. Her body is in the river. Jack derived no pleasure from any of this. He didn't even bother to ask her what she saw as she died. He wishes he would never have found that piece of paper. He can't get those people out of his head. It cannot be a coincidence that they had contact with two of these women. How many more do they know about? They must know something. But what?

twenty
six

the voice of god

I'm up late writing, and when I come to bed, Allison is long-since asleep. I remove my clothes and put them on the floor in one corner, then briefly flash the overhead lights so I can find my nightshirt. In the dark I put it on. I slip into bed. Allison doesn't stir. I whisper her name to see if she's awake enough to chat or make love, and she doesn't respond. We both have standing invitations that if the other wants to make love they can wake us up, but we almost never pursue that. There's always plenty of time when we're both awake.

I'm tired, but as so often happens the moment I lie down the muse begins to speak to me. She gives me words and sentences and images. This night she begins by telling me to listen to Nika. I don't know what that means, in part because I don't remember Nika saying anything. I keep picturing her reaching out. I keep feeling our fingers touch.

And then the images shift as I start to drift. I see the demons and I hear the stamping of their feet. I hear the director say in a hissing voice, "Choose."

I am asleep now, and I am dreaming. I am dreaming of the attempts to assassinate Hitler, and I am dreaming of the miracles that kept Hitler alive. In this dream I am wondering how we can possibly defeat the force that made—and makes—these miracles. I am wondering what miracles can possibly overmatch these.

I am dreaming of Stauffenberg's ring. And I am dreaming of rivers full of salmon, skies full of birds, forests and deserts and rivers and lakes and oceans full of lives. And then I am dreaming of my cat who died, the cat who made it back home from the vet's. She comes up to me. I tell her I thought she was dead, and she crooks her tail at me. I pick her up and she purrs and purrs. I see Nika. She reaches out her hand.

I see hall after hall filled with beautiful pieces of art. I see someone pulling them down, tearing them into pieces. I ask why. The person turns to me and says, "Because I can."

I see people operating machines. I see these machines pulling down forests. I see them erecting dams. I see them killing oceans. I see them sterilizing everything they touch. I look at these people. I don't even ask, and still they say, "Because we can."

And then I hear the voice of God. The voice says, "You cannot win. Don't even try."

And then I see Stauffenberg's ring. I see Nika. She is reaching out.

I see salmon going away. I see salamanders going away. I see swordfish going away. I see songbirds going away. I see apes and wolves and bison going away.

And then I see tiny salmon darting back into this world, smelling the waters, sensing if it is yet safe to come home. I see that lone ivory-billed woodpecker doing the same. I see passenger pigeons, wood bison, great auks. They all do the same. They are all waiting till it is safe to return. I see them all hiding. I see them all wanting to come home. And I know that if we—all of us, from seahorses to rivers to humans to muses to demons—do not stop this *wétiko* culture—if the God of stasis wins—they will never get to come home. And neither will we.

And I hear again the voice of God, saying, "You cannot win. Do not try."

And I see Stauffenberg's ring. And I hear the stamping of feet. And I see Nika. I hear her voice. She says, "Listen." I hear a hissing voice say, "Choose."

And I hear the voice of God telling me to turn back.

I awaken to the sound of the dogs barking. At first I try to ignore them. They don't stop. I try to wait them out, but they sound serious. I get up, walk across the darkened room, through the living room to the entry. Only then do I turn on a light. It's bright. The dogs are still barking. I wonder if there's a bear out there. I turn on the porch light, open the door. Nothing. I don't even see the dogs. But I can tell from the sound that they're very close.

I step outside, then around the corner and into the dark. The dogs are barking furiously. I hear the quick sound of three running footsteps on gravel, and in the dark make out the figure of a man. I raise my arms in front of me, but I am too late. I see an upraised arm, and the last thing I see is it beginning its descent.

I am falling and my hands are tied behind my back and the man walks into the house holding something in his hand. I get up, but I am falling, and my hands are tied behind my back. I follow him into the house but I can't find my gun and I can't even find a knife and he hits Allison too and ties her and carries her out, but my hands are tied and I am falling and I never do seem to hit the ground.

Someone is knocking on the door and I wish somebody would answer it because I can't get up. The knocking is in the rhythm of a heartbeat, and I am trying to sleep and I am trying to wake up and I can't answer the door because someone has tied my hands and my feet, and I'm not wearing any clothes.

I wake up. My heart is pounding in my head. Each pulse brings new pain. Metal cuffs around my wrists and ankles bind me to a table. The edge of the table comes to my lower thighs. My knees are bent. I open my eyes, see a man sitting on a chair staring at me. He looks in his late forties, with short brown hair going gray. Behind him are concrete walls: we're probably in a basement. The man looks across me to my left. I turn my head, see Allison cuffed naked to a chair. The chair is chained to a support post. Allison's chin rests on her chest. I can't tell if she's breathing. I look back at the man.

He says, "She's not dead. You go first."

Silence.

The man says, "I know what you're thinking. You're thinking this isn't really happening. You're thinking that this all seems like some movie that you can get up and turn off anytime you want."

He's right.

"It's not, though. This is the beginning of the rest of your miserable life. Everything you had before is gone forever. Just last night you ate your little dinner, just last night you pet your little dogs, just last night you pet your little woman, just last night you did your little routine before bed, and now it's all gone. Forever. Your body knows this. That's why you're shaking uncontrollably, like a woman, like a frightened animal."

I will myself to stop shaking, but that does no good.

He says, "Your body knows that your life is over, that now you belong to me. Your mind just hasn't caught up yet."

Silence.

He says, "And I know what you're thinking now. You're wishing you would have let the dogs keep barking, or that you would have brought a flashlight and a gun out with you. You're wishing you would have got the jump on me instead of me getting the jump on you. You're wishing you could have done one little thing different, and that one little thing would have made all the difference. But you didn't, and it didn't."

I still don't say anything. I don't know what to say, and even if I did I'm not sure I could speak.

He says, "I'm impressed. You didn't rattle the cuffs. You obviously know when you're beaten. And you didn't scream. Had you done that I would have made you stop."

He stops, takes a deep breath, then suddenly asks, "What do you know about Nika?"

Finally I speak, my voice trembling less than I would have thought. "I saw you hit her, by the Pullman Highway."

"Where were you?"

"There."

"I didn't see you."

"No, you didn't."

He thinks a moment, nods, then asks, "What were you going to do about it?"

I see no reason to lie. "I was going to stop you from doing it again."

"You didn't exactly succeed, did you?"

I don't say anything.

He asks, "And what do you know about Kristine?"

I don't know who he's talking about. I ask, "How many women have you killed?"

He seems genuinely pleased. He says, "Thank you for asking. No one has ever asked before, and I would be eager to show you my collection. You will be the first besides me to see it." He stands, reaches into the right front pocket of his pants, pulls out a key ring and a piece of paper. He tosses the paper on the table, says, "By the way, that's how I found you. Pretty stupid to put your name and phone number where I could find it. And even more stupid to be in the phone book. Why didn't you just walk up to me and ask to be cuffed?"

He searches his key ring, finds what he's looking for, walks to a cabinet on the far side of the room, unlocks and opens it.

I strain to look. There are probably fifteen jars on two shelves. He brings a jar to the table. It contains a pinkish-white cylindrical organ in some liquid.

He says, "Nika's uterus. Part of her sperm receptacle. She doesn't need it anymore. Allison's will be there soon."

He holds it close for me to see, like a trophy, then takes it back to the cabinet, which he shuts and locks. He returns to the table, says, "Don't look at me that way. This is nothing special. Go to any hospital in the country and you'll see these get incinerated with all the other medical trash. What's my paltry fifteen compared to seven hundred thousand per year? And doctors get paid for it. I should, too, for getting rid of these nasty, bleeding things."

He shakes his head, then continues, "Women think they're something because they give birth. But really, if they can give life and I can take it, who is the stronger between us?"

He keeps talking, but I am no longer listening. I say, "I understand."

He says, "I know you do. You're a man. That's why I'm talking to you this way."

But I wasn't talking to him. I was talking to the forest. I get what the forest was saying. I know what it must be like to be a forest, strapped down, facing death by someone who is insane, facing death for no good reason. I understand what it must be like to be a wild monkey shot by a tranquilizer gun, only to wake up in a cage knowing you now face the unspeakable. I understand what it must be like to be a river, to be shackled, me by steel and rivers by concrete. I know these things now. I knew them before in my head. Now I know them in my body.

I don't know how long the man—he finally said his name is Jack—has been talking. He talks about power, about God, about science, about control. He talks about the women he has killed, what he said to them beforehand. He talks about death, about wanting to know what is on the other side of death. He talks about his "scientific curiosity" that leads him to kill these women and ask what they see. After a while it all sounds the same. I stop listening. Allison has yet to move.

Suddenly Jack stands, says, "Tomorrow I begin to take you apart. I'm going to get some sleep. If you scream no one else will hear you, and you will just make me mad. If you make me mad things will go much worse for you tomorrow."

He walks up the stairs.

Soon after he leaves, Allison says my name.

I ask how long she's been awake.

"Long enough."

"I'm glad you're not dead."

"Me too, you."

Silence.

She says, "I'm sorry."

"You've done nothing wrong."

"If we wouldn't have come back we wouldn't be here."

Silence.

She says, "If I wouldn't have insisted we come back we wouldn't be here."

"If you wouldn't have come back you wouldn't be who you are."

Silence.

I say, "And you didn't insist I come back."

She thinks a long time, then says, "When you saw him dumping my body in the river . . ."

"Yes."

". . . did you see him dumping yours as well?"

"Yes."

She thinks, then says, "I'm sorry."

"I am, too. I don't want to die this way."

"We're not going to," she says. "It would all be too senseless."

"Lots of people die senselessly. The whole fucking world is being killed senselessly. That's the fucking point."

"We're not going to die."

I don't say anything for a long time. Then I say, "I don't know what's going to happen tomorrow . . ."

"Don't . . ."

". . . so I want to say thank you . . ."

"Don't give . . ."

". . . for being in my life."

"Don't give a eulogy on our relationship. Don't say good-bye. It's not over."

"Do you see a way out?"

"We're not dead yet."

"Show me the way out."

She's silent for a long time, then says, "Maybe the demons will come, or maybe something else will happen."

"I saw our bodies."

"That doesn't mean it has to happen that way. That was what the cemetery was trying to tell us when we made love there and it wasn't like what you had seen. Sometimes you see multiple futures. You saw the planet killed by God. You saw demons stopping the *wétiko* culture. You saw the possibility of us cleaning up the mess before the demons get here. Any of those could happen. The future is not pre-ordained. *Wétikos* want us to think it's inevitable. They want us to give up. So does God. But they're not going to win. We're going to stop them."

"We're chained here, Allison. I don't know what to do."

"I don't either. I'm just saying we shouldn't give up."

I try to stay awake, to share every possible moment with Allison, but I begin to drift. I dream again of Nika, who tries to tell me something. I dream again of the cat, who comes to lie next to me. I dream of Allison. And most of all I dream of what Jack is going to do to me in the morning.

I'm not going to tell you what Jack does to me after he comes down the stairs. I'm not going to tell you what he does with the pliers, the needles, the iron rods, the boiling water, the cotton-balls soaked in alcohol and set alight. I'm also not going to tell you all of my responses.

We all have ways we might hope or believe we would respond under the most dire or traumatic or painful circumstances, and we've all seen movies where the heroes retain their sophistication no matter their torment. But we don't so often see the entirely-to-be expected breaking down of façade after façade, the breaking of both body and psyche, the large and small betrayals of self that are ultimately the point of so much torture, the large and small betrayals of self that can be so very difficult to forgive.

I break. I cease to exist. I cease to care about anything but stopping the pain. If destroying the world would stop this pain I would destroy the world. If Jack would stop inflicting pain on me and begin to inflict it on Allison I would be grateful for the respite.

And when I think I can break no more, I break again and again and again.

I am no longer thinking that this is what it must be like to be a forest, or a river, or a vivisected or factory-farmed animal. I retain no space for any suffering but my own. And when it seems the suffering fills up all the space there is, it continues to expand.

Jack takes a rest. He puts several towels on the table, says, "You stink. You should be ashamed of yourself. You are so filthy. You disgust me."

He lets that sink in.

He continues, "You're going to clean yourself up. I'm going to uncuff one of your hands and leave another key on the table so you can uncuff your other hand. You will then use the towels to clean up your urine and feces, and then you will cuff your left hand so I can see it and gently leave the key on the table near your waist. I will be standing by Allison, holding this knife. If you do the slightest thing I don't like I will cut off her breast." He thinks a moment, laughs softly to himself, then adds, "Like a doctor, only I won't replace it with something bigger." Another pause before he asks, "Do you both get it?"

I nod. Allison says, "Yes."

When he uncuffs my hand I do nothing. When he leaves the key I uncuff my other hand, sit up—very shakily—and I begin to clean myself up. When Jack directs me to drop the dirty towels, I drop them when and where he says. When he tells me places on the table I've missed, I clean them up. And when he tells me to cuff my hand, I do, and I gently lay the key on the table, and wait for him to cuff my other hand.

When he is done with me he uncuffs Allison, recuffs her hands, leads her to a bathroom. He stands in the doorway looking back and forth between us as she uses the toilet, cleans herself up. She returns to her chair, and he binds her again.

Jack is standing over me. I hear Allison's voice say, "Why are you doing this?"

I hear Jack say, "Because I can."

She says, "That's not good enough."

He stops, stares at her.

She says, "You can also let us go. You can be different than you are."

He jabs the needle in the air, shouts, "This is who I am. There is nothing wrong with me." He stops, says calmly, "I know your game. You're trying to get me mad at you so I'll stop working on him."

"Your real hatred isn't toward women, is it?"

"Your turn will come."

"I mean, you torture them. You kill them. But your real hatred is toward men. You can't aim your hatred toward them because that would be too frightening. And your *real* hatred is toward God, because of everything *He* has destroyed, but that's even *more* frightening. You take orders from above, and you pass them on below."

He steps toward her.

"You're afraid to fight someone who can actually fight back, so you—"

He slaps her once, then again.

She continues, "And then you rationalize it with all your talk of power, of God. And it's all because you feel so very small."

He says, "I know how to make you shut up." And he walks back to me, picks up the pliers.

Allison stops talking.

Nika comes to me, sits next to me, tells me that things are going to be all right. She tells me she will help me with what I need to do. She says she went through all of this, too, and that soon it will all be over. She tells me I should tell Jack that she never made it home, but that she is happy where she is.

Jack is holding a knife. He says, "I am going to kill you now, and as you die you are going to tell me what is on the other side. You will tell me what you see and hear and feel as you cross that threshold. It's very important that I know this."

It's been so long since I used my voice to speak that I don't know if it still works. Finally I say, "You're going to kill me so you can find out what happens when you die?"

He looks at me.

"That's what this is about?"

"You finally understand."

"You're so stupid," I say.

He hits me.

"You can't find out anything this way. If you want to know what happens when you die, ask a dead person."

"I am, you." He presses the knife to my chest, says, "This is how you die."

Before he can push it too far, I say, "Nika told me what it's like to be dead. She wanted me to tell you she never made it home." The pressure on my chest stops. "What?"

"But she's happy where she is."

He looks at me intently.

I say, "And did you know she has willows growing from her hair, and wild roses on her breasts and hips?"

Jack lets me live for a little while. He asks me what else Nika told me. I tell him enough to keep him interested. He gives me more towels to clean up. I still don't make a move. I don't know what I could do. My legs are still chained and he's too far away for me to lunge at him. I'm not sure I have the strength to lunge anyway. When I'm done I try to snap the cuff only to its loosest ratchet so I can slip my hand free, but he catches on and makes a small cut on Allison's breast. I shut it. He finishes cuffing me.

He uncuffs Allison's hands from the chair, cuffs them back together in front of her, unchains her ankles. He helps her to her feet, leads her to the bathroom. I hear her sit. Jack stands in the doorway, moving his eyes from me to her and back to me.

Nika comes to me again, says one sentence over and over. I don't know what it means. I don't know why I should say it. I don't say a word.

I hear Jack say, "Are you done?"

I hear Allison say, "Almost."

And then I hear my muse say, "Listen."

And I hear the hissing voice of the director say, "Choose. Life or death. Choose."

And I hear Nika saying that one sentence again and again, with an urgency I've never heard in her voice.

I say, as loud as I can, "Nika says. . . ."

Jack looks at me intently.

"Nika says. . . ."

He takes one small step toward me. "Says what?"

"Nika says, 'Use the hammer now.'"

"What?"

"Use it now."

Jack looks confused, "What hammer? Use it how?"

And suddenly Allison is on top of Jack, hitting him again and again with a hammer. He falls. I lift myself as high as I can to see the hammer rising and falling, rising and falling. Again and again I hear the sound of metal hitting flesh, metal hitting bone. "Keep hitting," I cry. "Keep hitting."

She grunts with every swing.

She stops.

"Don't stop," I say.

"He's dead."

"Don't stop."

She keeps hitting him. Finally she stops. She finds the key to my cuffs on the ground where he dropped it, comes to me, releases me. I release her, too, then try to stand but fall. I crawl over to him, pick up the hammer in my swollen and bleeding hands. I can barely hold it. But I lift it up and hit him in what's left of his face. I hit him again. I hit him again.

twenty
seven

We call the police, then sit staring at Jack's body—making sure he doesn't move—until they arrive. They do not believe us at first. But we show them the cabinet full of Jack's trophies. Then they begin to believe us. They send other police to our home, where they retrieve our identification, and some clothes. Our statements make sense. They take us to the hospital.

Colleen is at her parents'. The telephone rings. Her father answers, calls her to the telephone. The caller identifies himself as a policeman, tells her he will be sending uniformed officers over soon. She asks why. The caller tells her the officers will inform her.

They arrive. Colleen meets them at the door. She asks why they are there. One tells her they found this address at her home in Spokane. She asks why they were at her home. The same officer tells her that her husband is dead. The officers ask questions about her husband, and about their relationship, and about when and why she was not at her home. In time she asks why they are asking these questions. At first they do not answer. They ask her more questions, and then more questions. Evidently they are finally satisfied with her answers, because they tell her why they were asking: her husband is suspected of killing numerous women. One officer says, "You should plan on staying here for a while."

She says, "There must be some mistake."

The officer responds, "No. The evidence is overwhelming."

She cannot stand. She leans against a wall, slides to the floor. She says, to the police, to her parents, to herself, "How could this be? I never saw anything. I never saw anything at all."

Several weeks have passed. Indian summer has given way to fall. Nights have gone from chilly to cold. We take a tour of the trees we planted for bears, and see ripe fruit dangling from tender branches. Where I saw Jack strike Nika we see that a tree overhanging the stream holds the most beautiful bright pink apples we have ever seen. We eat some of the apples ourselves, and leave the rest.

For a time we do not talk much about what happened. It's still too near, too raw: an open wound. My body heals quickly. The rest of me not so quick. I remain terrified of the dark, of dogs barking at night, of sudden movements. Shoes sometimes make me cringe because of Jack's last name. Right away Allison removes all the pliers and needles from our home so they won't remind me, but after a while I'm okay with them, and she brings them back.

At first Allison and I do not make love. We hold each other and do not speak. But soon we start up again. We do not resume slowly.

One day, sitting outside in the bright slanted sunlight, I say to Allison, "All those attempts to assassinate Hitler failed because of miracles. And this culture has overspread the planet because of similar miracles. Why were we able to win?"

She looks at me sadly for a moment before she says, "We haven't won. We've got a long fight ahead of us."

"Why did Nika help us?"

"Probably because you listened. I'm sure there are a lot of others who will help, if only we will listen."

"Enough others to bring down this culture?"

"Enough to bring down God."

How many times and in how many ways has God told us that He is a jealous God? Maybe God hates us so much in part because we can think for ourselves. Maybe He hates us because we can choose to walk away from Him. Maybe He wants to destroy the earth because we are part of the earth, birthed from the earth, and He doesn't want us to remember that. We are, when we are not too much like Him, wild and sensual like the earth, and if we have anything left of that sensuality, He wants to kill that. But if He hates us so much, and if He is afraid we will remember who we are and where we come from, does that not say something about us as well? That we are not as powerless as we think? That He thinks we are a threat? Otherwise, why would He even bother?

The night is cold. I'm starting a fire in the woodstove. The flame jumps from match to paper, from paper to kindling. I blow on it. It grows, reaches out to more and larger pieces of wood. Flames dance and hiss and pop, and sometimes I think I can almost begin to understand what they are saying.

Sometimes I see Nika. Sometimes she speaks. I thank her each time we meet. She smiles shyly and extends her hands. I take them in my own. Some time, she says, she will tell me her dreams. I tell her I would like that very much.

She looks beautiful, with willows growing from her hair, with ponderosa pines in her ribs, and with wild roses on her breasts and on her hips.

The cat comes to me in dreams, rubs up against me, asks to be held. I do. I am happy. So is she.

Snakes come to me, too, in dreams and when I am awake. I see them everywhere. I also see mice, and I see many others.

The director comes to me, too, tells me there isn't much time, tells me there is much to be done. This was only the beginning, he says. And he always says, "Choose. At every moment choose. Choose now."

Allison and I sit next to Hangman Creek, called Latah Creek before any of this all began, and to be called Latah Creek once again when it is all over.

I still fall through time. It no longer terrifies me. It is simply part of life, like breathing, like looking into Allison's eyes.

We come to the creek because I hope to fall back through time and see salmon run strong. It makes me happy, and reminds me what it is we are fighting for.

The sounds of traffic fade, and I know I'm falling. I hear the slapping of thousands of salmon tails against the water and I begin to smile. I see thousands of fins breaking the surface. I see the bottom of the creek disappear beneath the bodies of so many fish. I begin to cry, both at the beauty and because the fish are long gone. I wish the fish were still here. I wish I were seeing the future, not the past.

And then I see something I did not expect. I see an apple bobbing its way downstream. It is bright, and it is pink. It is the most beautiful apple I have ever seen. It takes me a few moments to realize where it came from and what this means.

Suddenly I understand. I have never in my life been so happy. I say, to the fish, to the creek, to the willows, ponderosa pines, and wild roses, to Nika, to the demons, to Allison, to my muse, and to myself, "There's a lot of work to be done. Let's go."

◉

Special thanks to the Wallace Global Fund
for their ongoing support.

About Flashpoint Press

Flashpoint Press was founded by Derrick Jensen to ignite a resistance movement. Our planet is under serious threat from industrial civilization, with its consumption of biotic communities, production of greenhouse gases and environmental toxins, and destruction of human rights and human-scale cultures around the globe. This system will not stop voluntarily, and it can not be reformed.

Flashpoint Press believes that the Left has severely limited its strategic thinking, by insisting on education, lifestyle change and techno-fixes as the only viable and ethical options. None of these responses can address the scale of the emergency now facing our planet. We need both a serious resistance movement and a supporting culture of resistance that can inspire and protect frontline activists. Flashpoint embraces the necessity of all levels of action, from cultural work to militant confrontation. We also intend to win.

FLASHPOINT PRESS
CRESCENT CITY, CALIFORNIA

About PM

PM Press was founded in 2007 as an independent publisher with multiple offices in the US and a veteran staff boasting a wealth of experience in print and online publishing. We produce and distribute short as well as large run projects, timely texts, and out of print classics.

We seek to create radical and stimulating fiction and non-fiction books, pamphlets, t-shirts, visual and audio materials to entertain, educate and inspire you. We aim to distribute these through every available channel with every available technology - whether that means you are seeing anarchist classics at our bookfair stalls; reading our latest vegan cookbook at the café over (your third) microbrew; downloading geeky fiction e-books; or digging new music and timely videos from our website.

PM Press is always on the lookout for talented and skilled volunteers, artists, activists and writers to work with. If you have a great idea for a project or can contribute in some way, please get in touch.

PM Press
PO Box 23912
Oakland, CA 94623
510-658-3906

Friends of PM

These are indisputably momentous times – the financial system is melting down globally and the Empire is stumbling. Now more than ever there is a vital need for radical ideas.

In the year since its founding – and on a mere shoestring – PM Press has risen to the formidable challenge of publishing and distributing knowledge and entertainment for the struggles ahead. We have published an impressive and stimulating array of literature, art, music, politics, and culture. Using every available medium, we've succeeded in connecting those hungry for ideas and information to those putting them into practice.

Friends of PM allows you to directly help impact, amplify, and revitalize the discourse and actions of radical writers, filmmakers, and artists. It provides us with a stable foundation from which we can build upon our early successes and provides a much-needed subsidy for the materials that can't necessarily pay their own way.

It's a bargain for you too. For a minimum of $25 a month, you'll get all the audio and video (over a dozen CDs and DVDs in our first year) or all of the print releases (also over a dozen in our first year). For $40 you'll get everything that is published in hard copy. *Friends* also have the ability to purchase any/all items from our webstore at a 50% discount. And what could be better than the thrill of receiving a monthly package of cutting edge political theory, art, literature, ideas and practice delivered to your door?

Your card will be billed once a month, until you tell us to stop. Or until our efforts succeed in bringing the revolution around. Or the financial meltdown of Capital makes plastic redundant. Whichever comes first.

For more information on the *Friends of PM*, and about sponsoring particular projects, please go to www.pmpress.org, or contact us at info@pmpress.org.

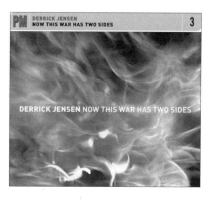

Also From PM Press

Derrick Jensen - *How Shall I Live My Life?: On Liberating The Earth From Civilization*

In this collection of interviews, Derrick Jensen discusses the destructive dominant culture with ten people who have devoted their lives to undermining it.

Whether it is Carolyn Raffensperger and her radical approach to public health, or Thomas Berry on perceiving the sacred; be it Kathleen Dean Moore reminding us that our bodies are made of mountains, rivers, and sunlight; or Vine Deloria asserting that our dreams tell us more about the world than science ever can,

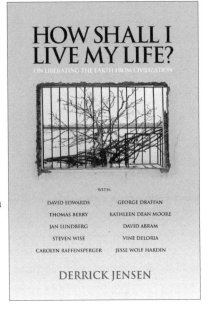

HOW SHALL I LIVE MY LIFE?
ON LIBERATING THE EARTH FROM CIVILIZATION

WITH:

DAVID EDWARDS   GEORGE DRAFFAN

THOMAS BERRY   KATHLEEN DEAN MOORE

JAN LUNDBERG   DAVID ABRAM

STEVEN WISE   VINE DELORIA

CAROLYN RAFFENSPERGER   JESSE WOLF HARDIN

DERRICK JENSEN

the activists and philosophers interviewed in *How Shall I Live My Life?* each bravely present a few of the endless forms that resistance can and must take.

Interviews include:

George Draffan	Jesse Wolf Hardin	Vine Deloria
Carolyn Raffensperger	Steven Wise	Jan Lundberg
David Edwards	Thomas Berry	David Abram
Kathleen Dean Moore		

Order at www.pmpress.org